# THE RUSSIAN INK

## Jake Armitage Thriller Book 1

### Simon W Clark

**SWC Press**

The Russian Ink

Copyright © Simon W Clark 2022

All rights reserved

PAPERBACK ISBN: 978-0-6455536-0-4

E-PUB ISBN: 978-0-6455536-1-1

For Scarlett,
showing me each day the endless wonders of life.

# THE RUSSIAN INK

# Chapter 1

Dusk had crept over an ink sky. In the cool Russian breeze, it triggered the clouds to form darkened orange clots across the coming night. Jake Armitage flicked the headlamp high-beam switch on his late model Hyundai Creta. The road illuminated in a blue hue.

Jake curb-crawled and scanned the street. He spotted a large letterbox sunk in a tall brick wall. Brown paint peeled on the timber face.

The address looked right. Armitage squinted as the light caught two numbers: first a six, then the one.

*I'm at the right place.*

Large iron gates wrapped each side. A gap appeared at the turn. The agent steered the Hyundai onto a built-up driveway. *It's open. No security.* The land sloped back from the road edge, receding into a thick canopy of trees. He sat on twenty miles per hour, searching the landscape for signs of life.

Not a staff member in sight. Nothing.

The path weaved to a gravel clearing. Tires crunched. A northerly wind picked up pace. The house sat further through the darkened treetops.

The agent returned to the boundary wall. He parked on a grass patch behind a thick cluster of tree trunks. The gates in his wake, six feet from the spot. Leaves swayed in the breeze. He positioned the vehicle behind dense foliage.

Gray clouds rolled. A sprinkle of rain tapped on the windshield. The agent pulled on his thin gloves. He preferred dexterity over comfort but tonight had exceptions from the usual rules.

Armitage checked his firearm. He pocketed a spare magazine, killed the motor and dropped from his Hyundai to the ground.

Shadows danced in the forecourt, offset by the building cradled deep in the grounds. Jake's eyes darted at each sound.

A static surveillance camera sat on a pole. The device pointed to the middle of the cement landing. Armitage stayed out of range, sprinted fifty yards to south of the circular parking lot.

The second CCTV was fixed on one position but could be wide-angled. The agent crawled around the edge of the opening, keeping within the cover of the trees.

Within five minutes, Jake reached the stately home.

The centuries-old mansion had a regal but neglected vibe. Saint Petersburg was filled with similar residential monoliths. It seemed to Jake that the city had only two types of abodes—Soviet-era apartments and massive gothic houses, both in no short supply.

*This is it: the safehouse. Is my information accurate?*

Inside this house, an asset represented the most important witness in the United States and Russian relations.

Ever.

The horizon transformed fast above the port city. Jake followed the boundary, his gaze locked on the windows. He loosened the zipper on his jacket, touched his P-96M pistol for reassurance. Tucked in a shoulder holster, his finger twitched, expectant of a quick draw.

An eerie silence floated over the flat landscape. The agent let the city blur in his vision. The lights of St Petersburg flared in reds and greens and yellows.

Old columns framed the front façade. Once pearl-white, time had faded and stained the surface. As Jake approached the squat, triple-story house, a knot formed in his stomach.

No movement from the house. Jake paused, listening for sounds. He crossed the compacted dirt path toward the weather-beaten timber slats.

Dark shapes hung over the large building as if the center of a black hole. Jake detected a smoky scent unusual to find in the open air. It smelt as if a recent discharge of automatic weapons had taken place. He knelt to one knee and picked a spent cartridge concealed in the grass. The agent squinted over the lawn and spotted four more rounds. He sniffed the spent jacket. It had been fired in the last hour or two.

Armitage approached the raised porch with stealth, eyes darting over possible ambush positions.

Twenty-four hours ago, Jake had intercepted a phone call between two Russian civilians. A broker and a suspected intelligence operative. A double agent. These men had engaged a team to eliminate a major witness in Jake's investigation.

The group had targeted a man in possession of incriminating evidence against the highest level of government. The president of Russia. This data could change the course of history.

Armitage had trailed the group for months but lost track until the crucial wiretapped dialog. The broker had contracted a private team to capture the asset who also possessed a memory drive. A storage device that had crucial evidence on political tampering between the U.S. and Russia. He'd discovered the asset was being held in an address on the outskirts of Saint Petersburg.

Their target disappeared a week ago, along with the evidence.

The asset had been presumed dead.

Until now.

The agent's tech surveillance had traced the caller's address to this large period house in the suburbs. Armitage ran a hand through his hair.

Trees cast long shadows over a garden. The agent assessed the front door, secured by a deadlock.

*Is this an ambush?*

The walls glowed unnaturally under the retreated light. Beyond the row of grimy window-panes, Jake checked a side path. Semi-broken steps reached an iron gate. He tested the handle, bolted from the inside. The old-fashioned lock required too much pressure and the expected noise might attract unwanted attention.

Jake's gaze drew back to the main entrance. An amber haze emanated from a single bulb. It swung from the ceiling.

The flooring creaked as Jake mounted the porch. He touched the holster packed against his ribcage and released the handgun. Silence. He disengaged the safety clip. The weapon echoed as if in stereo sound. His heartbeat pounded. Deep breaths, in and out, controlled his nerves.

In short steps, Jake inched to the door gap. A metallic waft carried by a gathering wind. His pulse raced as he fought himself to relax. He grasped the weathered handle, eased forward, pushed into the foyer zone.

An open window fluttered the raggedy drapes. Armitage took in the dated decor. The floorboards creaked and settled with the changing weather. He paced through an oak-lined passageway covered with scenic prints.

The decorations gave a homely, chic atmosphere to the place.

A corridor narrowed. Jake stepped around a plastic chair, the only furniture against the wall.

*This is too quiet.*

The air hung thick and stuffy. Nonetheless, Jake shivered. Adrenaline coursed through his veins. If a team of soldiers appeared, he'd blaze his way to a glorious end. Take as many enemies as luck allowed.

*I don't believe in luck.*

Armitage only trusted the speed of his draw. The fire of his weapon. One in the chamber. Fifteen in the clip, a spare magazine tucked in his jacket.

The corridor hit a T-shaped intersection. The walls narrowed and Jake turned right. A series of steps appeared in the gloom.

The stairs descended into a large dining zone. Jake flicked a switch, light pooled over a lounge settee. The rectangular room had high ceilings and furniture cluttered the space. Even the edges were capped with high shelves; books scattered the floors. Two sofas surrounded a broken coffee table.

*Not the place of a minimalist.*

The next step, Jake pulled to a halt, near losing his balance. He noticed a pile of furniture. Broken table legs strewn on other parts. Across the east corner, paper sheets were scattered over the floor. To his right, decorative glass ornaments glittered a path toward the far drywall.

*The operation is compromized.*

Armitage stepped sideways and edged toward the middle of the mess. He assessed the damage, calculating the cause for this chaos. A table for four sat against the south wall. The matching seats appeared buried within the chaos.

*I must take the asset and bring him to safety.*

A bird squawked. Jake raised his right leg over an upturned stool and planted his foot to the solid timber. A low table lay sideways, the surface split. He moved around for better visibility. The stack of furniture climbed more than half a yard high. As if a tsunami had wrecked the place.

An object caught Jake's eye. The agent picked a side table and placed it on the floor. He pulled away broken chair splinters. The pile collapsed, revealing a gap. He knelt on one knee and tossed a chair leg. With both gloved hands, he rummaged.

A shoe protruded in a right-angle, half-covered by a tan-colored chino. The agent's gaze traced the trouser leg upward, reaching the mid-section of the lower torso. His heartbeat banged a tattoo against his ribcage. A victim lay partially submerged within the pile of discarded furniture.

Among broken glass, a hand protruded from the rubble. Jake shifted the lifeless arm, creating a vacuum within the discarded carnage. He waited as more rubbish collapsed into itself.

Underneath the smashed pieces, a profile appeared.

His eyes ran down a bloodied corpse.

*The asset.*

With all Jake's remaining strength, he heaved the thick, wood furniture top. Shards of polished teak tumbled to the floor. He tossed the pieces aside. A drop of sweat dripped over his eyelid, ran down his cheek. When the stack cleared, he pulled the sole unbroken chair upright.

The agent sank back to take in the scene.

*Where did the killer go?*

The walls closed around. Jake leaned over the sprawled figure. Crimson liquid pooled in a medieval, crown-shaped pattern over the dead man's scalp. He performed a basic check on vitals. The skin was pasty. Armitage placed a finger over the neck.

No pulse.

Both arms splayed from the torso. The body lay spread-eagled, right side part-buried. Jake gained his feet. He stepped over the pile to view the victim from above. The right arm contorted in an impossible angle.

A break.

Jake's gaze moved across the face, dropped to the throat. He moved aside the matted strands on the nape, revealing a bloodied hole. It looked like at least a 40-caliber round. A large revolver seemed unlike a professional hit. In a close-range transaction, this weapon would be loud and messy.

Perhaps a kill by an amateur who's having a bad day?

With his right shoe, Jake nudged the shoulder aside. The body folded and arms flopped either side. Eyes stared lifeless at the ceiling.

Scenarios ran through Jake's mind. A struggle led to an execution. He reversed to the doorframe, the killer's first entry. Gunshot trajectory all but confirmed a surprise attack. The prisoner defenceless to a round fired from the rear.

Followed by another chest shot—double tap. A military-trained kill.

Afterward, the corpse had been deserted.

An execution, but why.

Wounds checkered the upper body, signs of trauma and torture. The victim's clothes were torn. Fabric spilt but not much blood.

Trace evidence should be everywhere.

The agent stepped backward and steadied his stance. He refocused on the broader scene, tried to capture every detail. If he missed a crucial piece of evidence, it could blow the mission.

Two different weapons and caliber produced half a dozen shots. The larger one came from a favoured Federation weapon. One invented and made by the Russians. Kalashnikovs were commonly referred to as their commercial name: AK 47s.

High-powered semi-automatic machine guns.

*Russia and the U.S. are not taking risks on this guy.*

Jake dropped to his knees, leaned over the victim. He spotted a bruise and laceration on the right facial cheek. On closer inspection, the blood had started to congeal.

# Chapter 2

The agent examined the mess as he hypothesized.

*A dead asset in a killing field, murdered by persons unknown.*

The floor creaked. Armitage crouched and balanced on the balls of his feet. He pushed aside loose bits on the upper torso. The most revealing sign: double-tap gunshot wounds, one each to the head and chest, caused instant death. Not enough extra blood surrounding the entry point holes.

A military-trained contractor who killed efficiently. Jake guessed these lethal strikes happened upwards of two to four hours ago. But not five hours as the blood would have dried. There's evidence of a violent struggle and additional bruises and marks.

Armitage rose, maneuvered around the corpse and skirted the scene. The dark slick expanded to a nearby dresser, stopped short of the edge.

*There's got to be more evidence.*

Over Jake's shoulder, the corridor plunged eastward with zero visibility. From the archway he counted three rooms on either side, paused and listened for movement.

*Not a sound.*

A dim tunnel flowed west. Jake pressed the firearm into his chest, nerves taut. Shadows flickered as he ventured into the unknown.

The boards changed to carpet as Jake progressed. Closed rooms on each side. His night-vision kicked in, adjusted to the lack of light. He touched the wall and used it as a guide.

Blood pounded through his ears. Armitage paused and inhaled slowly until his adrenaline rush balanced.

In the limited visibility, Jake ran his spare hand over a wall. He withdrew the smartphone from his front pocket. Inch by inch he stepped. He activated the flashlight app and pointed the beam toward the archway.

The agent faced the door opposite the one he'd entered. He cracked the jamb. The scent of stale perspiration and unwashed linen escaped. With his index finger, he exerted more pressure and it creaked two inches ajar. A second corridor glowed blue. It branched off of the main at a right angle.

Through the dimness, stairs climbed steeply into the shadows. The new passageway extended further than it appeared. He squinted left to right, attempting to make out the rectangular outlines.

Armitage eased under the archway and covered blind spots. He ascended the void, gripped the banister with his spare hand.

The sidearm pointed into black space, guided by the thin shards of moonlight from a window. Each time, Jake expected attack, an assailant to propel from the darkness. His pace quickened as he stepped over the worn carpet.

At the landing, Jake waited and listened. Nothing. The floor appeared uninhabited.

Shapes formed entries to additional rooms that punctuated left and right. In the first living quarters, the contents were ransacked.

An imitation Persian rug met the skirting board. Jake yanked the drape from the window. He stood at an unmade bed with sheets crumpled over the semi-exposed mattress. Stains marked the surface.

Light leaked into the crowded room, trickled around a desk. He contemplated the sort of person that would reside here.

Only someone desperate, or a prisoner.

These weren't sophisticated criminals and complex strategies at play. Traffickers working with or under organized crime.

European-brand pumps sat beneath a chair. The agent lifted one and read *Manolo Blahnik* in gold lettering on the inside.

*Just like a pair I bought for my ex-wife on our last holiday.*

*I wish.*

Armitage pushed a wardrobe open and discovered a row of black designer cocktail dresses. The top shelf had shoe boxes piled to the lowest shelving. A leather case on the dresser. He flipped the lid. A bent spoon with foil. Under a strap lay a hypodermic needle.

The drug kit for methamphetamines. Tweakers.

*But where are the girls?*

The agent zipped the case and tossed it on the dresser. He exited the messy hovel and headed south toward the corridor exit which led into a laundry.

A large basin sat next to cupboards with a pile of used towels stacked in a basket. Jake pushed open a connecting door and discovered a toilet. The tiles were cracked and mould-spotted, yellow with age.

Next door revealed a linen cupboard, most shelves bare. Folded sheets and towels filled the two lowest compartments.

These bedrooms all appeared as if they'd housed

slaves controlled by human traffickers. Evidence of drug usage and exotic female attire pointed to forced prostitution.

*What does this have to do with the asset?*

The agent's focus homed in on the end of the main passageway. He contemplated the weak, milky glow that escaped the north-facing room. In the silhouette, he made out the lines of a stove and linoleum tiles.

With his toe, Jake nudged a rug aside. He took a deep breath and zig-zagged toward the opening. At three yards from the entry, he gripped his firearm, ready for a showdown.

Through the door frame, Jake reached into the room, flipped a switch for an overhead fluorescent light. White flooded the grimy walls. A countertop with mugs ran the full length. Armitage led with the barrel first, trained on the far corners and his blind spot.

Jake started upon realizing he wasn't alone. His gaze fell on another body propped in a chair and slumped to the rear wall. The head dangled to the side at a near right angle, resting on the edge of a lower cupboard.

Jake crossed to the macabre display. The corpse had been made to look natural. As if a seated position would make a difference.

The man had medium-length brown hair. Thirties. Dressed in jeans and a button-down shirt. Scars and a five o'clock shadow. A typical henchman or Russian criminal. Behind the corpse, the plaster had four gunshot holes. Nine-millimetre rounds.

A spray from an automatic weapon.

Just like the other dead body.

It appeared as if the gunman had shot with a Kalashnikov from the archway, then positioned the body.

Armitage bent to check the man's pulse. No beat. The skin was warmish and the arm had started to stiffen with early signs of *rigor mortis*. Jake patted the man down for identity cards or a phone, checking the pockets. The others must have taken these items.

Smart.

On the right hand, under blood, Jake noticed a tattoo.

The agent searched the cupboards. On the bottom shelf, he found a roll of paper towels. He tore off a sheet. The door squeaked closed. He pulled the victim's sleeve to reveal the ink on his arm.

A detailed star with a dagger through the middle.

*One dead kidnapper. These guys don't work in pairs.*

The grubby tiles had turned murky green as Jake circled a worn table and chairs. He racked his brain on the ink.

Scuffed laminate bordered a sink, the ends hung over ground-level cupboards. Armitage lowered his weapon to hip level and reached toward the sink. He touched the countertop. The worn edges had been rubbed shiny. A half-filled mug of coffee sat near an aging kettle appliance.

*Must be a makeshift recreational zone for the minders and thugs guarding their female prisoners.*

The agent ran his index finger along the surface, detected a faint scent of disinfectant. He rubbed his finger and thumb. It had a moist film that clung to his fingertip.

A heavy-grade cleaner. The scent was fresh and applied by the killers to cover their tracks.

*Unless these guys have a maid. Or obsessive-compulsive disorder.*

The stuffy, dirty kitchen needed more scrubbing. The

rushed cleaning session indicated concealment and destruction of evidence.

Jake took a photo of the tattoo and the dead man's face with his smartphone camera.

The images began downloading through a satellite network to a cloud server. The agent preferred the security rather than using a local Russian telco network. At the same time, he activated data-matching software and connected to a secured outpost server.

Armitage pressed on into an adjoining hall. He plunged by more dingy bedrooms on both sides and aimed at a plain white panel.

The corridor snaked back to the first door. He paused at another bedroom and stared at a single bed shoved in the corner. Crumpled sheets cascaded to the floor. A tattered textbook on string theory, suitable for an astrophysicist, lay on a table.

*A smart female student caught up in a trafficking operation.*

Stale cigarette smell oozed from the furniture. The plaster was stained yellow, discarded ashtrays overflowing with squashed butts. In the last drawer, Jake found a silver pistol. He picked up the weapon and_pulled back the bolt. A 30-carbine caliber round in the chamber and a magazine packed tight. He shoved the weapon in a pocket.

With his right hand, Armitage slid the mirrored wardrobe open. Folded on a hanger hung pressed khaki pants, a casual shirt draped alongside. For the male guards. Travel baggage pushed under clothes on the wardrobe base.

*This pad was lived in but the inhabitants exited fast. They didn't pack or take their suitcases.*

The agent retreated through the passageway, double-checking doorways. Satisfied he'd missed nothing, he switched the lights off and descended the stairs.

At the bottom of the steps, the passage flowed to the family room from the south entrance.

The evidence overwhelmingly pointed to a local team. At least one perpetrator came from a military background. Jake's gaze drew to the holes embedded in the cabinetry. Too many semi-auto rounds fired at close range.

*Did the traffickers have a disagreement with mercenaries? But for what purpose and why?*

Armitage scanned the dated furniture, transfixed by the darkened floor.

*Think, think. Look at all the clues.*

The asset's corpse stared up at Jake, a macabre death mask.

He mumbled, "Must be something I'm missing."

The agent compared the holes in the wall with the magazine caliber he'd found in the bedroom.

Similar but not the same size. Not the upstairs pistol he'd found.

If Russian police or the Federal Security Service found Jake on the scene, they'd lock up a foreigner and bury this case in a mountain of red tape and bureaucracy.

Interpol would not be happy either.

The agent's mind scrambled across the chaos.

There were two dead bodies in a ransacked and trashed house, no clues or word from his handler.

This witness wasn't anybody though. He was the asset who could identify the agent that sold classified data to the U.S.

Armitage reasoned as he concentrated on the murder scene. Not only his handler, but the Department of Defence would want to bury this incident—and fast.

*That puts me in danger.*

The moon flickered his reflection as a ghostly face, one ravaged by twenty-four sleepless hours and counting. Frustration festered into anxiety. Jake inhaled and gathered his perspective.

Whatever motivated this homicide, he wasn't dealing with an average team of soldiers. The killers were dangerous opponents, educated enough to leave no evidence, even for experts. That means not your basic run-of-the-mill military contractors. These guys were more tactical, restless, ambitious and money-hungry than their colleagues.

The agent caught sight of the victim's left hand bunched into a fist. With a pencil, he poked until the index finger straightened. He applied pressure to the middle finger until it gave way and the palm opened.

Inside nestled a USB flash drive wedged in a death grip. Jake pried the miniature storage device loose, his heart pounding in his throat.

*I wonder if it's the missing data.*

Armitage shoved the digital stick into his inner jacket pocket.

A siren wailed in the distance. The cops could be on their way and if Jake got busted by the Russian police, they could pin this murder on him.

Jake gained his feet, inhaled, and hustled toward the front entry.

# Chapter 3

As Jake reached the living zone, he heard muffled voices and car doors clunked. The sounds emanated from the gravel beyond the porch. He spun, drew his weapon and backed against the nearest wall. The volume escalated as he strained to hear the words. In Russian he heard 'weapons' and 'secure'. Still out of range, he swivelled his head toward the drapes.

Through the window slit, Jake peered at the night. Silver basked the horizon and lit the fir-covered tips with a dull white glow. This provided sufficient light to assess the threat.

Three men. All armed. Military training.

The agent had the element of surprise, having parked his car out of sight. Whether this would be enough remained to be proven.

Boots crunched as rapid steps surrounded the perimeter. He heard the distinct click of the MP5 magazine slot into the weapon.

If they sprayed the walls with gunfire, Jake would be dead within three minutes. Blood rushed through his ears. He took a deep breath to calm himself. Stay focused on the target and completing the mission. He wiped his left palm on his jeans, repeated the gesture with his right hand. The P-96M handle gripped firm in his right palm.

The agent pressed back against the wall as a burst of light pooled at his feet.

A command became audible.

"Clear the rear. Go-go-go!" A deep voice in Russian penetrated the atmosphere as if in stereo sound. Military commands. It seemed as if the leader projected his voice on a loudspeaker.

*This could get dangerous and ugly fast.*

Jake angled his gaze at a crack. He could see movement; a pair of black shoes flickered near the porch. The first hostile stepped onto the landing. In thirty seconds, the leader would be over the threshold and through the front entrance.

More orders from the man in the black shoes. The instructions were to surround the house.

*But why so much back-up?*

The agent's heartbeat fell to its regular pattern as he prepared for the confrontation. Three to one. He touched the barrel to his face. The cold steel reassured him of a higher purpose. Any comfort will do in such a precarious position._

Two sets of footsteps scurried in opposite directions. They faded quickly as the hired help ran the flanks of the large house.

Their leader waited and let the grunts do the hard work.

The thugs wouldn't be an immediate threat yet. Armitage relaxed his posture for a moment. He gathered his strength and resolve.

Footsteps thudded on the stairs. One of the hired guns checked the top floor.

*I'll need to take the commander first.*

A clunk echoed through the passageway and sent a jolt through Jake's spine. He cocked his head down the hall toward the rear windows. Dim moonlight outlined a human silhouette moving behind the glass door frames.

Metal bracing clunked.

*Must be checking storage containers.*

The agent ran through his plan again. As soon as he took out their boss, the underlings would come running. Chaos would ensue and mistakes be made, but not by Jake. When most people are put under extreme stress, their emotional senses in their brain explode. Errors occur.

*Hand-to-hand combat, and only if absolutely necessary. No gunfire.*

Armitage positioned his feet apart by twenty inches, prepared for the ambush.

A second click of a magazine in a machine gun marked the boss's proximity. The main door creaked, groaning on its frame. Jake inched along the plaster, avoided the furniture dotted in his path. The passage boards moved under Jake's weight as he waited. He stepped slowly to make minimal sound.

From countless days in the field, Jake's stealth ability had reached legendary status. He paused at a cabinet, clutching the weapon to his chest with his right hand, his left hand open palm and ready to strike.

Armitage held his breath, counting down from five.

"Zero," he muttered. The agent pushed toward the entry as an athletic man with a clipped, black beard appeared in the archway shadow. From behind the door, the enemy waited, staring.

The overhead halogen light shone in the intruder's eyes, blinding him from Jake's presence in the shadows. It gave Jake an advantage but not for long. He retreated a step but maintained visual contact with the leader.

*Come on. Just step into the doorway.*

Braced against the door, Jake resisted the temptation to move. At the ten-second mark, a perplexed expression fell over the stranger's face. Both hands moved the firearm to hip level, a long, cautious and deliberate movement.

Armitage twisted to the wall edge, his right palm flat with the door's width. From the adjusted position, he could see the man's profile.

The leader of the intruding party flipped the hallway switch. It clicked and an overhead light transformed the dark. Light saturated the room, highlighting the sprawl of broken rubble and furniture parts. The agent's eyes took ten seconds to adjust.

Blackbeard's rigid posture took in the room, head swivelling in both directions. The agent could almost smell his target's breath. He heard footsteps on the living room rug leading to the peak of piled rubble. He pressed against the wall, a tightly wound coil ready to spring.

Through the gap. Jake followed the intruder's gaze.

The leader's eyes fell on the corpse. His face didn't twitch, as if a dead-pan expression had been permanently etched on the man's skin.

Blackbeard crouched and swore in Russian. Armitage recognized the word, having heard it before.

*These mercs must be the killers.*

A smartphone appeared from Blackbeard's pocket. The Russian rose and dialled a number. A terse dialogue began. The leader paced the room and returned to the archway.

Wedged in the shadows, Jake waited, holding air in his lungs. He assumed the thugs were occupied. If he could dispose of Blackbeard first, his chances of escape were much better.

Blackbeard terminated the call, returned the

smartphone to his pocket. Armitage braced as the intruder drifted closer. Counting down from five, Jake spread his feet apart. On reaching one he swung his arm outward.

Jake's arm extended with palm flat and struck the door in a fluid movement. The force of the impact shuddered through his shoulder.

The door smacked on the leader's face. A wet sound escaped. A groan. The agent stepped out to the hallway, turned his stance. Both his hands were clasped together and held at stomach level.

In times of stress, Jake's heartbeat slowed to allow maximum reflex speed. In this moment, he predicted the reaction.

Clear as clean glass.

Blackbeard's hands sprung to his face. The leader remained in a standing position. Blood spilled through his fingers and dripped on the floor. The agent stood and watched his assailant stagger.

If the leader was shocked, his face hadn't caught up with his emotions.

Open palm and fingers straight, Jake smacked the intruder in the trachea. The leader shuddered and clutched his throat. His lips parted in a soundless scream.

A blocked windpipe disabled all sound and function in the vocal cords. The leader shook, defenceless.

The strike hit the leader in the solar plexus. Armitage retracted as the remaining air escaped from Blackbeard's lungs.

Armitage braced his back and stretched both arms. The body went limp. Jake caught the mercenary mid-fall. He lowered the unconscious man to avoid noise.

# Chapter 4

With his right hand, he gagged the bearded man. Any intended sound Jake had muted by a cloth stuffed in the mouth. Unconscious and unable to breathe, Blackbeard's oxygen-starved brain would cease to function. A coma would result soon after.

Blackbeard had minutes to live.

The smooth timber floorboards allowed Jake to drag the unconscious body. He placed the corpse under a large dining table. Out of immediate sight. He switched off the main light.

*I've got two minutes to escape before the thugs find their boss.*

Jake placed a micro-transmitter behind a set of heavy drawers. He shrank back to the shadows, moving swiftly north to the porch. The agent slipped out on to the timber slats and slowly closed the entrance door.

The cool evening breeze hit his face. Armitage took in a breath and moved over the grass section. This avoided the stones' crunching sound. The thugs were disposing of evidence that may have bought Jake time. Precious minutes or seconds to escape the front room and muffle the sound.

Energy coursed through Jake's system again. He sprinted into the trees and rushed toward his car. The intruders' vehicle, a grey Toyota Kluger four-wheel drive, was parked on the circular drive.

No driver sat waiting.

*At least one lucky break for the night. Who had tipped these guys off? Or were they returning to the scene to destroy evidence?*

The agent paused and knelt at the wheel of the Toyota

Kluger. The tire cap unscrewed easily and he pressed the pressure valve. A hissing escaped as Jake tried to muffle the sound. In less than a minute, the rubber sat flat on the stone bed.

Armitage snuck around the other side, keeping out of sight. He repeated the process on the rear driver's side tire.

*These thugs aren't going anywhere.*

The license plates were registered in St. Petersburg, so Jake committed it to memory, though it'd probably be owned by an empty shelf company With an endless corporate trail leading to a dead end, or it'd be a stolen car which hadn't been reported yet. Either way, to have such details put in the NSA database could prove important in a later scenario or give him known associates of the owner.

The scramble down the sloped driveway took longer with Jake's upper torso bent. He crouched low to keep out of sight. On reaching his car, hidden by the thick canopy overhanging the perimeter fence, Jake turned to the old house. The large, square property appeared hung suspended under the mauve evening sky. Any time now, at least two intruders would reach their unconscious boss and come after him.

*I'll be long gone.*

It reminded Jake of just how many times the Russians had failed to capture him. In their own country. This occasion had come closer than most, but still Jake had outsmarted his enemy—the mother country.

The worn car fob key took two presses to unlock the vehicle. The agent yanked the door of his Hyundai. The keyhole showed no signs of tampering. He closed the door gently and pressed one headphone into his right ear. The receiver plug clicked in neat. Static crackled as muffled voices became louder. Jake sat for a moment and listened to the dialogue through the bug and receiver.

"Where did he go?" a thug yelled in Russian after smacking a piece of furniture. The other hostile swore in Russian. Footsteps crunched over the broken debris in the lounge room.

*These guys aren't quiet or subtle.*

Under the canopy, Jake contemplated the ignition button, conscious of the noise. With the escalating combat from the front room, the two mercenaries couldn't hear outside from thirty yards. Better to be cautious, just in case.

The gates appeared fuzzy as he grasped the steering wheel. They were still open.

*Maybe I do need those glasses.*

From the driveway slope Jake estimated one hundred yards to the gates. The two thugs appeared on the porch. Both men pointed at the entrance.

The lean, taller one had short, blond hair. The hostile reached over his shoulder, pulled a semi-automatic rifle and let off a spray.

*I hope he's too far to get a clean shot.*

The shorter, dark-haired man waved his arm. He held an assault rifle with a long magazine pointed at the vicinity of Jake's vehicle. A barrage of nine-millimetre bullets whistled in the air.

The agent threw his elbow out the open window and fired two successive shots. The bullets went long and wide as he gripped the wheel with his other hand. He intended only to distract the Russians rather than score a hit.

The hostiles fell to the ground to avoid eating lead.

Jake steered at the exit, gunned the accelerator.

The men staggered to their feet. The firing ceased. In the rear-vision mirror, the hostiles were waving their weapons in the air, gesturing at his escaping vehicle.

The agent gripped the wheel. The car swerved along the path, tires squealing on the remaining section of driveway. The engine screamed in response as the vehicle slid onto the section with smooth stones. Over the gate, the path bent sharply and he'd be out of visual contact in ten seconds.

The tall intruder had drawn what looked to be an MP15. From a stationary position, the man took aim and triggered in Jake's direction. More gun shots echoed, merging together. Most bullets went wide.

Armitage had pushed the car as far as it would tolerate. He yanked the wheel, losing traction on the right side. A branch scraped the window.

The moon hung over the landscape, lit the ground in a silver sheen. Jake squinted at the asphalt verge. Escape. The intersection lay over the property border.

Bullets hissed, peppering the air and flora. Pine trees glowed in the distance. Adrenaline coursed in Jake's veins.

The car swerved.

Armitage pumped the pedal to the floor. His flank was exposed to the attackers. Even for a brief moment, such a weakness could be fatal.

Both gates hugged the brickwork, sparks flashing on each side. The agent plunged over the median, holding the steering wheel straight.

*That's my exit strategy.*

The property boundary vanished in the rear-view mirror. Armitage leaned back in his seat and sighed. His Hyundai had taken a battering.

Shots ceased as Jake reached the open road. He squinted at the signals ahead, strained in concentration. The green lights went fuzzy. He somehow maintained control.

*A small vulnerable lapse could lose the battle.*

*Or lose my life.*

The engine revved out at sixty miles. Cruise control. Jake eyed the speed limit. He turned on the main avenue.

The agent took to deep breathing while he monitored the traffic.

A marked crosswalk appeared fifty yards ahead. The agent eased on the brake pedal. A throng of walkers stopped on the sidewalk.

Armitage sat in the slow lane at a safe pace, anxious to get away but cautious of attention.

The red blur of lights merged and snaked into the city. To get stopped by law enforcement or the mafia would be a death sentence. There could be an APB or alert out on his license plates. He concentrated on the cars and looked out for police cruisers. Or followers. Anything out of the ordinary.

The siren wail had disappeared.

A purple hue hung over the majestic, baroque buildings. Normally gaudy and gothic, Jake found them comforting. He savored the cool air rushing over his face. Every mile clocked put him further out of range.

As the road flattened, a blacktop rose on the horizon. Streetlights pooled over the surface, reflected the moving cars. One hundred yards away, the beginning of the metro suburbs formed a belt of houses. Colored spots flickered across the cityscape as citizens went about their evening rituals.

The agent's spirit soared, comforted by the knowledge that his getaway had been completed. The gun fight seemed almost absurd in such a tranquil, suburban setting.

The car hummed. Jake would change the car over and move this one. A necessary transaction to keep him off the radar, to blend in with the rest of society.

Armitage tuned the radio so he could join the rest of the world. As if hearing it somehow made life bearable and realistic. He steered on a straightened stretch as the tires gripped on solid asphalt.

The adrenaline subsided and Armitage hit a gentle pace as his posture loosened. A bump in the road knocked the SUV but it barely registered in comparison. He let out a breath he didn't realize he'd been holding.

The agent checked for tails but nobody pursued him— yet. He reached a fork in the road with three options. He took the middle road, skyrises dotting his line-of-sight.

Half a mile past the traffic lights, the lanes expanded. The car rose to a built-up junction of main arteries. High-density housing came into sight as semi-modern apartment towers cluttered the landscape. It reminded him of Paris.

Armitage took the turnpike and connected to the freeway.

Overhead a single CCTV camera pointed at the traffic. Recent government budget cuts meant many devices weren't operational. They sat unconnected, up for show or to dissuade.

Jake reached to the back seat. He pulled on a navy blue cap to further obscure his face should these cameras be working.

*My favourite cap. This has to be a good sign.*

Period mansions gave way to low-rises. As the vehicle

squared up, Jake pushed the pedal to the floor. Headlights blurred as the freeway traffic thinned.

Under the shine of the rising moon, Jake drove just under the limit, taking curves with ease. The suburbs below were lonely. Worker cottages mixed with hotels. He pressed the steering wheel and forced his eyes open.

The landscape flicked back to industrial factories again.

Blue lights lit up the skyline as Jake approached the city center and the main drag.

# Chapter 5

By ten P.M., the night opened to a vast blackness that enveloped the tallest high-rises. The freeway, courtesy of the city hosting the World Cup, climbed and dipped over a spider web of streets and lanes.

Jake contemplated his next move. In the hour since the confrontation, possibilities had caused Jake endless debate.

*Did the murderers return or did I stumble on another organized criminal sect?*

The high-capacity flash drive sat on the console. The agent wondered how many people had been killed for this device in the past week.

Or the cost for the pursuit of its contents.

*I need to work out who those mercenaries are working for?*

The pain in his leg had reduced to a dull throbbing.

Factories and Soviet-inspired warehouses flashed by, disused relics pre-dating the cold war. Armitage accelerated off of the turnpike, slowed toward a set of traffic lights, glanced in the rear-view mirror. He'd done so every five minutes since exiting the safehouse.

A clump of centuries-old buildings dominated the crest ahead, six cars spread across both lanes. Old mixed with new. Jake noted the make and model of each vehicle. None of them had tailed him for longer than a kilometer.

The lights ahead changed. No enemies in sight. Armitage settled into the seat. The gray, crumbling buildings grew taller. The city centre of St Petersburg flickered as if welcoming home a lost hero.

A prodigal son?

More like an enemy of the state.

Jake turned into a lane as the steeples of a Russian Orthodox church staggered across his view. The five-hundred-year-old Gothic monolith cast a jagged shadow onto surrounding structures, blocking the dark sky that threatened rain at any moment. He reversed to a concrete section that served as a parking lot for residents.

In a far corner, Jake unlocked and opened a garage door. Inside, a late model red Ford sedan glistened. He sat on the front seat and took the key from the visor. The ignition fired on the first key turn. He guided the vehicle into the night air.

A dog barked in the distance. The agent steered the Hyundai into the garage and fastened the padlock. With bullet holes in the chassis, he couldn't use it without drawing unwanted attention.

Beyond the open concrete lot, car lights bobbed through the gaps from the freeway. Armitage circled the Ford, his new runabout. The paint had faded slightly. A tarnished rear bumper. Used, not new: worn to the right degree. Perfect for blending in and being invisible.

Satisfied, Jake clicked the alarm, power-walked across the concrete pad into an obscured side entry.

The scullery door swung as Jake's shoes padded on a tiled zone. Long ago, the museum had been converted into a bustling restaurant and kitchen. He pushed through a red oak-paneled door. Trays laden with spoons, knives and forks lined the walls. A large head chef named Uri sweated over a row of stoves. Waves of heat and steam rose from a row of pots causing a hazy atmosphere within the confined space.

In long shifts, the morning meal service opened from seven A.M. and continued to midnight. With less than two hours to midnight, the dinner service was winding to a close. The broad-shouldered cook sliced fruit, his knife hitting wood that echoed through the chamber.

As Jake rounded the elongated, stainless-steel workbench, an assistant with a grim expression brought a returned dish. The timid waiter slowed as he neared the large form of his perfectionist boss.

*There'll be hell to pay for that mistake.*

The lounge part of the restaurant, ceiling covered with ornate Baroque carvings, carried Jake into a high-arched vestibule. From above, grotesque-faced bronze gargoyles leered and smirked as if sharing in a private joke. Underfoot, the tiles changed to smaller, greenish squares spreading into patterns.

Jake passed under large, stained-glass windows and approached a bricked archway.

Light bathed the wall mouldings from old fluorescent tubes bolted to the ceiling, highlighting various religious and political depictions, each intricate and beautiful. All reminiscent of past grandeur.

Moonlight shone on a large, stone, covered corridor. Jake ignored an assembly zone previously used decades ago during Cold War Soviet times Where people had lined up in the dozens for essentials such as food and household products. It now served as a connecting passageway and foyer.

This room opened to the building's heart. The agent passed by cement walls stained with age and stepped into a glass bay. He pressed the *up* button and number eight.

An elevator chimed, cables creaked and adjusted. Old electronic doors parted and whirred. Armitage noticed a flash across his peripheral vision. A neighbor named Mrs Bukin entered from his right as both doors slowly screeched shut.

Jake thrust his arm in the middle so they didn't close on her diminutive frame. The gap widened again as the metal clanged and protested. She shuffled forward into the center and turned to peer at the console. A bent finger pressed the fourth level button.

The look of disdain she reserved for him came forth. Her face scrunched like sucking on a lemon. The agent sighed under his breath. He ignored it, having grown a thicker skin since taking residence in the ancient structure.

An uncomfortable silence hung in the air. The elevator jerked and shook, rising slowly. Jake knew the older lady would exit at level four.

Armitage feigned scared and timid if the need arose. His acting extended to all waking hours of the day. A chameleon. The small talk he found difficult but a necessary part of fitting in with residents. With civilians the world over.

"Evening, Jake." The older lady leaned on a sturdy walking frame equipped with wheels to enable maximum free movement. Her Russian accent was faintly detectable, but impressive English for a lady that had never left the country.

"Lovely to see you, Mrs Bukin." Jake shuffled to a corner. "What brings you out at this time?"

The older lady brushed his comments aside with a flick of her frail hand. "I haven't seen you in more than a week." She studied Jake through thick glasses.

Their ascent in the Lenin-era contraption turned jumpy as the cabin jolted and shuddered upward to higher floors.

"I've been away." Jake smiled and added, "Work takes me to many locations." His arms braced the walls, one hand reaching the lady's frame to keep it steady.

"I see. Quite the traveller, aren't you?" Bukin nodded. Her eyes hardened as if little black raisins. "I've wondered what you get up to in my city." She shook her head from side to side, tutted as the frame swayed with her weight.

On more than one occasion, Jake had heard the recently widowed lady talking to herself in the downstairs restaurant. She'd been found wandering the ancient halls at all hours, engaged in urgent matters. Most of her nocturnal activities consisted of interrogating other residents.

The agent nodded and stared at the wall. The newer occupants sometimes didn't know how to take the old lady.

Since her husband died last year, Bukin had taken on the role of the apartment organizer. This gave her license and free rein to engage in her biggest love: being a busy-body. She always made her opinions clear, not only chairing the committee that oversaw the maintenance, but every single chore and duty relating to the high-rise complex.

Level four greenlit on the panel.

Armitage side-stepped, shifting from the door. It wasn't an uncommon occurrence for the widow to give a tongue-lashing to whoever found themselves within earshot.

Resident or not. Right or wrong. Nice person or not. She didn't mind who she delivered a serving to, or when.

The agent stared at the mirrored elevator walls, avoided eye contact, which seemed to work. He felt her eyes burning into his chest but ignored the sensation.

Doors creaked and retracted to the edges.

Jake stood aside in uncomfortable silence until the old lady disembarked. Again, Jake held his arm in the gap while she pushed herself over the threshold.

"Try to stay out of trouble, Jake, and find yourself a nice girl to settle down with." She raised her hand and slowly disappeared around a corner.

Armitage exhaled and slumped to a relaxed stance.

At his level, the eighth of ten, Jake unlocked his door and stepped into the dining and open-plan kitchen. In the thirty-second deadline, he deactivated a wall-mounted keypad, a basic system of concealed motion sensors and cameras. The system bleeped and he eased into the main living area.

Overhead, a rack of utensils and tools held suspended. Jake shifted to a cabinet drawer. He plonked a cutting board on the countertop and sighed. Visions of the asset's corpse flooded his consciousness. His narrow escape plagued him. He cursed not having heard the intruders earlier. The white-knuckled grip on the marble surface relaxed as he chanted a mantra.

"I am energized and fully protected."

These words calmed Jake in times of stress. He moved opposite the balcony door, sat cross-legged facing the sparkling array of city lights. He'd never tired of the beauty of this port city at night.

The agent cracked the window. He left ten centimeters. At this elevation, there were no snipers that could shoot from any conceivable angle. He'd checked and double-checked. The physics were impossible.

The wind flowed over Jake's skin and refreshed his weary bones. He paced his breathing until his heart rate dropped lower. The six-word mantra flowed from his tongue until his muscles completely relaxed. He repeated the phrase again and again. The world around him faded away. Negative thoughts disappeared. All the stress of the dead witness dissolved to insignificance. Five minutes of intense meditation brought Jake back to calm.

An exercise mat sat in the living room corner. The agent laid it out on the floor. He crouched to the mat, stretching his legs from the cramps of driving without a break.

Relaxed and calm, his mind returned to unfinished business. He moved into stretching, starting with seated butterflies. Each of his major muscle groups were hit. The tendons and ligaments became limber as he went from legs to arms, loosening each one by one.

Jake stripped his clothes and turned on the red faucet in the shower. He made the water as hot as he could stand. The heat seared his tired body and seeped into his cuts and bruises. It seemed to elevate the aches after a few minutes.

By the time Jake's feet touched the tiles and he'd towelled his body, the aches had dropped below his pain threshold.

On the sofa, Jake stretched his leg. On closer inspection, the wound on his right thigh didn't seem as bad. He cleaned the area again, applied antiseptic and a fresh bandage. The stinging sensation faded and he leaned back into the cushions. He sipped from a glass of whisky, replacing it on the table. A warm burn trickled down his throat: the familiar experience, and always reliable.

The agent sighed and closed his eyes. His mind crossed to the safehouse escapade. A messy situation, even by his standards.

*Lucky to get out of that situation alive.*

# Chapter 6

Moonlight struggled through the tinted lounge glass. Jake awoke with a start. He reached for his pistol. The dawn had already penetrated the city. Tips of the table surface glowed in the darkness. The agent kept the light off, pointed a flashlight to the wall. He conducted the first sweep of the living room. The balcony was the weakest point of vulnerability.

*Never lapse your counter-surveillance routine.*

The old maxim from training days had kept him alive more times than he could count.

On inspecting the street through the glass, Jake realized it was Saturday morning, but night-life activity on the sidewalk appeared to still be going strong. Heels clicked on the concrete. Music pulsated from multiple venues dotting the block.

The bedrooms and windows were untampered. Armitage closed the toilet door and moved through the passage. In the kitchen, Jake poured a whisky: neat, double. He stared at the laptop screen, flicking through the camera feed.

No intruders in the past hours of absence.

Armitage sighed and drained his glass.

Twelve months ago, Jake had returned to Russia for an assignment. The idea of working in Saint Petersburg had appealed to him. A one-year stint in the port city, seven years prior, had helped motivate him to take this mission.

That and Jake's marriage falling apart.

*I was a single NSA agent last time.*

This service seemed a lifetime away, but only yesterday in Jake's memory. The agency had improved in many ways since. A new data center in the States had motivated his decision.

*My aches and pains aren't getting better. I need another drink.*

Jake unfolded his legs and rose to his feet. In a large, green, decorative bowl sat a collection of citrus fruits. He grasped a lemon and carved three thin slices. He rested the knife and moved around the kitchen island.

The agent pulled a local Russian bottle from the fridge, opened the cap. He squashed the lemon piece into the neck and drained the bottle. The liquid washed down his throat and cooled his various pains and injuries. A tingle traversed his spine as he gazed at the kitchen.

Food crossed Jake's mind. He found bread in the freezer and put two slices in the toaster. Two eggs cracked over the saucepan caused a sizzle.

At the table, Jake tucked into his meal. He hadn't realized how hungry he'd become till this moment. All thoughts of the escape were put on hold until the dishes and cutlery were soaked, cleaned, and on the rack.

*I need to know what happened to the asset.*

Jake knew he may not be so lucky the next time. After a swig, he placed the beer bottle on the stone surface and powered up his laptop.

*Protect the asset at all costs.*

*I've failed.*

This thought ran through Jake's mind until his temple throbbed. The laptop blinked, a blue screen, as he stretched and arched his spine. His leg pulsed under the bandage, but this niggle couldn't compare to the catastrophe of the past four hours.

The death of the asset had hit Jake hard. He sat back in the chair and contemplated the window. The idea of retirement haunted his waking hours almost every day. A gruesome kill of their prime witness put back the assignment. The evidence had evaporated.

*How could I let this happen?*

Armitage stared at the hard drive prized from the murdered man's fingers. The device left indents in his palm. He hesitated in putting the USB into the computer, afraid a virus or malware might infect his computer or disable the larger NSA network. His pulse quickened and he loosened his collar.

*This situation was out of my control.*

The agent gained his feet and dug the cell phone from his pocket. He stood by the door, stared at his reflection in the glass. Slight dehydration had caused his skin to dry and go patchy.

*These nocturnal hours are bad for my beauty routine.*

The window formed condensation from the low temperature as Jake's gaze refocused. A young couple sat in the living room of a high-rise opposite. Over a round table, a hanging pendant lamp shone across two full dinner plates. Glasses of red wine. The woman laughed at a joke and they tapped wine glasses. A celebration of sorts; the kind of thing people did with a normal life.

The scene brought a knot to Jake's stomach, an ache in his chest as he pivoted at the next building.

*I need to retire and quit this career.*

The agent firmed his resolve and grasped his burner phone. He typed Chris Seaver's number into the device. The assistant director of the NSA was always on call.

Jake's index finger hovered over the call button, a decision that tempted fate again.

A final call had to be made on Jake's career. He drained the beer bottle and circled to the waste bin. The glass clunked on the plastic base. He paced the floor and finally pressed the touch-screen button.

The phone rang and rang. Butterflies moved in his gut.

"Hello, Chris. It's Jake Armitage." He paused to let the words hit home.

"Hi, Jake. What's going there?" Seaver's voice sounded crisp, even at eleven P.M. U.S. time. "You need something? Name it and I'll send it pronto."

"I wish it were that easy." The agent filled his lungs with oxygen, then continued. "The latest mission failed. Our asset is dead and I nearly got killed leaving the targeted address."

The reply came in three seconds. "I see. This can happen, Jake. We only gave you this assignment at the last minute. Don't be so hard on yourself."

Armitage rested his elbows on the ledge. He watched the blobs of light streak on the roads. Life continued on regardless, marching ahead, relentless and unstoppable. The agent pulled in his chest and made the announcement.

"I'm going to retire from active duty."

Silence fell as the assistant director contemplated his answer. Jake knew it wouldn't go any longer than ten seconds, maybe fifteen tops. His director always found words and Jake couldn't remember an occasion where the man had nothing to say.

"We need you, Jake," the deep voice resonated, impossibly calm and deep, even sent over thousands of miles and rerouting through multiple telco towers across the globe. "You're my only operative that knows Russia and has the network. You alone have the skills to get this assignment done."

Armitage sat and pulled a breath. Letting down the agency didn't sit right. "I'm not sure I'm a plus to this mission now."

"The director of the DoD insisted on you personally. We need to know who or what authority was behind the asset's murder, and why." Seaver paused and cleared his throat. "This is imperative to the agency's presence in Russia."

Outside, Saint Petersburg lightened to mauve. The agent examined the purple tinge that hung over the smog. Hundreds of lights weakened in the speckled dawn.

"We suspect there are American interests involved. Top government officials in Saint Petersburg."

In the distance, the ocean swarmed, vast and black as ink. Jake felt insignificant and helpless with the latest setback. His conscience grappled with the ramifications of quitting. The urge to complete this assignment tugged at his soul. His professional ego, and perhaps a little perfectionism, swayed his choice. Patriotism always won.

"Ok. I'll see what I can find." Armitage cleared his throat. "But no promises on how long I'll investigate."

"Thanks, Jake. We really appreciate your efforts. Stay in touch if you need anything and always use a burner."

The phone clicked and Jake placed the device on the table surface. He stared through the glass at the familiar, giant outline of neighboring structures. Even as the city loomed in purple blocks, the sight almost made him a touch sentimental.

# THE RUSSIAN INK

*Looks like I'm staying here a little longer.*

# Chapter 7

As Windows loaded, Jake ran through the organizations that could have enough intel and motivation to commit these murders. The Russian mafia were his first suspects. They had control of the house but were not strategists. Their involvement had to be motivated by greed and opportunism. For a higher power, this provided convenience and a great fall guy. The scapegoat. A house full of armed thugs, running a human trafficking outfit and other organised crime, provided plausible cover.

The team Jake had encountered afterward were not common gangsters. The leader had to be a private military contractor. Mercenaries, their presence alone a sign of higher financial interests. This could hopefully provide a sufficient trail of evidence.

An operation with this strategic and tactical magnitude had purpose and expertise. The military style of the killers pointed to an organized contract kill. A group recruited by sophisticated corporate psychopaths.

On the dead thug's left hand, Jake had seen a tattoo that extended to the arm sleeve. This could be significant. In Russian prison culture, an eight-pointed star indicated authority and rank. The interesting difference with this star is it had a dagger through the middle. An Internet search on the tattoo proved fruitless.

Jake slotted the USB drive into a port on his laptop. He clicked the mouse and surfed the contents. It contained locked files, so he applied decoding programs. He plunged the directory and ran basic security tests. Each file opened in succession.

This chewed up an hour. Stretching, he clicked on the

last file and found it had a different lock. Jake activated an encryption software and left the computer running.

In under fourteen months, Jake had converted the dilapidated Russian apartment into a comfortable but digital-fortified home. He'd changed the cupboards and flooring in the kitchen but left the first seven feet at the entrance in its original condition. Worn and patchy in the front zone, the drywall displayed peeling paint work. The floorboards were soft underfoot but appeared old and worn. Just in case a nosy tenant, or worse, came snooping. A coat of paint and the main bedroom became liveable. The bathroom had been modernized as well.

The blue screen silhouetted the beer empties spread across the table surface. The agent picked up the discarded bottles. It reminded him of a frat house after a big night. The portable drive whirred as the program sought to break the security fire walls. Metal clanged as he deposited the bottles into the trash.

No resident in Jake's block afforded such a lush interior. That's why he kept it hidden from neighbors and the public.

New people made life more difficult. From the street view, Jake's shabby stucco exterior appeared neglected. It matched the rest of the façade and provided a shield from prying eyes. If competitors spied the chic interior of his pad, unnecessary questions would come.

The agent paced the space between the kitchen and hallway. An inner zone of sofas and tables pointed to a feature wall. In the center, Jake had mounted a sixty-inch LED screen. He stood at the north-facing windows coated with full-strength tint.

The computer whirred in the background.

To add further deception, Jake had arranged an old

furniture settee on the balcony, which comprised an outdoor table and two chairs. The sun and rain made sure each piece of the furniture continued to fade. These elements added the final aspects that ensured his pad appeared as simple and poverty-stricken as possible. Such exterior cosmetic neglect ensured any onlooker couldn't tell the difference. From outside, his apartment presented as a dump—it, blended in with others, and nobody knew any different.

No one had a view into his apartment.

The shards of sunrise lit the kitchen back wall. Armitage placed the computer on his coffee table and settled into the cushions, typing on the keyboard. A cable hung from the primary monitor and he plugged into the HDMI port. The bigger screen flickered as it connected. He stared at the directory icon and waited for a file to open.

A message flashed on the screen:

*These files are classified and property of the Russian Federation government. Do not open if you are unauthorized.*

The agent exhaled and crashed back on the couch. Doubts flooded his mind as a vision of his NSA assistant director flashed.

A security prompt appeared asking for a password. Jake spent ten minutes punching in basic hacking protocols. The directory resisted his attempts to open the contents.

The agent leaned to a set of disks and inserted a CD. An old-school program but it worked a charm against many a system. His chance of retrieving this data was slipping away, but he persisted. The encryption program whirred in the drive but never failed to deliver.

A dead asset coupled with a highly encrypted flash drive made for a long day.

*I'm going to need lots of caffeine and alcohol.*

Armitage shed his shoes and took off his socks. The kink in his left leg sent more bolts of pain. He massaged the tender spot, kneaded and pushed the ligaments. A shot like a needle-prick fired north through his spine toward his brain. He wondered if his whole body needed new parts.

In the kitchen, Jake swallowed an anti-inflammatory tablet. The medication would take half an hour to one hour to digest and begin working its healing properties.

*How could any person outside the agency know about the latest asset?*

Besides Jake, only three people knew the informant's whereabouts—two of them were fellow agents. Mitch Gallows, a ten-year veteran of the NSA had covered the graveyard shift. Unmarried and lived in the Russian port city for over three years.

The keyboard sat flat on Jake's lap. He typed in the second contact's name. A profile flicked onto the screen, not that Jake needed this because he knew the details.

Paul Rooney, a dedicated agency worker in his mid-thirties had an unblemished record. Former Army intelligence and graduated to a field agent. First foreign assignment in Russia. Armitage had worked with Paul on another recent matter in Saint Petersburg. The intel Paul obtained was crucial to the success of this mission. In the past two years, the chances of this man turning on the agency seemed unlikely.

The third person was the NSA assistant director, Seaver.

One of their agents had to be dirty. A leak from an inside source, a tip-off, and they had a possible scapegoat.

*Me. Jake Armitage. The field agent in Saint*

*Petersburg.*

The agent swigged from his beer bottle and the lemon slice hit his lips. Its bitter texture swirled in his mouth.

Doesn't matter now the leak got out.

In the background, the hacking software worked its magic. Jake's eyelids drooped from sleep-deprivation. A stronger drop from the whisky on the shelf tempted him as he forced himself to go through the numbers again.

*What am I missing?*

A bleep sounded. Data cascaded the smaller screen in a vertical flow like flour through a sieve. Armitage shared his attention between the laptop and the monitor.

Near two hours into hacking and Jake's throat had dried as he contemplated the blue screen. He filled an empty glass with water and stared at the flickering numbers. The program breached the first layer but failed to break the protocols for the inner files. He sat up straight and ran through the code again.

*I can't find any more weak links in this security.*

A young couple yelled at each other below on the street. Jake closed the balcony glass. He punched in code, trying a few ways around the issue.

*A manual check on the back-end may be the only way to solve this issue.*

"Yeah, for a top-level hacker. I'm just a second-rate operator," he muttered.

The agent paced a lap around his kitchen island and racked his brain.

*This team couldn't be acting alone, so odds are that other members of the killer's people were killed. But who took the dead bodies?*

*The intruders were Russian but some spoke with different foreign accents. Perhaps a mixed bunch of mercenaries trained by foreign military outfits but with extensive experience and time spent in Russia. The leader had serious military training. Tactics and weapons-use at this level are not available to the common infantry. The other two men sounded as if they may have been European citizens who had learned Russian.*

As Jake waited for the encryption, he measured two cups of rice and put it on the stove. He found a tin of curry-flavored tuna in the pantry. The rice boiled and he sat down to a hot bowl for lunch. His watch read one-forty-two.

The laptop whirred. Armitage crossed to the sink and washed his bowl. He dumped the left-over rice and tuna in a container and placed it in the fridge.

A loud beep dragged Jake from his thoughts. The laptop chimed a second time. He leaned over and clicked the mouse. A prompt box appeared on the screen.

'File unlocked. Access granted.'

The agent clicked the mouse twice, which opened the directory layered with security. Icons flashed on the screen; an audio file with digital voice recording of a conversation.

He opened the first file named:

'Conversation 1: Campaign Advisor Ellard to President elect August 3$^{rd}$ 2016.'

Lines of dialogue confirmed that the transcript seemed real.

*It involves the president. My country. But does it prove who were the guilty parties?*

Armitage opened another directory folder labelled 'President elect emails 2016' with six separate documents in chronological order. He clicked on the first.

'Email 1: Campaign Advisor Bremer to President elect August 8<sup>th</sup> 2016.'

The document contained an email converted into an Office Word page. Armitage skimmed down the sentences. The content contained information about the Democratic representative who had ultimately lost the election.

Jake held his breath as he absorbed the words. The unauthorized emails from the Democratic representative contravened the law. Campaign advisor Bremer must have given this collateral to a Russian contact to be used in a social media slur campaign against the President's Democratic opposition.

*I cannot believe this evidence has surfaced now.*

The agent opened the next document labelled:

'Email 2: Campaign Advisor Ellard to Russian National One August 16<sup>th</sup> 2016.'

The screen blinked as Jake's eyes flickered over the transcript. This email had been in response to a request by the Russian party for synergy between the two governments. The union should be transparent and would come with further benefits for both countries if the U.S. President should be elected to office.

A bird fluttered over the balcony and landed noisily on the outdoor settee. The agent stretched in the chair and took time to reflect. His pulse pounded with the realisation that Seaver had helped Jake talk himself into this mission.

*I've sucked myself in with my perfectionism.*

Jake stood and arched his shoulders, his spine clicked, providing small relief. As he performed laps of the lounge, the new discovery swirled through his mind.

The ramifications of possessing this proof were

enormous. Jake stopped at the tinted windows that overlooked the balcony. The criminal trials against these two campaign advisors had concluded already with both Ellard and Bremer sentenced to prison terms. An outcome which had divided America and again placed distrust on all government, past and present. These emails, if revealed, may trigger a retrial and have far reaching impact on the American President and his tenure as the leader of the free world.

The sofa squeaked as Jake sat behind the computer. He examined the transcripts again, looking for anything he missed. Other documents within the encrypted folder had names of campaign advisors and dates of either a conversation or an email. Six in total. Jake's finger shook a little as he plugged in the headphone jack and turned up the volume.

It took a big piece of evidence to rattle Jake Armitage.

White noise static filled his ears. An American man's deep voice resonated—calm and smooth as pebbles falling on velvet. The advisor went on to request the suppression of classified emails. In reply, the other man, who sounded younger and had a slight European accent, confirmed this would be completed.

Armitage hit the pause button and leaned into the cushion. He stared at the screen. A dog barked somewhere close, breaking his concentration. The forecasted audience of the proposed media covered over seventy percent of the adult American population.

Most importantly, it reached ninety percent of the voting demographic.

The audio file icon flashed. The agent pressed play. The American with the smooth voice said this information could not be discussed on the phone.

"All will be revealed in due course." The American paused.

The younger European replied, "Our organisation is very interested in securing this project. We have all the necessary requirements in place and will do anything to secure it. Implementation is just a few clicks away."

Armitage tried to ascertain the exact origin of the second man's accent but the words became jumbled and faint. The audio recording hit the end. He replayed the same section, straining to make out each word. The rest of the conversation consisted of small talk and banter.

Then it struck Jake. The mystery accent had to be Russian. It was faint and diluted by years in Mediterranean countries like Greece.

The call ended on five minutes and thirty-seven seconds.

Armitage sent the information to his headquarters. The time read seven-nineteen P.M. He turned off the laptop and slugged the last of his instant coffee.

A cold beer sat on the top shelf. The agent swiped the cap and sunk into the sofa. He hadn't slept in forty hours. The liquid travelled down his throat and he relaxed.

He flipped the lights and climbed into bed. The clock radio numbers read nine-fifty P.M. He needed to get at least eight hours sleep before getting up again at seven A.M.

The evidence rang through his mind over and over. A mission that grew far bigger than expected. Agency heads demanded full disclosure on such sensitive data but Jake knew he had to be strategic on who he told.

*Can I trust Seaver with these files?*

And what he had told. Both to domestic and foreign governments. Everybody looked out for themselves.

*I have one clue. Zero help from U.S. home base.*

*What's new?*

In light of this information, Jake's handler and superior would be told of the drive's content in his own time. His mind reeled with the possibilities of this discovery as he dozed off into sleep.

# Chapter 8

Morning broke through the shades. The agent squinted and flexed his fingers. They ached from the recent gun fight. He pulled on a t-shirt and jeans and padded out to the kitchen.

The fridge had little in the way of edible breakfast food. A bowl of cereal with the last of some milk filled Jake's stomach. He'd left the balcony window open to allow fresh air into the lounge.

*Maybe I should call Melissa and ask her to check the new database. She's still a senior officer at Forte Meade.*

A headache formed as Jake thought about his ex-partner.

The agent limped to the balcony and peered across the gap. The breakfast staff started meals at dawn. A screech of tire rubber on cement floated up as a delivery truck shuddered to a halt in the alley. The driver waved a hand out the window. A door slammed and the driver jumped onto the landing.

Jake brewed an instant coffee, showered and towelled himself.

*I've hacked the flash drive but what do I do with it?*

The first line of enquiry, with a high-ranking colonel in the Russian army who investigated the mafia network in Saint Petersburg, would be the dagger tattoo..

In the elevator, Jake practised his speech to the colonel; a hard veteran who didn't sympathise about a single person. He wondered, and not for the first time, if the aging Russian had even cared about his mother. The doors opened as he sped over the old flooring and into the foyer.

The morning hung gloomy and overcast. Gray clouds let

only slithers of red break the horizon. Across the parking lot, a mist from the morning chill lifted with a westerly breeze. Armitage's view sharpened on commuters converging over Nevsky Avenue. Peak hour traffic appeared as if from the fog.

Armitage started the car and headed over town into the industrial zone, cutting past the old palace on the city limits. The bronze-colored walls of the residence towered over the freeway, favoured retreat of the President when he stayed in his birth city. Pigeons gathered at the base of a driveway fountain, squabbling over scraps of bread thrown by tourists.

The ramp ascended to the freeway and flowed into a bypass. Concrete columns held up the newly appointed arterial over the warehouse hulks and shipping containers. Jake floored the accelerator pedal, weaved in and out of the traffic. He glided over the smallest river in the city, the skyscrapers fading from the rear-view mirror. His appointment with the colonel of the Russian army was at seven-thirty and this was not a man he wanted to keep waiting.

At the next sign, Jake exited the freeway and cut through a cluster of large multi-story houses. Each with its own unique history, most predated the nineteenth century. Rural residential blocks dotted the landscape. Greens and yellows were painted on facades countless times over centuries, dozens of square windows dotted each structure. In his wake, a breeze swayed through the trees that hovered above the boulevard as silent, giant sentinels.

The hills dipped and fell, climbed higher as they came up to meet the horizon. Glimpses of sunlight broke through the clouds. Jake zipped through moist pastures saddled with silver sheds and tractors. Agricultural landscape surrounded a military base tucked away in the regional outskirts of Saint

Petersburg.

Streets narrowed as gravel replaced asphalt. The agent slowed at a junction and read the signpost. Stones flicked against the fenders. He took the next right. Overhead a turbine engine whined as a lone fighter jet descended onto a runway hidden beyond the rise. Jake calculated the base must be within three kilometers away. In the distance, he detected the rumble of other aircraft coming and going. He glanced at the GPS which issued instructions in a robotic voice.

Armitage steered right at a junction and drove up a short stretch of gravel. He slowed down to thirty kilometers per hour and turned toward a chain-link fence topped with razor wire protruding over the nearby ridge.

Lanky security personnel, dressed in a combination of various military fatigues, patrolled the perimeter. A man grasped an MP 15 rifle at waist height and looked ready to fire at a moment's notice. Jake pulled up and idled the car while shuffling in the glove box. He found the document that the colonel had given him a year ago. This registered Jake as an authorized civilian and allowed him onto the base.

"Here you go." Jake handed the paper over. His face defaulted to a neutral expression in line with the sombre mood of Russia. The guard spoke into a collar mike while he stared at the paper. A group of soldiers marched around a corner in the distance. They chanted a Russian military song. Jake looked back as the boom gate rose. The guard stepped up and waved him into a secured zone.

Over a hump, the ground levelled out and he could see a repurposed neo-Byzantine palace looming beyond the checkpoint. A green button lit up on a panel as he arrived at the intercom on a set of iron gates.

"Jake Armitage. Colonel Petrov is expecting me," said

the agent who switched to Russian when speaking to military personnel. A bleep sounded, followed by whirring as the imposing metal entrance parted.

Falls of light bounced off the faded mahogany desk of Colonel Petrov. The agent crossed the thick carpet to a solid credenza filled with framed photographs and trophies. The colonel sat behind solid timber overlooked by a large bay window.

Petrov shook hands with Jake. The large Russian stood over six-feet tall and tipped the scales at least at two-hundred and eighty pounds. A messy divorce had worsened the already shot nerves of this decorated officer.

Armitage sunk into a leather armchair across from the colonel. The walls were covered with military paraphernalia and not a spot had been left bare. Nobody had told the colonel that the major wars had passed. Perhaps the Russian didn't care to know. For in the colonel's mind, another battle raged somewhere in the world and usually involved the mother country. Jake stretched his legs in front while waiting for Petrov to begin.

"What do you have for me?" Petrov remained standing and cast a shadow over the furniture.

"There's been an asset murdered in a house last night. Three mercenaries came and did a clean-up soon after," Jake said and locked gazes.

"You haven't been running an operation in my country without full disclosure again?" The colonel paced by the window of his aging war-room.

The agent had contemplated the risk of coming here versus the value of not cooperating with the local forces. He had decided the former would produce success long term.

"Not a chance, Colonel. Sharing is caring." Jake smiled.

"Ah...huh." The Russian grunted. A cigar lay on the table surface and Jake suspected the Russian fought the urge to light up. On this occasion, Petrov resisted out of courtesy.

*That's got to be a good sign.*

"Once the FSB get involved, it's out of my hands." The officer paused at the glass and peered out at the cold mountains. Behind the imposing mansion, a row of steel sheds pointed north. A pasture of thick grass gave way to a line of runway. Ground staff, engaged in different tasks, dotted the landscape.

The agent nodded and rotated to face the Russian.

"I understand but hoped you might identify any of these guys I encountered last night before the FSB come on board." He hesitated before continuing. "This may benefit us both to get cracking early."

A huge globe mounted in an antique mahogany frame sat near the desk. Jake scanned the room as something new always seemed to grab his attention. On the wall a collection of medals hung behind glass that hovered proudly above a mini antique side-table. His gaze fell on paper, red and blue ink scribbled throughout, on a small table surface.

"As long as we don't break protocol...too much. What description do you have on this team?" Petrov moved around and stood opposite Jake.

Jake squinted to see more detailson the old-school color pin-boards outlining boundaries and territories. Other markers protruded through yellowed maps, littered on the major regions of conflict and battle scenes.

"A blond, tall thug that wasn't one of the mafia guys. No doubt this guy has serious military training. But special weapons and tactical stuff, not your regular troops."

The finer intent of such placements was a combat mystery that could mean something only to the large Russian. In between the whiteboards with permanent marker lines hung smaller sections of Syria, Afghanistan and Iraq. A different shade of blue indicated Northern Syria where various terrorist cells had taken over.

"Anything else?" the big man's eyebrows joined over his nose bridge like a caterpillar.

Armitage nodded. "The dead man in the kitchen had tattoos; a star on the right hand and full sleeve on the other."

The colonel bounced on his feet. A gaze narrowed to a squint, as if going through an internal checklist of possible suspects. Jake knew this body language cue. The Russian had more than passing knowledge on this mafia organization._

Petrov said, "Stars are common with Russian convicts and indicate rank or authority."

*You're not fobbing me off with that.*

The colonel paced toward his mounted world globe, throwing his gaze on Jake intermittently as if testing for weaknesses.

The agent always wondered if Petrov ever used these maps anymore. He considered the Russian's aversion to digital, and the mass of ink marks, and worked out the answer without asking.

"Yes, but this star ink had a dagger through it. It's different and new."

The colonel paused. "Are you sure?"

"I'm positive as I took him down myself."

A bottle of Smirnoff sat on a silvered tray as if the

prized elixir was calling its master from across the room.

Petrov poured the vodka into a glass. He stood and sunk the contents.

Jake watched a light sheet of rain batter the window. It caused a bluish sheen that reflected off the ground outside. He waited while the old Russian conjured his next sentence.

Petrov cleared his throat. "These tattoos are a hybrid version on the star ranking. A new criminal sect has risen within prison culture. The dagger through the middle indicates you'll die for your fellow members." The colonel squinted. "A member for life. Someone from my team took down one of them in an incident."

"A new form of radical belief for the average felon?" Jake shuffled in the chair.

"Yes, in manner of speaking. A person in this group will stop at nothing to complete a company objective or commandment. The level of commitment is fanatical. Like that of a death cult." Petrov's gaze found the markings on his wall map. "A member of this club is effectively a terrorist."

Armitage said quickly, "If we can work together on this matter, both countries will benefit, including your army as well."

"The problem is growing like a cancer through Russia."

"What now, Colonel?" Jake's eyes found the Russian as he circled the war room again.

"I need to convince my colleagues of your participation." Petrov pointed at the door.

The agent shook his head in the affirmative but stayed silent.

The colonel stared from behind his desk. "The FSB won't allow this murder you spoke of last night to go unchecked. Not as bad as the KGB, but many times I wonder. Someone from the department will take over and investigations give me a headache."

Petrov coughed out of a double-barreled chest. The gaze dropped again to the cigar protruding from a pile of paperwork.

"You know those things will kill you?"

Petrov shot Jake raisin-eyes so he pretended not to notice. The sooner this meeting closed the better.

*I wonder what the heating bill is on this fortress during winter.*

"I have activity in Saint Petersburg but I need complete autonomy with this investigation." The agent straightened his spine, wondered which ID he could use. "The price of capture is too high."

Armitage was a veteran of such clandestine meetings, always off the books for both sides. He reflected on the hardened Moyka River; it's blue-green surface disappeared at a base of rugged blacktops.

The officer paced and shook his head. "Let see how this plays out, shall we?"

A large statue, mounted on a marble base, sat on a ledge. Jake examined the group. A man in loincloth held a spear. The weapon pointed at a panther.

"I'll need something from your government. Assurances I have immunity should things get complicated." Jake rubbed his lumbar.

Outside, a wall of snow clustered the granite ridges, already dribbling truck-size portions toward the city.

The Russian noticed his gaze. "It's called 'The Hunt'. An original deco piece made nearly one-hundred years ago. A hunter about to spear the panther. Majestic and primordial. It reminds me never to be the panther. The prey."

Jake nodded and admired the workmanship.

"It's by Chiparus, the master of art deco." The colonel squinted at the mountain tops. "It will take time to process this authority." He bounced on the balls of his feet as if to relieve anxiety that clotted in the room. "You understand due process?"

"This request must be fast-tracked or the matter will be buried in administration." Jake shook his head. He leaned forward, placed his elbows on the desk. "The incident takes priority over all other projects."

Petrov's face flushed red and he punched the table surface with his palm. The old man swivelled to Jake, his eyes beady and black. "Let me get onto my staff and I'll call it either way by today."

The agent caught the powerful stare and maintained eye contact. Well practiced in staring down opponents. The two military superpowers, his country and Russia, had been in regular standoff and conflict since the Second World War.

Now an endless Cold War. This conflict wasn't any different.

Armitage scribbled a number on a piece of paper and pushed it across the desk. "That's where you can reach me."

An oily sheen reflected off the colonel's head. It might be another fifty years of tense relations. What could he do?

Petrov stared at the number and nodded. "We can talk soon."

Fog spiralled through the air, as if a wayward spirit

seeking closure, tinged phosphorescent by slithers of light breaking the thick morning air.

The old soldier lowered into an armchair, sighed as marching cries echoed from a distant parade. At any given time, a major military event unfolded somewhere within the Federation borders. Impending sleet, snow, and minus-zero temperature did little to slow these dedicated patriots.

The agent turned and faced the exit.

"Don't do anything we haven't approved of first." The Russian typed Jake's number into his smartphone. "I've called your number just now so you have my new one as well. Meeting at the base may be off-limits until further notice."

"You know me, Colonel." Jake arched his arms out.

"That's why I'm saying this to you." Petrov shook his head. "And Armitage..."

"Yes."

"Don't be the panther. Ever."

An American spy colluding in a Russian officer's suite —sacrilegious for both parties. These European military outfits took only themselves seriously. The rest of the world were lesser peasants who existed in the enormous and charitable shadow of the mother country. For Jake, this discussion must occur as a necessary evil. The motive was two-way, that much he assured himself.

The agent ignored the negative ideas that swam in his head. He'd have to get moving before the evidence trail went cold.

From the window, framed by limited sky, Petrov rose. The leather groaned under his movement.

"Thanks for the information, Colonel."

Petrov nodded and locked gazes. "I'm serious about this; FSB can't know too much as they'll try to take over the investigation."

"Got it. I'll be in touch through the burner phone." Jake walked out and pushed through a door that led into the fire escape.

He longed for a power nap, to drift off for even thirty minutes.

Too much to do.

As Jake climbed the concrete steps, the realization dawned that the colonel might be setting him up.

*What did he mean by the panther comment?*

*I'll find out soon enough.*

# Chapter 9

At near noon, Jake plugged the address of the city's biggest media company into the GPS. He merged with traffic and took off southwest toward Nevsky Prospekt. Russians called the major roads Prospekt. The route took him into the cobbled lanes that ran along the Fontanka River.

Thin slivers of yellow beams parted the gray chunk of clouds, faux biblical. Jake lowered the window halfway. A brisk breeze floated in the car as the sidewalks clicked with street hawkers and pedestrians. Gathered on the riverbank, the sellers had a similar array of products.

Armitage passed by the tent canopies. The displays, of fridge magnets, babushka dolls, key rings and models packed on shelves, blurred. Sightseers swarmed the walkways, haggling and taking photos. Cameras clicked at the multi-colored domes of the *Church of the Saviour of Spilled Blood*.

Despite the recent departure of the World Cup festivities, walkways and parks pulsed with supporters. Citizens donned their team colours. The walls were covered with posters depicting paraphernalia of football.

The agent turned onto Nevsky Avenue as a band of buskers pumped out English cover songs. A crowd gathered around the musicians, live vocals and music overpowering the rushing water and traffic.

The colonel's information on the ink put Jake on a new path. Low level thugs needed a leader. These guys were being guided by an organized faction.

*I need to find out who.*

It bothered Jake that he didn't know the colonel's motive yet. Petrov gave crucial intel but he knew the colonel could not be trusted.

Armitage watched the building numbers and heard the chants and cries of a generation echoed along the river. The memories of his time walking this street seven years ago flickered out as Jake focused toward the neoclassical structure ahead.

A mid-eighteenth-century mansion with its original façade loomed into view. The style, brought from Western Europe over two-hundred years ago, had left its mark on the port city.

Armitage eased behind a black SUV and killed the engine. He pressed the car fob as he waited for the double-glass door with a bell symbol splayed onto the surface. It opened into the most well-known and oldest print media outlet in St Petersburg.

The agent reached the far corner on ground level. A stainless-steel panel displayed the floor numbers and office tenants. He pushed the button for Bell Media Group and stepped through the doors.

At level three the elevator pinged. Jake pressed on over the linoleum-tiled flooring and observed the pace of the publishing house. A line to a large coffee machine snaked around the side, disappearing behind a corner edge. He glanced over the partitioned cubicles that separated each employee, scanning the workers for his contact.

A sea of faces bobbed over the phone pods and workstations. Dozens of conversations created a cacophony Jake could almost see hovering overhead. He moved through the employees and pivoted to avoid bumping and collisions.

Down the corridor, a bottleneck of journalists crammed in the main corridor to a capacity greater than appeared possible. Armitage waited for a woman in a power-suit. She grasped a mug in her right hand and was deep in conversation with a bookish, middle-aged man. The two reporters angled toward a corner office.

"I'm after Katerina Venski, please?" Jake asked a young man who didn't slow his pace. The staff member pointed to a cubicle at the end of the next aisle.

Venski's cubicle sat wedged against a far wall at the end of the middle passage. A patchwork of frayed carpet marked the office entrance. Jake snaked his way through desks and bodies, narrowly missing various media employees.

Makeshift glass panes comprized the top half and were joined to fabricated divider bases from waist height. A name plate tacked to the frame displayed *Katerina Venski* in faded gold lettering.

Jake halted at the edge of her office. Venski inhabited a walled-off corner position neater and more organized than most of her colleagues. Jake waited for her to acknowledge his presence. She chatted on her mobile and typed with one finger on a keyboard. He cleared his throat after standing at the desk for two minutes.

The maverick reporter swung around to face Jake and gestured to the only seat. He lowered into the swivel chair opposite her worn but organized desk. The reporter's voice dropped as she raised her arm.

After Venski threw more hand gesticulations with the rise and fall of her chair, his host terminated the call and placed her smartphone on the in-tray. Her lips formed a grin as she looked him up and down and grasped his hand in a firm shake.

"Well, Jake, what can we do this time?" She spoke English with only a hint of a Russian accent remaining. "Normally you call in your questions. A personal visit, huh. This one must be really important."

Jake smiled. "Hope you're well, Katerina. I won't take up too much of your time. Can you please get information on a story your media covered two years ago here in St. Petersburg?"

"This sounds intriguing." Her hazel eyes sparkled. "Which one are you referring to?"

Before Jake began, he eased forward. "It's about how the Kremlin became compromized by a massive cyber-attack. I need any information on the hackers involved as well."

Katerina nodded, "Don't worry; no one can hear you with this noise. I'll see what I have."

*Amazing how any worker can concentrate with so much activity and noise. Must be something you get used to.*

"When a new story breaks, we have to get it first." The Russian journalist sighed and flicked between two monitors. She brought up an old archive and began speed reading.

"That day you're asking about, the President was rushed out of Moscow." She glanced at Jake. "I remember this story."

"That's the one. You were nearby when he exited the mansion?"

"I missed it." Katerina turned to her screen and clicked the mouse. "Here we go. I went across town to cover another story and couldn't make it before this matter unfolded."

She called up a file.

"Let's see what I can find."

The Russian reporter pivoted the screen toward Jake. The cursor dashed across the platform showing newspaper articles. She clicked on the date in a drop-down box, first the year, followed by the month.

"Here we go." She pointed a slender finger at a calendar entry. "This article here I wrote myself. It was a Saturday and overcast that day. Funny weather for late summer." The journalist paused and chewed on the end of her pen. "I wrote the smaller article but it got closer to the front cover. It's position, not size, that counts in the media business. We both scrambled to press to score the biggest piece of the year. For a moment, the editor thought my story had been the only one to make print. Afterwards the freelancer trumped the larger article, but I had the real detail."

The journalist's eyes sparkled at the thought, a wistful expression on her face. She shook herself from memory lane. "Check this out. It's an interview I did with the whistle-blower that never went live or to print." She aimed her finger at the section.

Jake nodded as he concentrated on the screen.

The sentences were in a large font. The agent skimmed and digested the content. The whistle-blower claimed the cyber-attack on the Kremlin was the first part of the strategy. Two months prior, another political outcome had been tampered with through a sophisticated network of Russian hackers. The coders and hackers had infiltrated a foreign government system and influenced results through social media. Jake's stomach lurched as the detail unraveled.

In the transcript, Katerina had asked if the information had been published or released anywhere. The interviewee answered that his source had been silenced.

*How did this story stay supressed for so long?*

More than five minutes lapsed as Jake finished the

fourth page. What started as a threat had escalated to mammoth proportions. A network of Russian hackers that held the President of the United States to ransom. A tampering conspiracy to end all and trigger the impeachment of the leader of the free world.

If it could be proven.

Venski had unverified evidence.

The last paragraph revealed the source worked for a government contractor and the business had inside and first-hand knowledge of transactions.

"Who was the contractor?"

Katerina said, "SPG Partners were the consultancy firm the whistle-blower mentioned...but off the record."

"So, according to your source, this did happen. His company, SPG Partners, were in deep." Jake leaned away from the screen. The possibilities flooded his mind.

"Someone leaked this story to the media so I got there first." She crossed her arms and smiled. "But I kept the interview confidential as I didn't want to risk putting myself in danger. It's very easy to become a target in this business."

"Wise decision." Even though the temperature gauge read fifty-nine degrees Fahrenheit, Jake's palms were sweaty. He wiped his hands on his jeans.

The journalist watched him and nodded. "It's not hundred percent proven that they hacked the US political system. This scandal came during a depressing and gloomy economic period. In fact, this sentiment has been lingering for years. It lightened the public mood, if only briefly. People were distracted for a moment with thinking Russia may return as an economic superpower with global influence." She chuckled, but a sadness reflected in her eyes.

The agent took a deep breath and straightened in his chair. "Can you please print me a copy of this? The English version is preferable."

"Normally I couldn't, as you know." She paused and stared past him at the office noise. "But because you gave me the first break on the Ukrainian arms dealer a few months back I'll do this for you. Give me two minutes and it's done." She tapped the keyboard and headed to a large printer set up against a wall.

Through the glass, Jake tuned to the mad rush of media employees. Although spying was dangerous for your health, this new threat would destabilize the peace of the free world.

Venski returned and handed Jake the printouts. "Here you go, but Jake, this cannot leak to any outside media. OK?" She shot him a serious expression. "Don't show this to anyone."

"I understand. Please trust me, it's safe, and again, thank you."

"Maybe we get a drink later?"

"Sure. Do you know anywhere good?"

Katerina shook her head. "There's a bar two blocks from here. On a street that runs off Nevsky. I'll meet you on the corner at eight P.M."

"Look forward to it and thanks for these again."

She smiled. "No problem."

Armitage stood and maneuvered into the working frenzy. The elevator bay had cleared since his arrival. Three people waited in the bay.

The seriousness, and the players in this conspiracy, had clicked up a level or two. Jake stared at the paper copy of the transcript. As the elevator descended, Jake considered the possible danger for Katerina.

Visitors waited in single file at the reception desk. The agent handed in his tag, signed off and exited the large, automatic doors. He glanced at the papers Venski had given him. She could be risking her life by showing them to an American agent. A protective emotion swelled inside him as the risks ran through his mind.

Jake left the lobby and faced the exterior. Strangers rushed past on the cracked cement. The frosty air penetrated the layers of his coat. He pulled the zipper up to his throat.

Merging with the pedestrian flow, Jake shoved the folded transcript in a pocket.

# Chapter 10

In the gathering night chill, Jake turned the corner. Katerina waited under the glow of a streetlight. The Russian reporter wore slim jeans and two-inch heels. A chic jacket to keep out the cold. Casual and stylish. Her eyes, copper-hazel in the semi-darkness, were framed by shoulder-length brown hair.

"You're looking beautiful tonight," Jake said.

"You make a girl blush." She laughed and pulled him to the curb.

Nevsky blurred red with a stream of car lights. She took his hand and guided him along a side street. A Gothic building with a market cast a shadow over the asphalt.

"The club is over the next intersection." Katerina pointed to a sign overhanging the sidewalk. Music pumped from the spot, the beat volume increasing as they neared the venue.

For a moment, Jake forgot to check for watchers. Lost in the moment, his paranoia vanished.

Voices sounded from different directions. Jake glanced over his shoulder at a group of three young people clustered in an alcove. Blue smoke trails rose from the shadows. Chatter and laughter followed. The dress code was smart casual. Fashionable. Garments had no sign of concealed weapons. No one made or avoided eye contact.

Katerina paused under the club's neon sign. A small line waited to enter. She nodded at a bouncer. The muscle-bound giant waved as Jake followed under the rope and down a flight of stairs. They spilled onto a black dance floor. Lights flashed and bass vibrated through his feet and up his legs. The bar wrapped around to a set of toilets. A DJ on a raised mezzanine section had one hand on turntables, the other waving at the patrons.

"Let's go to the bar. I need a vodka." She angled into a wall of patrons. The smell of beer and vodka fumes clouded his senses. Armitage remembered to check faces as they forged a trail to the bar.

The female bartender winked at Katerina as she poured vodka into two glasses. Straight up and one-by-one. Liquid flowed from the bottle and swelled over the ice. The bartender inclined her head and backed away. A hand grasped the second spirit tumbler.

The agent paid and they sipped the beverages in a corner. The music flowed as a warm sensation filled his stomach. It took the edge off the day. His stress started to ease and take a back seat.

"Nothing like vodka to warm your insides." Jake smiled as they bunched closer on the padded seats. The décor was simple and rustic. Timber planks lined the wall, painted with a basic black mix. A night club didn't need a five-star interior to succeed. Only patrons willing to buy drinks.

"Come with me." Katerina weaved away from the bar.

Armitage trailed behind her to the dance floor.

"I need to tell you something," he said as she turned.

Katerina swung her hips, swirling with the beat. Strobe beams curved over her lithe figure.

*I can't concentrate when she looks so good.*

"Tell me later," she said, spinning on one foot.

Jake read her lips as the music drowned out her words.

The next drink loosened Jake some more. They took spots on the edge of the dancing zone. Strobe lights spun in his eyes as he concentrated on Katerina.

A sudden niggle began in the base of his neck. Jake examined the patrons. Couples gyrated to the beat, concentrating on each other or off in la-la-land.

The gut instinct never failed. Jake's gaze reached the far wall. Groups of tables and stools sat in a zone thirty feet from their position. He scanned the individual faces, never stopping longer than a second. Most were in their twenties, absorbed in the hedonist atmosphere.

The agent smiled at Katerina, who spun on the spot. He swept the west side of the partition.

A man waited alone. Loose jacket over a button-down shirt that could conceal a weapon holster. Worn jeans. Sturdy but light-weight boots. The subject looked in his mid-thirties. Erect posture. Lean and fit: not too much bulk. Assured and confident. Brown-hair. Six-one. Out-of-place in this environment. The clothes were wrong. The man tried too hard to blend.

*This guy is a watcher. He's been made.*

Armitage covered the south end. Watchers work in pairs, the partner probably a female. His gaze reached the far wall. A pair kissed in the darkened corner.

Katerina dragged Jake to the bar. The bartender leaned and shouted over the music. She ordered two more vodkas. The agent scanned the spot he'd seen the brown-haired watcher. A woman swayed drunkenly in the same position.

No military guy. The stranger had disappeared.

*Were we followed and by whom? How could they know to identify us already? I knew my counter surveillance wasn't up to standard tonight.*

Armitage worked backwards. He'd seen Katerina at the media company offices. The route back to his apartment had been in busy traffic. He'd applied super-vigilance as always.

*Unless they stalked Katerina's place.* A chill went through his spine. *How much do these guys know? Who are they: mafia, Russian intelligence operatives or military?*

The music tempo changed to drum and bass. Trance-type music was not his favorite but he swayed along as his mind raced. Katerina smiled and spun. If their enemies had traced Jack over this short period, Jake would need to get Katerina out fast.

"Are you having a good time?" Katerina said.

Armitage's eyes came into focus.

*I must look crazed, staring into the distance.*

"Sorry, Katerina. Yes, this place is pumping. I have a lot on my mind." Jake time put the vodka glass on the nearest tabletop. He placed his hands on her hips. She held his hips as they swayed. Over her shoulder, Jake gazed at the seating zone again. The man had to be near, unless he'd recognized Jake and retreated.

In an hour, the club became packed with twenty-something Russians having a night out. The atmosphere elevated with music. Aromas of alcohol and sweat stifled the air.

At the bar, Jake declined another drink.

"Would you like a vodka?" he said to Katerina.

The Russian reporter shook her head. "Do you want to leave? I'm feeling light-headed after that last dance."

The agent nodded. They weaved around the floor and climbed the stairs. A waft of cold air blended with cigarette smoke greeted them. He could see smokers on every corner.

"I'll walk with you to your apartment."

Katerina smiled. "I'm five minutes away."

"I won't take no for an answer."

The watcher in the night club would remain Jake's secret. For the time being anyway. He didn't wish to alarm Katerina unless absolutely necessary.

A light drizzle coated the buildings with a fine mist. Streetlights reflected in puddles. Jake scanned the late revelers for familiar faces, the watcher he'd caught out in the club on his mind.

Katerina pulled the hood of her coat over her head. The night life hummed, groups converging on nearby bars. Larger crowds made it easier for stalkers to slip through undetected.

The agent looked for signs. Unnatural behaviour. Things out of place. A trio of women stumbled in high heels. One collapsed across her friend's shoulder. Harmless youths out for a night of partying.

More drunks stumbled across the uneven concrete. He stared past the females at a woman powerwalking. A building shadowed a slab. The single woman was distracted by a cell phone in her right hand.

*I'm sure I recognize her, but from where?*

On the opposite curb, the lights turned green. The agent walked over the lines, anxious to check the mystery woman's face. She got close.

Armitage maintained visual. Blue eyes and dark brown hair. Buzz cut. He turned his gaze at the last moment. It hit him. A sledgehammer to the skull. The military guy's partner he'd spotted in the club.

*This watcher team are professionals. Not the best, but above average. Don't do anything to stick out or draw attention.*

A public fight would showcase Jake's skills.

The Russian reporter pulled his arm sleeve.

The agent shook his daze and focused on Katerina.

"Sorry, what did you say?" His breath condensed fog. Shadows flickered over the window edges and arches seemed to close in.

"I'm feeling better in the cold night air." She did a twirl in her heels."It's liberating."

At the corner, Katerina pointed to a faded yellow stucco building. "This is me."

"Thank you for a lovely night, Katerina."

"My pleasure." She leaned forward and pecked him on the cheek. "Let's do it again. I'll be in touch about the transcript soon."

"Thanks again." Jake released her hand. He waited until Katerina had unlocked her door and disappeared into the entrance. The breeze tugged at his jacket. He regretted dragging her into this conspiracy, despite her investigative profession. Such a level of danger put her in a compromized position.

The dim lights of Nevsky Prospekt shimmered in the distance. Jake watched the door creak to the jamb. He let the stress and worry drain from his body. The night air bit into his skin as he walked back to his car. He liked the cold as it kept him alert, focused on potential danger lurking in every shadow.

Armitage flexed his fingers. He didn't wear gloves, preferring dexterity over comfort. Drawing a concealed firearm took speed. The finger can get caught on the trigger. In a confrontation, a second could mean the difference between life or death.

The apartment appeared different: surreal and foreign. Weariness fell over Jake's body. He pulled off his jacket and tossed his jeans on a chair. The pillow bounced as his head swam with images of faces. Enemies were everywhere, even in his dreams.

*I've got to find a new career.*

# Chapter 11

*The floor came up hard. Jake's cheek pressed against the canvas. His head swam. Pools of sweat and blood. Palms pressed as he pushed to his knees.*

*Sweat trickled into his eyes. A bare foot swung out of the fog. Arms blocked instinctively.*

*Where am I?*

*Armitage pivoted and swept his leg at the figure. His ankle connected. Whoosh! A body crumpled.*

*Voices screamed. A language Jake knew. The smell and smoke. A fevered atmosphere.*

*Bangkok.*

*Training camp.*

*"You won, kid."*

*A hand lifted Jake's arm. Propped between two shoulders. The breeze cooled his face. Noise faded. A mattress underneath.*

*The van door slammed. Darkness. Bumps in the road.*

*Brakes creak. Doors opened.*

*"See you, Armitage. You're done."*

*Gravel hit his check. The agent stumbled to his feet. A dirt road. The orange sun burned overhead. His feet ached. No choice but get to the locker and the airport.*

The agent woke to the sound of footsteps echoing within the bowels of his ancient residence. He sucked in air and realized his heart hammered against his ribs. The morning rush of the restaurant serving early-bird patrons. He switched the alarm to silent and climbed out of bed.

The stone benchtops lit up like burning coals as Jake zipped his carryall. Rare weather for this time of year, he decided to go out. He managed to avoid other residents in the elevator, much to Jake's relief, and reached his car without incident. Five hours of sleep would have to suffice. He thought of the body aches, both new and old, and hoped the anti-inflammatory medication he popped at breakfast kicked fast.

Downtown Saint Petersburg swelled with a steady stream of office commuters. Jake merged with the traffic flow. People marched relentlessly across the city and the main avenues were full of shoppers no matter the time of day.

Armitage parked and took out Katerina's interview transcript. The impact the hacking scandal had on Russia had been as big here as the U.S. Solid evidence like this was gold and very hard to locate. He looked over the sheets and digested the words, reading between the lines. Page one started with a brief introduction. In the second, she launched into the one-line questions.

Speed reading pages three to seven, her questions turned bold. The Russian reporter drew out the interviewee with an effective investigative style.

A talent in its own right.

Commuters rushed past Jake. He maintained concentration on the document. There had to be another clue that pointed to something useful.

At the bottom of the last page, Jake found the interviewee's name: Mark Forest. Katerina said Forest had been an American consultant that dealt with the U.S. secretary of state for the first two years of his term.

Marginal lines of light poked through the gray morning

in pink slithers and warmed his neck.

*This guy's answers had to be on the level, but what if he wasn't? I need to check the consultant SPG out before I chase this lead.*

Armitage switched on his laptop. He searched the local Internet on Mark Forest but found little.

*A deep dive into encrypted storage maybe more useful.*

He cracked the layers of law enforcement when he couldn't get any hits on public domains. The second level entry to the DIA database, a sister department to the NSA, gave him superfluous data. The file opened to a collection of documents.

As Jake flicked the pages, he swigged from a water bottle.

Forest had an interesting resume which included lucrative arms deals with Russian, European and Gulf countries.

A long association with questionable parties and transactions showed a degree of guilt. Most of Jake's U.S. expats were white collar executives and consultants with loose practices.

These operators lived on the moral fringes, sociopaths who carved out a profitable career advising other like-minded, rich and powerful entrepreneurs.

Armitage closed the laptop and eased back on the seat. The hardware at his home base had more capability and power to data dive. He stretched and supported his aching lower back._

*Forest may have commanded the hit on the asset himself, therefore pulling the trigger.*

The possibilities were numerous and Jake needed more proof. He placed Katerina's papers in the glovebox.

*I'll ask questions and network until I get a lead.*

The agent started the car and steered into the gap between lanes. He rode the wide avenue past two bronze monuments that depicted military and political figures. The high canopies swayed, creating shadows over the wide highway lanes. Many of these figures were immortalized by sculptors not recognized in their time. Those of royalty or of the cloth had special treatment. The country had a rich cultural tapestry that spanned over a thousand years.

The last block piled up with stationary cars. Armitage slotted behind a line, the front of which disappeared over a rise. A large bus screeched to a halt and the smell of brake fluid reached his nostrils. Jake exited the main drag and descended over the pedestrian walkways. The street curved after a set of traffic lights. He squinted through the windshield, searching the signs for the exit the GPS told him would come up soon.

A cacophony of noise rose from the foreground below his apartment. Jake studied the source. Across the river canal, a group of protestors had congregated at an intersection. For a few hours, this had limited the traffic flow as police struggled to manage the signals properly.

The traffic jam had obstructed the entrance to the parking lot. Additional demonstrators flocked from the south. Signs bobbed in the air as the mob chanted their rights in Russian and demanded action and answers.

Armitage bypassed the bustling protesters, stepped over the pitted cement that overflowed into the marble-floored lobby. He nodded at the empty reception desk and kept moving rapidly toward the corner.

The elevator doors closed with a clang. He crossed the

steel landing and eyed the worn wood panels affixed on the walls. A deep sigh escaped as he sussed out any potential danger.

The strata management refused to update and modernize the décor and furnishings. Jake glanced at the cheap, gold-colored mirrors in the passageway.

*Tacky. Good for remaining unnoticed.*

Armitage deactivated his door sensors. He placed a burner phone and his keys on the countertop. Dust flickered in the sparse light. He settled behind the laptop that fronted the window view of the city. A study desk lay hidden under mountain-sized stacks of paperwork.

The notification chimed as Jake sunk into his keyboard. A mild flashback of the day's events interrupted his concentration.

The agent rose and gazed through the glass at the flurried movement below. A city that pulsed energy always hid a multitude of sins. The dead man's face appeared in Jake's thoughts and he grappled with the possible guilt of involvement.

*If someone was trying to get my attention, why would they leave evidence on a dead body?*

He struggled against the fatigue and drowsiness. Limbs ached. Joints cracked. His work ethic and solving a new dilemma dragged him back to the laptop.

Lines of code streamed. Armitage read as they flashed in number sequences. The scroll bar clicked as he tried to make sense of the data.

Armitage flicked between the laptop and surveillance monitoring in various key locations. He found footage of a bikie bar that could be relevant. Two suspects in a covert conversation. A guttural voice echoed. He adjusted the audio as a potential suspect banged on about a mission that never unfolded. Jake's programs had sorted information from the top sources. He hoped at least two of the biggest suspects would have links inside this information.

The latest mining programs had sifted thousands of files of data communication intel. These had the capability of access to the most accurate information through the major Telcos and satellites.

That's the prime objective of the NSA.

For the second time that week, Jake placed on his gray hat and hacked into the highest security level of the DoD through a backdoor. His own agency. Jake had entered the network the hard way as headquarters wouldn't give him clearance quick enough.

*I'm the one sweating it out in Russia.*

Inside the billions of data bytes, Jake located the target's profile. A large digitally encrypted file popped up marked classified. He circumvented the safe checks and broke the code surrounding the information. It took another ten minutes to disarm the firewall without leaving digital footprints.

This avoidance took the most time and was basically impossible to leave untraced. There would be some temporary evidence of his presence. The justification matched the means; a valuable asset had been murdered.

Armitage never left an easily traceable trail, even hacking his own agency's database. The IT bureaucrats back at Fort Meade, Maryland would discuss clearance and red tape access in their own time.

In six minutes, Jake clicked on the file directory and opened the contents.

The heating pushed warm air into the room as Jake

logged into the database. He clicked into the tables. Local mobile numbers matched with keywords in the database. The first layer.

Jake's second layer would match numbers based on key words and locations. The software improved itself. Artificial intelligence. Next-gen technology had advanced.

Ten years ago, at Red Bull, this process was cutting edge technology. The hacker Jake had worked with on cyber security had showed him how to create the software to evolve and mimic thought.

Mark Compton.

*I wonder where he is now.*

The last Jake heard, the hacker had avoided prison.

A shiver went up Jake's spine.

*We are all living on the fringe of civilization.*

Some more than others.

The agent drilled for specific aliases that connected the murdered victim's description. The program he'd helped implement cross-sectioned information and notified the user if they got a hit.

The search continued for over two hours. Jake completed a file. He rose to relieve a cramp as a notification pulsed. A rumble in his stomach gained traction.

Armitage sighed and repeated his mantra.

*I am energized and fully protected.*

Outside, a noise lifted from a cluster of people. Jake watched at the window, observing the scene unfold. A man in his sixties staggered over the loose asphalt. The clothes on the stranger were thick, but very old. Holes showed in the sleeves and pants.

*A homeless person needing food.*

The agent recognized him as a man who loitered around the kitchen downstairs. Once he'd given the man one-thousand Russian rubles. The man nearly collapsed and Jake thought he'd made a terrible mistake giving him money. He'd convinced the homeless man to buy food, instead of alcohol or drugs, and even escorted him to the nearest supermarket._

The computer beeped at Jake again, so he opened the notification. He clicked the icon and an audio file of conversation number seventy-eight from last Tuesday filled his ears. A person of interest had made a call to Saint Petersburg on the tenth of June, forty-eight hours ago. The number had been tracked to source against a target's last known address. One of the main reasons this dialogue flagged was they mentioned the words 'asset' and 'safehouse'.

The caller, AKA Manny Popov, had been ordered to get a crew together for a hit. No motive yet. The target remained anonymous but the receiver of the call was a known associate of a high-ranking Russian crime figure. These individuals were under heavy surveillance since last week, a team on the ground changing shifts, plus round-the-clock monitoring via drone and satellite.

In the data pool, Jake found the caller's name: Manny Popov. He scanned the list of priors that appeared with basic-level hacking of local law enforcement.

*Popov is a busy boy.*

The rap sheet extended for years. Popov had a dozen serious assault charges, the first in the nineteen-nineties. The Russian beat a murder charge and had convictions for attempted murder. Arms dealing and drugs weren't mentioned but no other convictions were recorded beyond his capabilities either.

Interpol had flagged Popov on a special watch list.

Armitage loaded a photo of Manny Popov. A mugshot taken near two years ago on arrest for attempted murder. He'd gotten off using a great lawyer and probably corruption. Ink extended up Popov's neck, visible in an open t-shirt. Jake scanned through and found another shot that showed his bare upper torso. Tattoos covered most body parts pertaining to prison culture ink.

A dead look in the eyes told him of this enemy's psychotic tendencies.

Other smaller marks, like scars, lined his face. Jake's gaze fell on the right hand. He froze.

On Popov's hand was a star with a dagger through the middle.

*He's one of them.*

# Chapter 12

Armitage zoomed in on the image of Popov's hand until the pixels become blurry and near unreadable. He reverse magnified two times. The image sharpened resolution.

A star and dagger tattoo that represented a new underground sect. The cell secretive enough that few knew it existed. The agent leaned at the screen, calculating the odds of finding these people.

The Russian mafia had targeted the most important asset in decades, if not ever.

*If they had the intel, who else knew about their guy?*

Jake clicked the mouse, lost for a moment in a trance.

Two superpower countries at loggerheads. One influenced a presidential election in the other. But which one?

The screen blinked. A thug's simple prison ink represented such a powerful message. Organized crime and mercenaries chased a flash drive right under their noses? An international matter concerning a foreign government. The power to bring down the leader of the free world.

This had potential to blowout to a global crisis. Armitage exhaled and stared at the screen.

Setting the computer to sleep mode, Jake circled the island bench. This didn't make any sense to him.

*Who would hire these thugs to do such a serious hit?*

He stood at the window. Across the plaza, startled seagulls took flight from the base of a statue. Breadcrumbs lay scattered in their wake. His gaze followed the birds fluttering into the afternoon breeze.

*Unless the contracting party wanted subterfuge to hide*

*the real motive of the murder.*

*Hang on. That's it.*

*The backroom accommodation at the safehouse.*

Jake straightened.

*A dead thug's corpse in the kitchen. In the same house with the asset. The catacomb of bedrooms and bathrooms. Syringes scattered over the floor. The female clothing, drug paraphernalia and other tell-tale signs.*

*The human traffickers were baby-sitting the asset and realized what they had. By that time, it was too late.*

*Part A solved. But what else am I missing?*

*The local mob ran other criminal enterprises. They took the asset to a secure location. But that still didn't explain why they agreed to this complex contract. Perhaps the payoff had been too lucrative to resist. Maybe the mafia heads didn't care who they went up against.*

The agent returned to search mode. He examined other links that explained the association. Another source reported the ties Popov made in his long stretches in prison. Armitage found a loose connection with a politician. He opened the file. The scanned newspaper article flickered on the screen.

A Saint Petersburg politician had been sleeping with a young female hooker. The story reached the media through an anonymous source. One morning the woman's body washed to shore on the banks of one of the rivers. An extensive enquiry ensued after investigations linked her to the politician. The Federation Council voted Adrik Lebedev out of office.

Armitage clicked through the article. He found a report that implicated Popov as the main murder suspect. The case made preliminary hearing but once again the trial was thrown out due to lack of evidence.

Popov has been a lucky guy—so far.

The broader checks on European ties and major terror incidents proved a dead end. The Interpol database had a brief description and a warrant if Popov set foot in an EU country. A deeper profile check revealed two known aliases. Armitage compared the two documents. Great fakes. This group had a sophisticated network of people creating authentic and quality passports by the order.

In two hours, Jake produced little more than a number of possible associates. A tight organization. In all the data correlation and playing Big Brother, he'd searched dozens of emails and calls with key words for Manny Popov. The cursor scrolled through a call bundle and he clicked into the main menu. On the interface, he switched to a digital communications folder, search function activated again.

The list of emails appeared endless, streamed from one of the world's largest data-collecting centers. Mega virtual storerooms, many hidden five-hundred meters subterranean, were managed by the National Security Agency.

In the early days of his training, Jake had descended Fort Meade into the million-square-foot facility and walked the catacombs in awe. Hard drives mounted in enormous racks stacked seven meters high to the open, steel-beamed ceiling. A massive warehouse full of memory. As far as the eye could see, a horizon of endless data memory storage. Millions of bits of global communication data between people and organizations. The previous year he'd heard a rumour that the facility had maxed out the Baltimore-area power grid.

On that day, Jake had reached a central room contained in a glass-like vault. Bullet-proof, reinforced

Perspex protected a super-computer believed to be the world's most powerful. A carpeted lane snaked around the machine, dotted with three operators on swivel chairs.

Part of Jake's tech arsenal included track-to-source technology. He stared at the screen. The telecom signals, even from disposable phones, could be scooped via aerial scanning, recorded and archived. Armitage opened the next parcel of communication data.

The NSA employed advanced drones to comb concentrated pockets of interest. Targets in foreign cities were picked from public transport, streets and cafes, all via facial recognition. Open space no longer guaranteed privacy and security as prying government agencies plucked your conversations and data from the air. Not to mention social media and search engine giants such as Facebook and Google.

A key-word search narrowed the pool to seven calls in the batch. Jake leaned and tipped the chair back against white-washed walls, eyed a kettle over the workstation. His hands shook with a self-inflicted caffeine overdose, but he craved another.

Both knees cracked as Jake rose and stretched his lumbar, padded to the countertop and flicked a switch. He spooned two full teaspoons of instant coffee and remembered he was out of milk.

*Black it is.*

After small sips from the mug, Jake adjusted the speaker volume. As drowsiness seeped in and blurred his vision, he forced himself to focus. Jake opened a new batch of calls dated two days ago, clicked on the first file. Each conversation sounded like the last, blending together in a hazy succession. As the next file finished, he shook his head to brush off the nodding.

*I need exercise, and fast.*

The agent walked around the island bench. He circuited the lounge furniture, determined to remain focused.

Theories flooded his mind, none more interesting or feasible than mafia links.

*Someone had pulled the strings here in the Federation Council, and for far too long. A politician or a high-ranking military position, that's the authority required to pull off this caper. Perhaps Adrik Lebedev still had influence and power, even dead.*

The beep interrupted Jake's exercise, a prompt flashing. He bent over the screen. His advanced protection software had picked up a tracker. Someone had tried to trace his calls. He didn't want to give away his position. The IP address location bounced to an apartment block at the other end of his street. A second ping to a house twenty kilometers northwest in the suburbs.

People were always watching and listening.

An IP address source came up. Jake recorded it and sent the trace on its merry way, travelling down the network to land at the wrong IP address. If it wasn't the NSA or another American enforcement agency, such as the CIA, someone had advanced cyber skills employed at work.

Such an attempt caused Jake to think, not for the first time, that the murdered asset smelled like a set-up.

*Why would the unknown party set up a contract kill just for him? Who bothered to dig this deep to fool a foreign agency?*

*Unless to smoke-out the real guilty parties.*

Armitage's blood turned to ice.

*What if these killers wanted his location? If his operation or the asset had been targeted by Russia's government, it opened a whole new set of threats.*

*And implications.*

Jake picked a red apple off the table and took a bite.

*Does the DoD have a white hat hacker on me as well?*

The agent came to his senses.

*The Department of Defence, of course, is likely monitoring me day and night.*

*They spy on the world and store billions of digital communications.*

*If it is a rogue hack...*

Armitage scanned the apartment walls. A decent hacker can turn any device into a ransomware machine. He turned and spied his coffee machine. A medium quality model with enough smarts and it had WIFI Internet capability.

These thoughts plagued Jake as he tried to calculate the probability. Regardless, he had to clear his mind and focus.

*If they want me dead, let these people come.*

*If I'm a target, I'll use this to my advantage.*

This question beckoned Jake to his laptop and he crunched data files with renewed enthusiasm. As he flicked through the conversations, he reached one from last Tuesday. This dialog started with the usual code words. A date preceded the intended location, both speakers careful about every word they spoke. One slip-up and their position would be compromised by eavesdropping.

The notification beep echoed in the darkness. Jake

bolted upright in the chair, weariness driven from his mind. He examined the prompt. The jackpot surfaced with an exchange occurring near midnight.

A call alert that identified Jake's key words. The suspect had called from downtown Saint Petersburg, a hotel on the eastern side of the main river.

Armitage clicked on the player. A deep, accented voice spoke in Arabic. The commander. A second man replied. The two men's heated dialog explored an opportunity. An address and an asset. He struggled to translate some words. Static and poor telco quality rendered the conversation patchy.

The audio file beeped. Jake pressed stop. He exhaled and rubbed his left trapezius.

*These men are connected and had known about the asset.*

This discovery of a dialog between Popov and former politician Lebedev created the most solid lead yet. The plans were sketchy but Jake's confidence of intercepting the target increased.

*It's not a simple mafia hit.*

The last known address for Popov came up through the system. An old, Soviet-built block ten minutes across the city, his location during the day, when not fulfilling a contract or errand, identified as a two-level bar. This venue had a reputation of violence and criminal associations.

The agent sized up the location on Google Maps. The building sat near the southern bank of the Neva River in the central zone of Saint Petersburg. Canopy trees shaded the black, churning water. Public cobblestone paths ran wide giving a long line of sight. Not much privacy. Many exits dotted the shoreline; half were useless. An open area presented security challenges. The agent stretched but stayed focused on the screen.

A well-known high-ranking mafia boss named Kalef owned the establishment. Jake had heard many rumors about the extent of this character. Low-level operators such as Popov were foot soldiers. Mafia stooges. Expendable and used up by bosses like Kalef. His research found that the police were wary of this place and thought twice about entering. The law enforcement that hadn't been paid off by Kalef.

Armitage grabbed his keys and locked the front door. The elevator nearly closed as he jumped inside, clicking the button for ground floor. He headed straight for the car and took off onto the side street.

Nevsky Avenue had started to receive the peak afternoon traffic. Jake steered west toward the Neva River and crossed at the nearest bridge.

*I'll need firepower to stake out the bar.*

# Chapter 13

The late afternoon clouds rolled, streaking the horizon in red and gold, a distant firestorm over the landscape.

A throng of tourists pointed and clicked cameras at the unusual architecture surrounding the block. Jake found the address and parked. He strolled past the targeted establishment. A drunk ambled out the door. Feral drinking hole.

The agent broke away from the sidewalk and took a narrow alley, hugging the edge. It spilled into a dilapidated carpark. Weeds broke through cracked concrete. A chain link fence covered the south end.

The parking lot behind Manny Popov's place of employment had a mix of different cars. A high-end, blue Mercedes sedan represented the most luxurious automobile brand. Crime pays well. At three-hundred thousand U.S. dollars this vehicle made an impressive statement. It also gave away the position of one of the employees. Such a display of ill-gotten wealth exposed a weakness to their enemy—Jake Armitage.

Armitage took in a breath. He knew either Popov's boss, Kalef, owned this Mercedes, or Popov himself.

There was a smattering of other cars parked. An older model Toyota owned by one the security staff.

The agent circled to the mouth of the entrance. He didn't want to get caught scoping. He noticed the other mid-range, gray four-wheel-drive looked only two years old. Full-tinted windows all round indicated a likelihood of nefarious activity.

A bird fluttered in an overhead gutter spotted with rust.

The agent checked the rear entry and roof eaves for cameras. There were none in the lot, which he found unusual considering the business activities of the occupants. A coughing noise echoed around the cement block.

Three casually dressed men smoked on the sidewalk. Armitage scanned the streets for watchers. The drunk patron out front stumbled off toward a *Fresh* restaurant and nearly fell head-over-ass. A siren wailed in the distance. He waited until the lot cleared of people. The smokers dispersed and headed in different directions.

When everybody had left, Jake drew out two micro-tracers and secured one on the Mercedes.

His SUV was parked opposite a jewellery shop five minutes away. Jake walked back through the alley that ended a block from the club entrance. Cars banked up as peak-hour traffic clogged the clearway zones. He waited across the road in a café and scouted for patrons and employees coming and going to the bar.

A waiter at the café came to collect Jake's order, a strong double expresso. She brought it hot, so he blew on the top until it cooled.

The small black handset had a black screen. Jake switched it on and lit up a grid. Red lines showed the roads. Black dots for the GPS signals. The transmitters on the cars were stationary.

Armitage sipped his coffee and watched the club.

The main bar operated during the day and catered for an interesting clientele. So far, the patrons ranged from under-age to at least fifties. The roar of motorcycles blared. Two Harley-Davidsons were parked side-by-side. The bike tanks sparkled and chrome glinted despite the limited afternoon rays. A person could see their reflection in the polished metal.

It must be a bikie meet.

"Let's do this inside." The main speaker spoke with an American accent. A bouncer disappeared inside a shard of glare.

*I don't think it's a coincidence this dump has a tight security team.*

A second bouncer shook hands with the first. This gorilla had walked to work with a female: a tall, attractive blond in her mid-twenties. She could be helping behind the bar. Or waiting on patrons for drinks and snacks. She smoked a cigarette and chatted with security. The conversation ended. She threw a finished butt at the asphalt and the pair trudged inside.

That left three cars in the rear lot unaccounted for. The agent applied his high-probability elimination. The blue Mercedes had the highest price tag. His eyes found a dinted Ford sedan made in the nineteen-nineties: the barman's or bouncer's.

Armitage paid his bill and stepped off the curb. He weaved between the traffic. The escaped air from the bar carried the scent of stale beer and smoke. He took in the dingy, low-lit establishment. The walls were grimy with patches of damp mould. He scanned the patrons. Seven in total. Each milled within reaching distance of the barman.

Contaminated air flowed from the patched entrance. A drunken man wobbled on his feet. Everybody ignored the drinker, who mumbled to himself. Staff readied the venue for a larger crowd.

The owners mingled with customers making it harder to eliminate potential candidates.

Jake fastened a blue sports cap on his head. The visor made it difficult to take clear surveillance images of his face from overhead cameras. He hadn't shaved that morning so his dark-brown whiskers cast a five-o'clock shadow. A worn jacket and faded jeans completed his disguise.

The agent stepped up to the long timber bar that ran along the back wall. The security nodded from the shadow of a booth set-up in a gap to take door charges at night.

On the right, three pool tables surrounded a bay of toilets. The pair of heavy-set men in their forties played a game of eight-ball on the nearest table. A dense blue fog of smoke hovered above the green felt surface. Balls clacked. A coloured five dropped into a pocket. Pot glasses of beer surrounded a half-empty jug resting on a round tabletop. Jake noticed both men wore full black leathers.

The two bikies.

A back wall busy with dated beer advertising and mirrors. The agent shifted casually along the counter. He checked the numerous taps and badges. The nearest barman grunted and rose from a stool. An overhead lamp reflected off the muscular man's shaved head, years dedicated to the gym to achieve his physique.

"What can I get for you?" The hulk spoke English with a heavy Russian accent.

"One pot of the Russian lager with the gold and white there." Jake pointed at a nearby tap.

"Nevskoe Imperial." The bald barman grinned. "You want to be Russian, huh?"

"Something like that." Armitage employed a mixed European accent. No particular language. He used his peripheral vision to scope the nightclub section. A rough-hewn timber booth stood against the east wall. Inside lay a simple seat for collecting the door entrance fees. Shards of artificial light fell in the cracks on the neglected tiled flooring.

There was minimal spend on a seedy club business.

The bar man wiped the counter with a rag and held a glass under the spout.

Speakers gave off static as old-school beats pumped. Armitage glanced past the bikies. A toilet door swung open as a man exited.

"Here you go." The bodybuilder plonked the glass on the bar. Armitage watched the froth overflow the rim.

The lager tasted strong and bitter. The agent sipped slowly, small quantities. The barman held out his hand in the air.

"That's twenty-five rubles."

"Thanks." Jake pushed ruble notes over the sticky surface. "Keep the change."

Pint in hand, Jake wandered around the tables, deciding on a position. Music blared from speakers that hung from the ceiling in brackets. A younger couple wandered from the back room and sat at the bar. The man had a mohawk and a full-sleeve tattoo. His female company had a short skirt and appeared streetwise.

Hairs on the back of Jake's neck raised.

*I can feel someone watching.*

Armitage swept the room with his gaze. In the corner, he found his mark.

One bikie stared at Jake. The man started coming toward him, straightening as he drew closer. A sneer formed on his face.

Armitage broke eye contact.

The shorter bikie shoulder-nudged his friend, nodding at the agent. He pivoted toward a small table.

A hard nudge to the shoulder came as the bikie reached level. The man was around Jake's height, but stockier. Jake stood firm. An intimidation tactic.

The agent ignored the shorter bikie and wandered to the far side. The men withdrew and sat at the furthest stool from the bar. Their colleague stepped away, head hung low. Jake sipped his beer. He kept the two in his peripheral vison, circled to the toilet doors.

Jake leaned against the bar, relaxed and casual. An arch at the south end of the bar marked the threshold to the night club. It led into a large oval dance floor beset with three podiums. He scanned the room. No irregularities.

Armitage watched the staff preparation. He peered across at the DJ booth. Curved around the edge sat a second stone-topped bar. That could be trouble. At the opposite corner, a roped area marked the VIP entrance and stairs that disappeared to the next level.

Taking a sip of the lager, Jake carried the glass to a vantage position where he could press his back to the wall. This delivered a view of the arch and the second bar. The young blond woman, who had entered with the bouncer earlier, arrived at the VIP zone. She cleaned and arranged the shelf in a collection booth.

The agent sat his burner on the bar surface. He swiped the screen pretending to look busy. A cash register clicked and the blond employee bagged all the takings. She bundled the cash into a small canvas bag. An older man with thinning slick-back descended to a lower nook. She passed the cash. He smiled and whispered in her ear. The man wore an expensive European suit.

*Must be the owner, Kalef. I've seen his mugshot.*

99

Above the VIP zone, a camera angled to the foot of the stairs. Jake checked for digital surveillance inside the pub and saw another lens pointing to the front bar. It had limited range and was old tech, so was not concerning. He'd seen this camera on entering and turned his back when ordering the beer. This obscured the view and his face.

The bikies playing pool paused and placed their cues against the wall. A serious huddle formed as the men chatted about a strategy. The game appeared abandoned as various tasks had to be completed. The leader yelled across at the barman to bring another jug. A bouncer materialized and started a conversation. He seemed to know the men. Armitage sipped on his glass of beer. The amber liquid tasted a little stale.

*I bet these thugs work for Popov and the mob.*

In his peripheral vision, Jake noticed movement in the VIP area. He slowly drew his gaze to land on Popov at the rear bar. The blond worker became animated again, chatting happily and flirting. All the while, Popov stared at her chest.

The older man in the suit took the bag and left through the rear exit.

A third man entered and joined the bikies. Diminutive in height and middle-aged, the newcomer wore faded sweat pants and joggers. A lighter flame flickered and a fresh cigarette sent a blue wisp of smoke curling.

The bikies broke ranks. Each one shook the middle-aged man's hand, grouping in a ring. As they talked, the newcomer scanned the room, eyes darting at each person. His gaze fell on Jake who casually diverted his eyes.

*Don't be memorable.*

The sweatsuit man's lip twitched.

A door swung open from the toilet. The newcomer

scratched his arm. Armitage spotted a sore, red rash inflamed.

*Tweaker: methamphetamine user.*

The smaller bikie led the buyer to the restrooms. A drug deal was about to go down. This place fits Popov's profile to a tee. Jake sipped his flat lager for effect, waited a few minutes and pretended to play with his smartphone.

The agent placed the unfinished glass on the benchtop. He headed to the front entrance. As he walked, he pulled his cap closer over his eyes and stared at the window. The bouncer had taken a bathroom break.

Step by step. Focus.

The door swung open. Evening had darkened the sky.

Foot traffic on the strip had increased. No one paid attention to him. He disappeared down the alley and used shrubs and bushes to hide his exit path.

Armitage relaxed his shoulders and powerwalked to the corner. At the turn, he scoped the street. He examined eyes and expressions. People strolled in the receding daylight, going about their business.

A mother scrambled to gather her child. Peak-time workers swarmed the sidewalks and road. Armitage circled around to the parking lot.

The clouds formed thick bunches. A storm front gathered in the west. At his SUV, Jake unlocked the door and settled behind the wheel. He turned on his blinker and moved into the traffic. Pedestrians swarmed the crosswalk as a red-tinged dusk split the horizon in stripes. He changed lanes in a gap. The smell of beefsteak with strong herbs wafted out of a restaurant.

The next set of lights flashed red; Jake considered his next move. Popov could be tracked. The criminal's next destination was crucial to the mission.

Club staff and patrons were typical lowlife. Jake waited for the tracking device fixed to Popov's bumper to alert on the console. The screen lit up blue. He adjusted each of the dials, checking they were on and working.

Once the tracking icon moved across the GPS grid, Jake would have sights on Popov. A waiting game. Time to get some shut-eye.

# Chapter 14

Armitage staggered into his apartment and locked the door. His gaze caught the microwave numbers glow: one-ten A.M. The city lights shimmered through the lounge glass. Shadows flickered in the apartment. He drained a glass of water and headed to the bathroom.

The toilet flushed noisily as Jake wondered if the plumbing issue had returned.

Leftover rice was still in the fridge. The agent heated the meal and took the bowl from the microwave. His stomach filled quickly as it had shrunk with irregular meals. He had a quick shower and towelled himself briskly. The chin stubble had started to grow into a beard. A quick trim and shave changed his facial hair into a goatee.

The tracking monitor sat on the table. Jake took it into the bedroom and climbed into bed. He tossed and turned and soon drifted off, too exhausted to dream. The tracker alert beep woke him from slumber.

Armitage rolled over and grasped the console display, focusing on the grid. A blue dot pulsed across the screen and confirmed Popov's car was on the move.

Basin water gave Jake's skin goosebumps. He dressed and headed to the kitchen. Dawn broke over the horizon. He grabbed two ripe bananas.

Jake hurried to unlock the car. He started the engine as wipers scraped the ice off the windshield. He turned the demister onto four. As soon as he could see, he took off checking the transmitter signal. The blue icon flashed at a slow pace. He locked the location into the GPS and finished the second banana.

The seven A.M. chill bit his fingers as Jake wound down

the window. A cold breeze kept him alert.

Traffic had yet to reach capacity. The agent changed lanes, conscious of speed and followers. Russian police were the last thing he needed.

The target reached a destination on the edge of the industrial zone. Jake parked four buildings back on the opposite side. The man stepped out and approached a multi-story apartment block.

High-density social housing. The structure loomed over a block of warehouses.

A truck rushed past. Dawn splintered through Jake's rear window, lighting up the dusty console. Popov appeared in the foyer, crossed the sidewalk and paced the waterlogged asphalt in front of the neighbouring warehouse, an overnight bag in his hand.

Armitage adjusted the seat and stifled a yawn. Effective stakeouts consisted of patiently waiting. Hours of sitting got to some people. Not him. Patience was crucial to Jake's success and survival.

A cat scurried across the road and stopped, staring at Jake with large green eyes. He slugged the remaining liquid in a water bottle and watched as the animal grew bored and continued on its way.

A passing truck threw water on the windows. Armitage left the car, pulling on his generic red cap, a trademark accessory, and headed for the corner. The gloomy day began with a dark roll of clouds on the horizon. More rain. He walked a pedestrian crossing with lights and strolled by the high-rise.

The structure had been hastily erected in the sixties, the agent guessed for price, not quality. A setback of at least twenty meters separated the opening from the worn foyer. The stucco had run long ago, a pattern of splotches like tiger strips. Bricks on the ground level wrapped the Soviet-style box. Bars marked the windows.

A low metal fence with an opening for a gate dotted the perimeter. It climbed one meter high in most parts. Armitage looked for a way to reach the entrance without drawing attention.

*I've got an hour to get in and finish.*

The orange sun struggled behind a storm front. Jake weaved into a dilapidated lot wedged between the apartment and the warehouse. Fir and birch trees grew in all directions. Jake hoped the canopy foliage hung low enough to provide cover from the occupants.

In the distance the agent heard muffled voices. He sprinted behind a row of thick hedges. The block loomed over the grounds, shadows driving miniature vermin back into the undergrowth.

A break in the boundary timber fence led to a basketball court and communal recreational area. Armitage squeezed past a hole in the hurricane fence. He gazed up at a ball ring hung from corrugated iron, the backboard split and stained. Neglected swings and a slide surrounded a grass patch.

An office cabin made of cinder blocks climbed from the concrete. It sat tacked to a larger structure: a dispatch zone.

The chill in the breeze picked up pace. Jake stepped along the flank. The temperature had dropped to five degrees. His black jacket retained some heat.

A forklift reversed, emitting a beep. Jake flattened against the wall, frozen. Silhouettes moved as the drapes flickered. He felt his heartbeat rise.

The agent eased closer to a dusty pane. He ran his

finger down the groove. The angle gave a partial view of a rec room. An old fridge and a dining table surrounded with rickety chairs. Sofas pointed to a TV.

Seated opposite two other men, Popov stared at a stack of paperwork. A case lay open on the surface, bundles of cash stacked in neat piles.

One of the men opposite Popov stood. A clump of blond hair shook as he laughed. Tall and excellent posture. Super alert. Ex-military. Armitage couldn't see the man's face, obscured by a large bookcase. A side profile showed European features. Slavic.

The blond man moved around the room, throwing his hands in the air. Armitage angled at the pier edge. A conversation or argument; Jake couldn't be sure.

The window ledge jutted out two inches from the wall. Light streamed through the pane, spilling onto a bookcase. The agent pulled himself up to the gap. He peered into the room. Popov sat with his face turned, following the conversation. The blond guy paced the carpet closer to the window.

Armitage shifted to avoid being seen. The third man with dark-brown hair was shorter. Jake watched as the last occupant disappeared through a door.

A dog barked in a nearby yard. The agent pressed against the cinder. Overhead a pigeon rustled in leaves. The blond startled at the noise and marched to the window. Armitage dropped carefully to the ground.

In Jake's peripheral vision, the drapes parted. The mercenary's reflection appeared in the glass, revealing patches of grime on the pane. Retinas were red.

Armitage pressed his spine to the brick.

The blond guy's eyes darted back and forth, taking in

the grounds. The agent hid just out of sight, but if the thug opened the window, he'd see him. The mercenary appeared at the glass as the bird took flight in a flurry.

Gazing at the flapping birds, sun captured the mercenary's features. Jake caught a glimpse of the man's profile in the descending light. He suppressed a gasp.

*It's the tall shooter from the safehouse. Contract killers are in league with organized crime cells.*

Armitage inched further from the glass pane, careful not to get too close to the next opening. The drapes fluttered again as Jake hugged the wall. His P-96M pistol concealed in his belt, one second from drawing. The smaller caliber weapon held eight in the magazine, one in the chamber.

Right hand poised over his belt, Jake resisted the urge to draw and fire. Left hand fingers grasped the cinder block, body frozen and flat. Thirty seconds dragged on as if one hour.

The blond guy's face vanished from sight. Both drapes fell and settled against the frame. He exhaled and waited to detect movement from inside. Distant chatter started in the rec room.

A buzzing sound came from the sectional garage door southside. The agent squeezed out of sight. He waited. None of the thugs came to investigate. A light truck honked, cruising from the opening.

This network needed to be taken down but he required a strategy. No point going in, three guns versus one, with military-trained opponents. A firefight may draw attention from neighbors and created other avoidable issues.

*If I retreat and return to the car, I'll never get back here in the light.*

A black Toyota Land Cruiser sat in the lot. Jake recorded the registration and considered attaching a tracker. The vehicle's spot meant sprinting to the opposite boundary fence.

Armitage calculated his odds on being spotted out in the open. In current conditions, with three men in the lounge, the probability of success was less than fifty-fifty.

A distraction. Jake spied a bank of small stones that lay scattered in the lot, two meters from his current position. He crawled around a tree and picked the top rock. Warming up his shoulder, Jake pivoted at the roof.

The stone sailed high over the eaves. He watched and listened. A clang on metal followed.

*Bingo: hit the gutter.*

The next thud indicated it hit the rear yard, bounced on dirt and rolled.

A second toss. The stone hit a solid plastic rainwater tank and ricocheted into the grass. Voices came from the warehouse. Footsteps sounded in the room. Popov yelled words in Russian. A door slammed over the far side.

Positioned at the front corner, Jake sprung and sprinted past the drawn drapes. He threw the third stone across the roof to the driveway side rear. It clanged against and skimmed along the concrete.

The agent listened. More voices.

Footfall changed direction as the blond-haired assailant reversed his steps. Through the drape, Jake saw Popov alone, fingers wrapped on a Beretta. A drop of sweat ran down the thug's forehead.

Armitage edged toward the north end, a thick timber door in a frame. Jake counted down to three, tried the handle. It turned easily in his grip. He cracked the door and slipped into the opening.

A wall separated the lounge. The agent appeared in the archway.

"Hey! What are you doing?"

Armitage spun as the shorter thug appeared from behind. He unclipped his weapon and pointed his P-96M from a four-meter range. Silencer attached to the barrel.

The Russian fumbled over the weapon, stammering swear words. His safety seemed jammed.

*I need cover—and fast.*

A side door stood three feet away. The agent leapt and plunged through the gap. He landed at a recessed section near a study cubicle. The silhouette of the blond-haired assailant flickered past the window. The agent clicked the safety and unleashed the P-96M at the window. Glass smattered in the yard near the Russian's last position.

A barrage of rounds punctured the wall. Armitage dived onto the laminate floor. Plaster chips flew, showering the furniture and dropping on Jake's head.

The blond mercenary bobbed up at the bare window frame, grasping an AK 47. A handgun only did so much against a semi-automatic rifle.

The agent squatted against a table. Glass crunched underfoot. Jake checked the corridor. Clear.

Staying low, he followed the passageway. It dumped him in an open-plan kitchen at the south end of the property. Footsteps hit concrete.

A noise from a doorway. Armitage tried to get his bearings. The last door swung open as a round whistled past his ear.

Glass shattered and fell, shards tinkling on boards.

Jake shot high to distract, throwing his body. It bought him a few seconds. He landed near a bench. Two shooters bobbed up, taking turns to fire.

*I'm pinned down from both sides.*

Armitage crawled to the space. Rounds punched the air. He returned fire blind. Paper sheets exploded. The shooter kept him distracted with double auto sprays. Jake's pistol aimed low, he snapped three consecutive rounds.

The air thickened with drywall particles. The agent's elbows burned from the crawl. He found a smaller storage room. This provided temporary cover. He tumbled at the opening and hit a shelf.

Out of range.

Breaths came slow as Jake inhaled deep. He rolled on his stomach, took visual of the entrance. Boots trod lightly.

Two hostiles came up fast.

The blond-haired thug appeared in the frame. Armitage lay parallel to a three-seater sofa, P-96M pointed at the target. Plaster dust floated in the air, fogging his visual.

*Where's your boss?*

A sudden burst exploded from the wall. Kalashnikov rounds chipped the table above his head. Splinters exploded, brushing his face. The air churned white powder. A breeze from the smashed panes pushed a cloud over visuals.

*This lower visibility will work to my favour.*

The agent flattened on the hard surface where the air was clearest. A mist swirled in the room. The black-haired Russian scrambled in the chaos. Armitage took aim low at the thug's thigh. A grunt and a thud.

The vibrations of steps through the boards announced the next assailant's arrival.

Armitage waited. The floor creaked.

A silhouette appeared through the haze, framed by strands of fluoro. Jake aimed at the dark hair mass and punched out a shot. Footsteps clicked. A door slammed.

*Popov must have bolted.*

The dust dissipated with a breeze from the open door. The agent circled the furniture. He listened for sounds. A bird chirped in the distance. The short thug groaned from the corner. Jake tied the man's hands behind his back.

A car engine fired to the east.

Armitage bolted toward the opening. He faced the exit. The black Toyota Land Cruiser reversed out of the lot at high speed and skidded onto the asphalt. Smoke billowed from the tires.

The Land Cruiser bumped over the gravel and out onto the street. Armitage ran with arm outstretched and pulled the trigger, keeping his finger pressed. Bullets sprayed the trunk.

Rounds missed, going wide. The mercenary ducked, accelerating blind. A tire blew and the rear brake light shattered. Plastic tinkled on the asphalt.

The vehicle gained speed, reaching five-hundred meters. Staring down the barrel, Jake cleared the road.

Tires skidded and the vehicle fishtailed. Rubber burned. The smell of acrid smoke reached his nostrils.

The agent knelt, hands on knees. He pulled air into his diaphragm. An orange disc faded behind a gloomy sky. He watched as the vehicle spun off into the receding tree canopies.

*And I didn't get a tracker onto that car.*

# Chapter 15

The agent crossed the graveled grounds and took in the dispatch zone. Through the rec room, the dark-haired hostile lay trussed up on the floor. Jake navigated the mess, passed into the kitchenette. The table was tipped, sheets lay askew, and rounds had peppered the walls.

A basic, old model Nokia cell phone lay on the table. He flicked through the menu. No contacts and three calls over four days.

On the dark-haired thug, he found the same model android phone and, again, no contacts.

*Did someone's boss have a bulk deal on old brick burners?*

These guys were smart enough not to leave evidence of their identity. In a jeans' pocket, there was a wallet with cash and no identity cards.

From a crack in the drapes, Jake checked the landscape. The setback had to be thirty meters. This provided cover and some buffer from the noise. A couple of onlookers had gathered, staring through the fence at the playground.

Armitage waited five minutes and peered down the asphalt from the warehouse. The two people moved on, chattering to themselves.

Conscious of additional curious spectators, Jake took the corridor to the rear lot. Hurricane wire marked the boundary edge. He threw his jacket onto the razor wire and climbed to the top. His fingers found purchase as he avoided the sharp ends.

Jake landed in the disused basketball court. Empty and still. No occupants appeared as he sprinted over a stretch of cracked concrete.

The far side of the disused playground had a bluestone boundary. At least there's no razor. Armitage fell to the dirt. A low timber fence surrounded a patch of yellowed grass that cushioned his fall. As he landed, his legs buckled. Needles shot through his knees into his calf muscles. He rolled to disperse the energy, which helped ease the pain a little. His fitness had taken a back seat in the last two weeks.

The agent stretched his right hamstring. It would be the only allowance he'd give his battered body. Jake had little time and the clock ticked.

Another warehouse led to loose stones on a long driveway. Thankfully no gate covered the entrance. Armitage slipped from the property and reached the road at a brisk pace. His exit position sat a block away from the scene. A hundred meters at least. Lucky these Russians live in massive houses. With the recent commotion, he had to create distance from the gun battle.

A band of commuters had their backs to Jake as he neared the car. The trees swayed with a faint breeze.

On the main road, Jake avoided eye contact and walked slowly toward a bank of trees.

In the distance, a police siren wailed. The agent walked fast, but not too fast to look like fleeing. The whirring sound closed in fast. He guessed an ETA of five minutes at most and they would reach the warehouse.

Jake reached his car, partially hidden on the low tree canopy. Nobody turned or looked as he unlocked the door and settled behind the wheel.

No strollers occupied the sidewalk.

Armitage reversed carefully over the curb and drove

off in the opposite direction from the property. He checked the rear-view mirror.

All clear.

On the main avenue, Jake drove at the speed limit. The first police cruiser sped past three minutes after leaving the scene. A mugginess increased as his shirt stuck to his body. Fatigue kicked in and body parts ached. He drove toward the city center, carving by a cluster of mid-eighteenth-century mansions.

By eleven o'clock that morning the gloomy sky had cleared, reducing clouds and the usual darkness. The temperature read nineteen degrees Celsius and traffic deepened with the improved climate. For a spring morning, the port city seemed extra vibrant as he ran through the morning's gun battle in his mind.

In a quiet lane, Jake stopped the car. He pulled out the first cell phone taken from Popov's hideout and checked the dialled numbers. A burner for sure. The first call registered on the device had been to the night club. The agent recognized it from the flyer he had kept in the glove box. The two remaining numbers might be crucial to his next lead.

Armitage noticed a public phone at an intersection one-hundred meters away. . A user clunked the receiver and left. He inputed the number on the burner.

It rang and rang before diverting to voicemail.

"This is Uri. Leave a message after the tone." A message in English with a strong Russian accent.

The second number rang only twice.

"Zdravstvuj" A deep man's voice answered in Russian. "Hello."

The agent's stomach lurched. He waited as the person

repeated the greeting in louder volume.

"Who is this?" the Russian said.

A breeze carried as Jake remained silent. He watched a horde of people enter a Hungry Jacks. The place teemed with eaters lining for orders.

The man swore and yelled an obscenity into the phone. After ten seconds, the call cut out and Jake replaced the receiver in the cradle.

An idea simmered in his brain.

*I recognize that voice—but from where?*

Armitage hurried to the car, cell phone in hand. He ran through the possibilities, trying to recall the connection.

*Who does that voice belong to?*

A young woman bobbed on the crosswalk, a small, white dog in tow. She paused and watched while the pet lifted a leg on a signpost. Jake stared at the pair, thinking all the while about the man's voice. The dog owner ran a hand through her long, blond hair as the air caught the strands.

Blond hair.

It suddenly dawned on Jake.

The man on the other end of that call was the tall mercenary. Contract killer.

The agent nearly ran and hugged the stranger and her dog. Now he had the mercenary's vehicle registration and his cell phone number.

The phone might be a burner but hopefully the contractor retained the device for the next forty-eight hours.

# Chapter 16

The freeway exit fell hard and steep, descending to the other end of Saint Petersburg's industrial zone. Jake hugged the turn and veered right into a narrow single lane. He flicked past Government administration buildings that sat in various degrees of exterior neglect. The bland colors flashed by in his peripheral vision.

Armitage slowed into the left lane, eased up to a gated office suite. The Saint Petersburg branch of Russian Interpol. The office had been set up, some said in haste, five years ago. Many people in the know thought it came as a direct order of the President who wanted a branch in his home city.

A truck emerged from a roller door, honked to oncoming vehicles. Jake stopped at a brown building that crested a concrete forecourt. A once-grand fountain shot recycled water in a vertical arch from a cupid figure. Pigeons surrounded the nearby slates, picking at food crumbs. The birds scattered to flight as Jake walked across their feeding ground.

In the foyer, Jake followed a carpeted zone. Imitation fittings were abundant in this dated office. Overhead he noted standard coverings. A basic pine table was a further homage to limited budgets.

The agent crossed the near-deserted waiting room and nodded at the token receptionist.

"I'm here to see Zima."

She smiled in return and pointed at an opening. Armitage pushed through the door into a cream-coloured space. An aisle ran down the middle, offset by rows of generic cubicles. Not unlike an airport lounge, each slot had all the standard USB ports and sockets.

Fake plants, dotted in intervals, added no more ambience to the sterile setup. The agent counted the doors on the east side and stopped at number twelve. The handle dropped as he knocked and entered.

A thin, middle-aged man with a comb-over sat behind a modest timber desk. Officer Leonid Zima wore a button-down shirt under a maroon cardigan. A conservative dress sense even for a bureaucrat. The cream chino trousers completed the bland ensemble. Every time Jake met the officer, it always reminded him of Woody Allen.

Officer Zima stood and shook Jake's hand. "Mr Armitage, what can we do for you?"

"I've had a run in with one of your top five wanted list."

Armitage yanked a chair and sat down.

"This is serious." The officer's brow furrowed. "How did this come about?"

"A necessary evil this time, Zima." Jake crossed his legs. "You are aware of our safehouse asset we put under protection?"

"Yes, of course. A complex arrangement, to say the least. Did something happen?"

"The asset was found executed."

Zima crossed his arms. "Did you identify these people?"

The agent shifted in the seat. "I think so. A team of professional contractors returned to the scene when I had secured the location. At least one is a mercenary and military trained."

"Interesting. And the house?"

"Russian Mafia, I think." Jake steepled his hands under

his chin. "The leader is named Popov. Both these sides don't play well together."

Zima exhaled and leaned his chair. "How can this be going on under our noses?"

"On the dead kidnapper, I found a particular ink. Same one Popov had, which linked them together," Armitage said.

"What's the tattoo?" Zima's eyebrows rose.

"A star with a dagger through the center."

The Interpol agent nodded. "It's a new sect of Russian criminals, as you may know. We've been chasing this group through all law enforcement; police, agency, and even military."

"I've heard. Any information you can provide would be appreciated, and reciprocal as always."

"You know my policy is quid pro quo. What specifically do you need from me?" The bureaucrat crossed his arms.

"If you could please check your databases for an ID on this blond guy. He's at least six-one tall, lean, muscular build. Thirty to forty years old. Ex-special forces, I'm guessing, and he may be Russian. If not, European, but lived here for years. He speaks Russian almost flawlessly with an unusual, deep voice. That's why I could pick his voice easily."

"As you're aware, Armitage, I'm just a data-gathering officer. Limited field scope. A bureaucrat, if you will, and with no enforcement powers. We can only help police and agency to share information," Zima said and bit his lip. "I can send reinforcements if you need, though."

"This I know, but please. The access you have to Interpol's international database could prove vital in this instance. And this guy is going to keep committing serious crimes if we don't stop him and fast," Jake said.

A dated beige PC tower lay on the floor. Cords ran up the side to a twenty-inch flatscreen monitor.

"Give me a moment," Zima said and tapped away on his keyboard.

"Thanks, Zima, much appreciated." Armitage grabbed a disposable cup and poured water from a filtered tank in the passageway. He slugged the water and refilled the cup. As he paced outside Zima's office, the enormity of the force against him hit home.

A climate control unit hummed overhead, the single dominant sound besides irregular faint typing in the background. Back-up might be necessary, but hard to know who to trust.

The agent reached the corridor end. With Popov gone and the shorter henchman from the morning dead, this left the blond assailant.

At this stage.

More associates would come once Jake continued his investigation. He didn't know who was paying for these contract kills. Or all the motives hidden behind these actions. Besides greed and money.

As Jake stared out the window, the Russian bureaucrat poked his head out the door. "I think I found your suspect."

Crouching over his desk, Zima turned his screen to face Jake. A headshot loaded of a blond guy in khaki army uniform.

"This the guy?" Zima asked.

Jake glanced at the monitor. "That's him alright."

"His name is Bohdan Kolisnyk: born in Ukraine on September 1982. He's got an interesting resume. You were right, Armitage; this guy is Ex-Spetsnaz. Russian Special

Forces. He got dismissed from the military two years ago. Started making up assignments and killed a prisoner in Syria on a tour. Just executed the civilian in cold blood and in front of witnesses. Also suspected of torturing, and other kills not sanctioned." Zima cleared his throat. "That's what we can see. Kolisnyk's classified military files cannot be released to Interpol. But the agency can do this if a citizen is committing serious crimes on home soil and has specialized training."

"Charming individual. That's enough to get started, thanks." Armitage crossed his arms. "Any other information?"

"I can show you this whole file, but you need to memorize. Or come back. Sorry. No hard copies allowed."

"I understand."

The Russian turned his screen. "I'll make a coffee. What do you have?"

"White with no sugar, thanks."

The agent scanned the data on the blond mercenary. His known associates had included Popov, among others. The Ukrainian had links to Gulf Nations—Syria and Afghanistan. A large uranium buy, that went south four months ago, listed him as personnel for the seller. A psychotic mercenary adding an extra zero or two to his pay packet in private enterprise. Armitage wrote down the last known address. He memorized personal details and two main associates.

"I found Popov's warehouse. I don't think he'll be an issue now," Jake said and reclined in the chair. "He escaped on foot."

"Bohdan here will be more difficult. How do you plan to take him on?" The bureaucrat rose to his feet. "Wait. On second thoughts, don't tell me. I don't want to know. Just keep the public incidents to a minimum."

Armitage shrugged. "Will do my best."

"I'm sure." Zima's eyes narrowed. The desk phone rang. This saved Jake from a second admonishment. Zima shook his head and answered in Russian. He told the caller he'd be out in a moment.

"I'll leave you to it, Zima." Jake stood. "Thanks for the intel."

"Please try to keep the body count down and stay in touch." The Russian came around his desk. "I hope this information helps."

"I'm sure it will. Thanks again."

Zima nodded and replaced a file in a drawer.

At the reception desk, Jake waved to the woman busy on a keyboard. He exited the elevator and crossed the tiles. The fountain's feathered residents had returned in greater numbers. He circled around their feeding frenzy.

The car alarm chirped. The agent sank behind the wheel.

*Bohdan Kolisnyk wreaked havoc with his associates in the criminal underworld for what? To get their asset's USB drive with data on a political conspiracy? There had to be more.*

Armitage reversed from the parking bay. Everybody wanted this flash drive. Jake's enemies had a lot of both man and firepower. The mafia guys are expendable to the politicians and oligarchs pulling the strings. But a military-trained sociopath such as Kolisnyk will be more of a headache.

A lot more.

*To take him out, I'll need a plan.*

A red serpent of brake lights blurred to the next intersection. The car fell into a rhythm as Jake checked his surroundings. Any followers would be a minimum of six cars behind.

The agent remembered Katerina's mention of SPG Partners and checked online for their address. The company in Katerina Venski's interview may be connected to this political conspiracy. A firm that consulted campaigns for politicians had a definite motive to get this drive.

He flicked the turning indicator and weaved into the outside lane.

The robotic voice of the GPS filled the interior. It instructed Jake to take the next left. The headquarters for SPG was three minutes away. Armitage glanced at his glove box that hid his pistol.

*My day is starting to get interesting.*

# Chapter 17

A corner street sign pointed west as Jake slowed at the intersection. Number sixty to seventy-two appeared stamped in large, glittering silver across the metal-framed glass frontage. He stared at the intended address, an ultra-sleek twelve-story tower that shadowed neighboring structures. On the left, a nineteenth-century hotel that needed a facelift and a single-story restaurant on the right.

*That's the address the company listed online.*

On the front window, the words 'SPG partners' appeared in large red and blue letters. Steel and glass covered the façade, doors giving way to stone pillars and marble counters.

The light turned green. Armitage pulled up opposite the high-rise. Out of habit his mind clicked into counter surveillance mode. Every building had its weak spot, no matter the security. Jake scanned the ground floor lobby, evaluating the entry points. The immediate exterior area had public bench spaces and decorative garden sections.

The agent sought mounted cameras on either side of the revolving doors. He counted three lens, old technology with limited scope and range. Across to the south end, a small utility room for staff had a bulky, old-fashioned padlock.

Two glass revolving entries spun with a steady flow of visitors. Armitage lowered the window a crack to get a better view. Once inside, the guests reported to an elaborate marble reception.

One overweight rent-a-cop strolled the lobby. In thirty minutes, the uniformed guard drank a coffee and raided the vending machine for snacks. The guy looked ready to puke if he had to run twenty feet. Jake's gaze drew over the elevator bays.

From the paved square, walkers spilled across the double lanes of Nevsky Avenue. Jake settled in the car seat and observed the sea of faces. For reasons unclear to him, every Russian wore a serious expression. Each person appeared in a perpetual state of aggression. It had taken time to get used to, and even today, he still didn't understand the propensity toward this apparent hostility. He thought perhaps their history of dictatorships, oppression and communism contributed to such a serious collective state of mind. He shifted positions to alleviate the numbness in his behind.

The DoD database had a backdoor that Jake used to hack in anonymously. Armitage fished the laptop from a carrycase. He powered up the Windows screen and opened a browser. Blue light flickered in his lap as he scanned intel on the business.

A stray dog with brown patches scurried past the curb. The canine appeared to be ownerless, unusual in this high-end, inner-city zone.

The clouds dispersed to allow flickers of warmth in the car. Jake peered up at level seven, taking in the plethora of commercial activity. A parent company leased the whole of seventh floor. In all probability, level six below had been rented and disguised under a different shelf company. His research revealed the CEO created a business trade in the same consulting practises for both six and seven.

There had to be considerable money laundering and illicit trade. The agent sat patiently as he assessed his options. From the multi-level parking lot, the view would be perfect. The height of the opposite building provided the perfect angle for a sniper shot. Jake's marksmanship had been in the top five percent of his core.

Hours and days of painful and cramped conditions on assignments paid dividends. Armitage's ability to sit motionless didn't go unnoticed by superiors and commanding officers. To pick off a target from up to two kilometres. with the right scope and rifle. proved something he could perform, and regularly.

The light reflected from the broad glass façade of the structure and made Jake squint. He angled the laptop screen down to read about the company. Further intelligence reports inferred that level six, the lower one, conducted most of the shady deals. The primary business of mining consultancy appeared to attract the majority of revenue for SPG. All the questionable operational procedures funneled into a complex financial deception. Shelf companies owned by another company in a chain of empty trading names that ensured it led nowhere in the end.

Noise increased outside. The foot traffic thickened. Armitage typed in SPG and deep-dived the DoD hard drives. His search covered historical data from a period of ten years. Shelf company on shelf company leading to dead ends.

Jake scratched his head. Organised criminals and sophisticated white-collar executives were involved in this conspiracy together, and he couldn't deny that. The mafia stooges were soldiers and expendable. They also provided a good distraction from investigations and law enforcement.

The real puppeteers were these guys upstairs who committed the crimes. The biggest crooks were wearing designer suits and gathered in plush offices, living in plain sight and getting wealthier by the hour.

A blind opened in the boardrooms on level seven. Jake watched as heavy-set corporate types filed out the door. It provided evidence of these elitists. The most educated and powerful controlling the wealth from their ivory towers.

The agent sunk into the car seat. He contemplated the best approach. On the laptop, Armitage loaded up the SPG Partners' site. A consumer-centric home page that presented a convincing front of integrity. Under the corporate activity section, it listed as *consultant of business services*.

An impressive website. The company appeared as a bustling hive of professional presentations and transacting. Suited-up men and women continually shuffled by the street-facing windows. From a central corridor, meeting rooms branched off, packed with long tables and speakers connected to audio visual equipment.

The agent studied the intel files. The company resumé became vastly different as the complex story unfolded. These corporate pretenders were associated with cases involving extortion, blackmail and solicitation of contract kills.

The engine turned over. Jake drove around the surrounding block, surveying the landscape. A cluster of Mercedes, BMWs and high-end luxury cars circled the streets. He curb-crawled in low speed around the next bend to stall for a view of the street.

A red supercar turned into the street. The six-hundred-thousand-dollar vehicle growled to a halt.

Through the eclectic architecture, sunlight glinted off the steel structures. Old styles, such as Baroque, contrasted with new as if the city couldn't decide which era would dominate.

From this vantage point Jake monitored the flow of people, looking for a break.

The crowds finally thinned as four o'clock drew near. Jake checked his firearm, adjusted his cap.

Armitage bleeped the car lock and crossed the road.

Through the automatic doors, he scanned the high-end contemporary art suspended overhead on invisible wire. He strode into a maze of marble and steel. The high counters wrapped around a row of seated receptionists. He paused for a second before leaning over and clearing his throat. An impossibly gorgeous lady smiled up at him like a long-lost lover.

"Welcome to our building. My name is Lily." She extended her right hand and waved in the air. "Who are you here to see?" Her teeth were so perfect they appeared painted.

"I'm here to see Mr Victor Bollov." The agent straightened and smiled.

The woman paused, evaluating his face. "Please let me check if Mr Bollov is free. Is he expecting you?"

"In a manner of speaking, yes. Tell him it's concerning a mutual acquaintance of Manny Popov."

"Back soon." The statuesque Russian rose and power-walked toward the rear. Her heels clicked on the stone. She vanished behind a high-end wall covered by contemporary art. Men and women carrying briefs stormed by, absorbed in conversations.

Armitage discreetly gazed at the window. The movement angled his face away from the cameras. Less exposure the better.

The receptionist returned in three minutes. "He'll see you." She motioned toward the back section. "Please come this way."

Jake followed her to the elevator bay. After punching in a code, the Russian stepped inside. She scanned an ID card on a console and gestured to enter. The expression on her face remained stoic.

On level seven, plants surrounded the bay: half were fresh, the others made of plastic. Designer sofas with fancy side tables lined the corridor. Armitage took in the décor, reminding himself of the probable source of this wealth.

The receptionist strode through an open area and into a passageway. Red doors with gold plated numbers stretched both ways. The agent counted four on each side and one at the end. In his mind, he created a virtual map of the structure. The receptionist didn't slow her pace but seemed to float above the plush carpet.

As Jake scanned the surroundings, a foreboding sensation overcame him, like trying to hide from wolves while stuck in their den. The financial control this organisation had extended well beyond the murder of the asset. This was becoming increasingly more apparent.

She led him to a room at the far end: number twelve in gold plate. The receptionist paused and cleared her throat.

"I'll leave you here." She knocked twice.

The clicking of her heels receded as a voice said, "Come in."

The agent pushed open the door and entered. A long, cream table stretched to the rear. More contemporary paintings dotted the walls at intervals. The table could seat at least twenty people. At the other end, a white board sat on a stand. Two men in designer suits sat near the table centre with broad smiles on their faces.

A middle-aged executive with streaks of gray hair stood and offered his hand. "Hi. Jake, is it? My name is Paul Greenwood. I'm the managing director here. Please take a seat."

Greenwood spoke with an American accent and no hint of Russian. With foreign executives, the firm had obvious roots in America. A link Jake hoped to uncover, and quickly, before they could trace it back to him.

Armitage sat opposite the two men, close enough to chat easily. The second man, with light-brown thinning hair and larger waistline, angled across the table, hand outstretched.

"My name is Bollov. I'm a senior partner here." He spoke English well, but with a distinct Russian accent.

"Thanks for seeing me at such short notice." The agent sat upright in the chair and placed his elbows on the arm rests.

"You mentioned the name Manny Popov to our receptionist?" Greenwood said, pouring water into a glass. "Would you like some?"

"No, thanks. I'm a freelance photographer and journalist." The agent looked back and forth between the men. "A few days ago, a man named Popov called my media group with information. Apparently he had a big story and wanted us to break it first."

Greenwood and Bollov shared a glance. The Russian adjusted his tie. The American leaned in his chair and shrugged.

"We haven't done business with Mr Popov in near six months. I can check with our calendar on his file, if you like."

As Greenwood pressed the numbers on the handset, Bollov chimed in with a raised hand. "Do you know what information he offered?"

"No, because we never made contact. Mr Popov didn't attend the arranged meeting." Jake paused. "Now he seems to have gone missing."

"That is strange, isn't it…" The Russian let his words

hang as if a thought suddenly occurred. "We have limited information at hand, so it's difficult to help you with this matter at the present moment."

Greenwood pressed a button and spoke into the receiver. "Hi, Elena, can you please check the system for a Manny Popov. I need to know his last billable transaction. Please call me on the conference line, thanks."

The agent looked at Greenwood and pivoted to the Russian. "Appreciate both of your cooperation."

"Happy to help an ex-country man, if I can." Greenwood sipped from his glass. The American gazed at Jake as if trying to read his mind. "But we cannot divulge the nature of our dealings with Mr. Popov. Client privacy and all that."

"Of course. I'd expect this," Jake said.

The handset rang and Greenwood picked the receiver from the cradle.

After listening for thirty seconds, the American said, "Thank you, Elena," and hung up. "Mr Popov's last communication is dated nearly six months ago. That's all I can confirm."

The agent smiled. "Thanks for confirming. I'm probably barking up the wrong tree. We don't like to let a story go if we can still get the scoop."

"I'm sure," the Russian said. "Was that all?"

An overhead clock read five-twenty. Jake stood. "Thanks again to you both for your time today."

Bollov nodded and shook his hand.

"Let me walk you to the elevator, Mr Armitage." Greenwood gestured toward the passageway.

Armitage followed as the American director guided

over the carpeted corridor. Fancy artwork flashed by as Jake thought about all the money that funnelled through this company.

At the stainless-steel panel, Greenwood pressed the down button and smiled.

"Thanks for coming in." The director reached into his suit pocket. "Here's my card and please let me know if you require our services."

The elevator door pinged and opened smoothly. Jake shook Greenwood's hand. He pressed the ground floor button and waited.

# Chapter 18

As Jake passed the reception of SPG Partners, he saw the rent-a-cop patrolling outside the building. Attached to the man's belt hung a holster with a forty-caliber handgun.

*A big weapon for a security guard.*

The sky dimmed and Jake hovered at the driver's side of the Hyundai. He checked the time on his watch as near six P.M. and closed the door. A late model white van, side windows covered, signalled to turn from the nearest lane. the driver parallel parked in front. Two men in their thirties jumped to the sidewalk. Both were dressed in slacks and shirts with suit jackets. The men moved with straight spines and good posture. Their confidence and body language became more apparent as they readied for action.

*More muscle. This is getting more interesting by the minute.*

Over the wheel, Jake assessed the men. Signature lumps in their jackets indicated they were armed, and with decent-sized weapons. The driver, a stocky bodybuilder of medium height, gazed at the windshield. The agent lowered his head. The cape visor and window tint would obscure his features.

The more Jake watched the two new arrivals, the more convinced he became about their intentions. Each movement from the security men had purpose. They circled the foyer and surrounding structure from opposite sides.

*A disciplined sweep. Impressive.*

The men doubled back and met at the entrance. A wave from the rent-a-cop implied a signal. The uniformed guard continued his laps. The pair examined the passers-by discreetly as they faked a conversation. Again, each person appeared to be sized up and evaluated.

*A slick military outfit: why does Greenwood's office need so much protection?*

Pretending to play with his smartphone, Jake took in the drill in his peripheral vision. He left the interior light off in the cabin. The driver had noted Jake's presence and was aware that the occupant hadn't left yet.

Armitage memorized the registration and the men's physical description. He started the engine and merged with the traffic flow.

A sign for takeout coffee beamed bright neon above a restaurant. Streetlights flickered to life over the curbs, the afternoon near dark. The agent found a parking lot in a side lane. In desperate need of a caffeine shot, he entered the serving area.

The evening meals were churning out, waiting staff everywhere. In the main section, customers were shown seats and the tables were filling fast. Jake watched as staff scribbled orders, pushing bits of paper to the chefs behind.

Armitage ordered a double-strength latte. He waited near the register. A young female brunette called his ticket number. Jake paid and gazed over the selection. With the aromas of baking in the air, his stomach protested about a liquid-only meal.

The morning bananas had been the last food he'd consumed. An assistant noticed and raised her hand.

"Would you like something else?"

The agent nodded. "I'll take that turkey sandwich with lettuce thanks." Armitage paid and headed to the car.

A breeze gained strength as Jake slid onto the driver's

seat. He sipped the takeout coffee, scalding the tip of his tongue. With his other hand on the wheel, he placed the cup in the console holder to cool.

The meeting at SPG Partners still rolled around in his head. Their chat today could only be described as fobbing him off. It appeared more than dubious business associates and consultants with dodgy dealings.

Greenwood appeared a slippery character used to talking his way through problems. If that failed, the American probably threw money around or hurt people.

Bollov provided the cultural and local network. The Russian likely mixed this with a healthy dose of highly lucrative fees via illegal financial transactions processed for the mafia.

Jake presumed SPG partners must be the party that hired Bohdan Kolisnyk and mercenaries to kill the asset.

*Is Greenwood a middleman?*

Armitage chewed his sandwich. The complexities of this network deepened with each development. He blew on the hot beverage and sipped.

The sidewalk thickened with foot traffic. People eager to get home from a day's work. The agent's burner phone vibrated. Only six people had been given the phone number. A familiar local caller ID flashed on the screen.

Armitage pressed the call button. "Hello."

Static filled his ear from a bad line. A faint voice. Female.

"Jake, it's Katerina Venski." She spoke fast, breathing raggedly, her voice a pitch higher than normal. Jake couldn't hear the usual chaotic sounds of the media group in the background. *A different noise, like a pay phone. She must be out somewhere.*

"Katerina, is everything alright?"

Silence for a second. She blurted the words, "I'm worried. Last night I thought someone followed me and I took another way home. When I got inside, I locked all the doors, and the deadbolt, which is very rare for me. I alerted my apartment's security team. They check everyone coming and going in the building." She stopped and caught her breath. "Anyway, staff escorted me to my car this morning. Everything seemed fine at work but I still felt nervous."

"Please try to stay calm and tell me slowly," the agent said, his mind racing at the possibilities.

"I received a message today. A note appeared on my desk. It's a death threat. They mentioned about the..." She cleared her throat. "The story we discussed. These people accused me of talking to foreigners. An American, in particular, but didn't give names." Katerina's words slowed as her breathing returned to a calmer rate.

"Where are you now?" Jake levelled his voice and supressed the rising panic.

"I'm in a place called Café Singer. It's a block away from my apartment on Nevsky Avenue." Her beathing became laboured. "The place opposite the cathedral fountain entrance. It's open and above ground level, so I'm safe for the time being. I think I lost these people. For now."

"That's a good position. Don't move. Please stay in public and around people. I'm coming to get you. Keep your phone on in your pocket so I can hear, just in case."

The static noise background filled the car. He heard shuffling as Katerina clicked the end button.

Silence enveloped the cabin.

The agent pressed the ignition and eased into traffic. At the intersection, the light sat on red. He yanked the steering wheel and pulled a hard U-turn. A car on the opposite side slammed on the brakes. The horn blared, rattling his teeth.

*I've got to get to her before they do.*

# Chapter 19

The café sat on level two of a corner building named Singer. Patches of grime dotted the neglected façade.

A line of cars banked up to the lights. Neon lit up the building edges. Armitage slowed, peering up at the glass frontage. The options for a getaway, if necessary, were limited. He reversed into Griboyedov embankment lane and left the SUV in a parallel parking bay.

The water in the canal behind him churned and sloshed against stone banks. Jake opened the glove box, grasped his P-96. He attached a full magazine and thumbed off the safety.

A fire escape sat two meters from the vehicle. Jake tested the door. Unlocked. Good escape route.

The agent entered from the commercial customer side of the building.

Taking two steps at a time, he reached the reception zone of the open-plan restaurant. He noticed a bar behind a stand. A young woman offered to escort him to a table.

"Thank-you. I'm meeting someone," the agent said, scanning the patrons. He saw Katerina and pointed, moving around the tables to reach her.

The glass walls wrapped around the façade. A direct view, across Nevsky Avenue, of Kazan Cathedral lit up the darkening twilight.

Katerina grasped his hands in hers. "Thanks for coming so fast Jake."

Armitage smiled. He sat opposite. "That's fine, Katerina. Don't worry. I can't have anything happening to my favorite journalist." He gazed into her eyes. "Has anyone acted suspiciously since we spoke?"

"There's a man across in the corner, against the glass. Black hair and a brown coat. When he arrived, he searched the tables as if looking for someone." Her knuckles turned white as she squeezed the table edge.

The agent shook his head. "I saw him. Keep talking, please." He nodded and scanned the room subtly. Katerina sipped a cocktail to ease her nerves. He didn't check the direction of the man straight away. The chair forced his posture straight. Motioning Katerina to lean forward, he angled his head.

In his peripheral vision, he saw the brown-haired man staring straight at her back. The watcher appeared to be another mafia stooge, but Jake never assumed. Many Russian Special Forces' guys had dozens of tattoos all over their bodies.

"Here's what we're going to do. You stand on the count of three and go first. I'll come straight behind, and we'll walk together to the register. Do you have cash?"

She nodded.

"Great. Use that, please, instead of a card. Take it slow. You do the talking: light conversation. Anything: discuss a topic and smile. I'll answer every so often."

Katerina nodded.

"After you pay, continue to the lobby. Take the fire exit stairs which comes to the sidewalk. My SUV is parked two meters away."

She sipped her drink and looked up. "I'm good to go."

"OK. On the count of three. One, two, and three." The agent held eye contact.

Katerina stepped toward the reception. She held a

laptop bag over her right shoulder. Jake flanked her from the window side. He smiled.

The brown-haired watcher flinched.

Armitage clenched the P-96 grip, staring ahead.

The Russian journalist reached the bar and faced the hostess. She opened her bag and pushed cash over the counter.

Jake gazed over the patrons as the transaction processed. He stood behind Katerina, monitoring the watcher's elbows. The watcher had a cell phone to his ear, talking fast and low. The hostess handed the change and receipt to Katerina and she thanked the lady in Russian.

As they turned toward the escape, the brown-haired man jumped to his feet suddenly. The cell phone disappeared and he reached into the brown jacket.

A firearm.

The agent placed his hand on Katerina's shoulder. "He's up. Take the red door exit there." He shoved the key fob into her spare hand. "Unlock the car and get in the passenger seat."

Katerina hurried toward the landing.

*I hope there's no one waiting downstairs.*

The watcher produced a semi-automatic weapon. Time slowed in Jake's mind. He lowered around a large furniture piece. The gun barrel followed. A nearby female customer screamed. The blast lasted two seconds. Pot shots.

A waiter startled as a serving plate sailed over the tiles, the shards rebounding at shocked patrons.

The exit banged shut. Katerina disappeared. The agent exhaled, moved behind tables.

An overhead light blinked and extinguished.

Armitage drew the pistol with his right hand. He swung and aimed, checking there were no innocent people obstructing the way. None. Fired a single shot. It sailed over a plant and a table setting. The round hit an inch from the watcher's heart. On impact, the brown-haired assailant tipped. Jake ducked. A table toppled. The watcher groaned as the force of the momentum pushed him toward the floor-to-ceiling glass wall.

A second table collapsed, plates thrown asunder. Jake stepped forward, arm stretched and gun straight. A waitress hugged herself, crying. Two more male patrons hit the floor and crawled between chairs.

The agent fired a second round that hit the target square between the eyes. As he pivoted away, the glass panel shuddered. The watcher's body slammed the wall with his full dead weight and momentum. Spiderweb cracks formed in the wall, spread like a road map. A female patron's scream pierced the cafe followed by splintering shards of glass falling.

The shooter's body disappeared over the edge. A scream. Glass collided with the cobblestones outside. Yells from bystanders below. The wind sucked in through the gaping hole, the night air whipping the tablecloths.

Armitage pocketed his weapon. The exit door flung open. He sprinted over the stairs, two at a time. Blood pounded between his ears. Katerina's face flashed in his mind. He reached ground level, spilled onto the sidewalk. The corner hid his appearance. A cool breeze hit his cheek. Relief as he gazed into the car window.

Katerina slammed the passenger door. The agent slid over the hood. She reached across and released the driver's side latch. He tumbled into the seat and started the engine.

The car faced toward Nevsky Avenue. He gripped the wheel.

"Put your belt on, please." Jake clicked his seat belt, pumped the accelerator pedal to the floor. The car launched off the concrete.

In front of the café, onlookers huddled in a circle. Glass shards lay scattered on the cobbles. The shooter's body lay face down, dark-red pools puddled in the cracks.

The agent navigated through pedestrians, trying not to hit anyone. He reached the curb and sat waiting for a break. The crowd surrounding the dead shooter grew to three layers. An old lady fainted. Katerina stared straight ahead, ignoring the spectacle. He grasped a red cap from the rear seat and fastened it on his head. The next set of traffic lights turned red.

A figure appeared from the throng. The tall male in a dark brown jacket stared at the window. Armitage activated the handbrake aiming at the nearest lane. Nevsky Avenue traffic thinned out since peak, a smattering of vehicles in each lane.

*That stranger has to be one of them.*

The traffic from the red light bunched, leaving room at the end. He waited a second for the right moment, releasing the brake switch. The tires skidded and the car fishtailed into a gap.

A horn beeped as Jake flicked the turning signal.

The moon poked above the Kazan Cathedral, bathing the tall man in light. A glint of a weapon as the shooter aimed at the receding traffic. The agent changed lanes, weaving around the drivers. The assailant couldn't get a fix on their car.

In the rear-view mirror, Jake saw the man vanish in

the passing commuters. He checked for any tails but at this stage there seemed to be none. A siren sounded close. The police would be there in less than five minutes.

How did they get the shooter in the café so fast? He must have been tailing Katerina.

Jake increased speed, leaving Singer in their wake. The speedometer hit sixty. He eased off to stay right on the limit and squeezed Katerina's thigh.

The side of her lip turned upward, as if the beginning of a grin. Katerina nodded, a glazed expression in her eyes.

*She must be in a bit of a daze.*

The journalist turned to him. "What an exit, Jake Armitage. Are your evenings always this eventful?"

"Only if I'm lucky." He smiled and concentrated on the road ahead.

# Chapter 20

One streetlight illuminated the parking lot entry behind Jake's apartment block.

"Stay here for a moment, please. I need to do vehicle maintenance." Jake popped the trunk lever.

The agent found his screwdriver. The new plates went on easily. He dumped the old plates in a dumpster.

"You're an old hand at this game, aren't you?" Katerina said as Jake leaned behind the passenger seat. He placed a Beretta he'd taken from Popov's gang in a small carryall with the burner phones.

"I've had a little experience. Come through here. You'll be safe."

Jake led around the side entrance and into the kitchen. The chef gave him a glance. Jake waved and pulled Katerina after him to the elevator bay.

"I hope we don't run into my neighbor, Mrs Bukin. She's quite the busybody."

"Yes, we have one of those." She grinned.

The elevator ascended through the spine of the old building. To Jake's relief, no residents entered the elevator.

"Home sweet home." A double deadlock clicked and Jake stepped aside.

Inside the apartment, she raised an eyebrow at the first passageway but remained silent. At the kitchen, she nodded.

"This is very nice once you get inside." She walked around, glancing admiringly at the settee and kitchen.

"I can't have the neighbors getting too jealous. Must keep up appearances." The agent winked and put down the keys. He shelved both Berettas in the cupboard.

Katerina opened the balcony door. Wind blew her hair. She placed a hand on the rail and inhaled deeply. Armitage ran over and gently pulled her back inside.

"Sorry, but you need to stay out of sight. If you're a target, these guys might have drone technology or access to geo-positional satellite coverage." He pulled the sliding door shut. "That's why I installed a heavy industrial tint on this glass."

"Understood, Jake, and I know you're taking care of me. But I'm not completely defenceless, you know."

"I'm sure. That brings me to my next question." The agent picked up his firearm. "Have you ever shot one of these at a target before?"

"Yes, but at a shooting range. Self-defence purposes, not a live target. Yet. A lady can't be too careful."

"That's good; at least you've handled a weapon before, which will come in handy."

Armitage slipped behind the kitchen island and cracked open the fridge. He pulled out strips of raw beef.

"It's only simple food but it's all I have in the fridge. Haven't gone shopping yet." Jake smiled. "You know. Killing bad guys and all that. Would you like rice and beef stir fry?"

"I'd love food, thanks, Jake. Too scared to eat much at Singer."

Jake cooked the meat. He chopped vegetables, added to the pan. The sauce went in at the end, served with boiled rice.

The agent laid out plates on the table and they ate in silence. The evening's events ran through his mind. He blocked them for the duration of their meal.

"This food is good." The reporter took a final bite and placed her cutlery on the plate. She looked across at Jake and gave a half-grin. The expression seemed to indicate she had a lot on her mind.

Armitage reached for her plate. "If you're finished."

"Yes, thanks." She gained her feet and Jake touched her hand.

"It's ok. I'll take care of these."

"I'll help you with the cleaning," Katerina said, picking up a towel. "And a great meal too. Thanks for making it."

"Least I can do after your ordeal this evening."

The agent washed the dishes and Katerina dried. When the kitchen was sorted, they moved to the living room. He clicked on a wall-mounted heat system. The warmth began to flow straight away. Katerina curled her legs underneath her and turned to Jake.

"Do you know who these people are that are chasing me?"

Armitage adjusted the office chair and slid the wheels next to her. "I'm not sure yet. We located an asset that went missing. He was being held captive by a new sect of the Russian mafia in a house. The whistleblower offered evidence that the Russians interfered with the U.S. presidential campaign." He paused and took a breath.

"It's been an eventful forty-eight hours." Jake rubbed his neck.

"I'll say." Katerina grimaced and shook her head. "Now they tried executing me in a public place. Unbelievable the mafia would get involved in a contract kill of this magnitude. Even for Russia, this is strange."

"That's what I thought too. This operation looked like

human traffickers and other organized crime. But I'm not sure if they were paid to hold him. Or if there's a third party who set them up to make it look that way."

"What do you mean?"

"With the dead asset, I found another corpse from the same mafia sect. They have a star ink with a dagger through the middle. Three guys came back after the kill. Not sure why. Maybe to clean up or maybe they weren't the murderers." Jake shrugged. "But these guys were ex-soldiers and armed."

Katerina gazed thoughtfully at the reverse cycle. "I can tell you the history of the sect with the tattoo. Its foundations lie in prison culture. A convicted criminal named Uri in the notorious Jaka hellhole. One of the worst prisons in Russia. Uri had a falling out with a mafia boss. Started his own branch and they've been at war ever since."

"That clears up the origins. But the network is bigger than these criminals. The restaurant shooter looked like a contract killer. I've come up against at least one military-trained mercenary. Slick operator."

Darkness blanketed the walls. Lights flickered outside.

"Now we know this connection, we need to work out who's managing the criminals and paying mercenaries," Katerina said.

"And why..." The agent stood and stared out through the floor-to-ceiling glass. Streaks of amber sparkled across the baroque-marble architecture.

Jake angled his gaze at the Griboyedov channel, its waters reflected gold on black, like a royal passage leading to the Church of the Saviour on Spilled Blood. Colors shimmered off the onion-shaped domes. His contemplation rested on the canal that flowed through to the Moyka River.

Katerina loaded her laptop. She typed as the blue hue lit up her face.

Turning from the balcony, Jake said, "I'm more concerned about this Ukrainian contract killer. His name is Bohdan Kolisnyk, a former Russian Special Forces soldier. Interpol gave me his resume and it's not pretty. Came up against him this morning with two more dagger-and-star guys."

"What happened?" Katerina crossed her arms.

"I tracked Popov, a mafia thug I'd been tailing, to a worksite. Three guys were covering their tracks and making plans for more payoffs and contracts. I managed to eavesdrop for a while, but I decided to break up their party."

The Russian reporter's gaze rose. "You're having me on, Jake."

Armitage shook his head. "Let's just say that Kolisnyk had an AK 47 and I was outnumbered and out-gunned. After a friendly neighborhood shootout, the Ukrainian escaped in an SUV. I got the vehicle registration but I'm sure it won't point back to him. There's a bit of damage. Should be easy to identify if he hasn't ditched it already."

Darkness blacked out the windows.

"You're a one-man army trying to take on Russia's underworld." She sighed.

"Don't I know it." Jake smiled.

"I feel safer with you." Katerina restored her composure and gazed at her laptop. "Is the WIFI safe to use? I have some work to do to help our cause."

"Yes, I've got advanced security protocols with airtight firewall that bounce the signal to other URL addresses. No one can track you here, even with serious cyber technology."

The agent moved behind her. "Let me show you." He typed in the password in the prompt and connected her laptop.

"Thanks. I'm going to raid my server at work and see if I can find anything on this group."

She tapped away for twenty minutes as Jake made two drinks. Through the glass, he saw the lit drawbridge open over the main river canal below. The sight never ceased to amaze.

"It must be midnight already. Time flies when you're having fun."

"I didn't notice." The Russian reporter chuckled. She'd become engrossed in the screen, flipping through logins and databases.

Armitage carried the mugs to the sofa.

Katerina took a sip. "I've deep-dived all day and found some court trials for Manny Popov, but not much else. Tomorrow I'll get started on this Bohdan. We'll see what else I can dig up on these guys."

"Sounds good. I'm going to get some sleep." Jake yawned and pointed at a two-seater sofa against the wall. "This sofa folds out to a bed. I can sleep out here and you can take my bed."

"I have a nightie and some underwear in my bag. I've been dodging these people for days and had to be prepared."

"You can have a shower to freshen up. Bathroom is through there." The agent gestured at the corridor. "Second door on the right. You'll find the bedroom opposite."

"I need that. Thanks again."

"Don't mention it." Jake said and collapsed the sofa

end to the floor. He laid down a fitted-sheet and a cover over the top. A sheet and doona went over to keep out the chill.

The living room dimmed. Armitage grasped the blind cord as the city lights disappeared. He took a glass of vodka while Katerina finished her shower and dressed. The day's events ran in his mind. He supressed his anger. Involving the Russian reporter was the last thing he wanted.

In the bedroom, Katerina helped as Jake made the bed up with fresh sheets.

"Thanks again for your help, Jake." She touched his hand and he took her fingers in his palm.

"It's no problem. I feel responsible. I'm happy you're in one piece and alive." He grinned. "But it's not over yet."

She nodded sleepily. "Yes, I had a bad feeling about that."

"I'll be up at six A.M. When you wake, let me know and we'll discuss the next phase." Jake released her hand and trundled into the living room. He closed the door gently and padded to the foldout sofa.

The sheets were fresh and gave off a pleasant fragrance. The agent lowered his head and fell asleep as soon as his head touched the pillow.

# Chapter 21

The alarm started music at six A.M., Jake awoke from sleep. He rolled off the sofa bed and took in the lounge ceiling. In the corner, he'd set up a stationary bike. The usual routine consisted of twenty minutes but he did ten this time.

Sweat rolled over Jake's brow. He opened the shower and flipped the faucet to hot. As the water ran over his body, he thought about Kolisnyk's cell number he'd recorded from Popov's missed calls. The burner might still be in use and it gave Jake an idea. Arrange a meeting in a public place to draw out the rest of his party. This might also reveal the motive behind the Ukrainian's actions and who else was involved besides SPG.

The blue numbers on the microwave read six-twenty A.M. Armitage locked the door and jogged over to the convenience store. He bought two large cartons of fresh milk. In the basket he added a bunch of bananas, apples, and a bag of oranges. He found a carton of eggs, a box of muesli, and oats. In the final aisle, he picked up a loaf of bread.

On the journey home, Jake took a longer route. He checked for followers but couldn't detect any unusual behaviour. In the lobby, he found little activity. The kitchen started later on Sundays. Jake entered the apartment and stocked the cold goods in the fridge. He emptied the other items in the small pantry.

Armitage ate a bowl of muesli with sliced banana. The meal went down quickly after the work out and yesterday's hectic activities. He took five oranges and squeezed them. Eggs blended with milk were poured into a pan and placed on the stove.

By the time Katerina emerged from the bedroom, Jake

had toasted bread sitting on plates.

"Morning. You've been busy." She smiled and sat down at the table.

"Hi, Katerina, you look rested. Would you like scrambled eggs?"

"Yes, please."

The agent tilted the pan at the toasted bread. He took the plate and the fresh juice to the table.

"Excuse me for a moment."

"Of course." The Russian journalist picked up a knife and fork.

Out on the balcony, Jake closed the sliding glass door. He took out the number for Kolisnyk's cell and dialled from a new burner.

"Zdravstvuj," a man's deep voice answered in Russian.

"Hello, Kolisnyk. How are you on this fine morning?"

"Who is this?"

"I'm surprised you don't know. My name is Armitage and we had a scuffle yesterday morning at your friend's warehouse."

"So, you're the one." Kolisnyk chuckled. "You've got balls, American. Do you think you can win a fight against me?"

"I'm aware of your resume. It doesn't concern me in the slightest. You left in a hurry though; I couldn't say goodbye."

A slight pause. "Manny no longer works for me."

"I'm sure. This foreplay is fun and I'd like to do it all day. But I'd rather we meet up to have a chat and swap intel."

"An exchange of information? Name the place."

"How about the Marketplace on Nevsky Avenue? There's a café at the south entrance. What about ten A.M. today?"

"See you there, Armitage." The phone cut out and Jake pressed the off button.

The sparse sunlight cracked through the rolling clouds. A bird fluttered off the balcony and soared over the edge. Armitage slid open the door and slipped into the apartment.

"I'm going to meet Bohdan Kolisnyk in a restaurant along Nevsky."

"Are you crazy, Jake?" She shook her head. "This guy is a psychopath!"

"I want to look him in the eye and ask the questions face to face. That way I can see his reactions, and if he's lying or not." He paused and reached for her hands. "Katerina, it's better if you stay."

"If I stay here, you'll be out there alone?"

"No, I've got an idea. Stick with me." Jake dialled a number. The dial tone rang and he waited.

"Leonid Zima. It's Armitage."

"What can I do for you, Jake?"

"That Ukrainian mercenary we discussed named Bohdan Kolisnyk. He's going to be at a café called Pyshechka at ten A.M. today. It's on the Griboyedov channel embankment."

"I know where it is. Are you certain of this information?"

"I'm positive. Can you get law enforcement people

there on short notice? They'll need to be military."

"Leave it with me, Jake. Next time give me more notice?"

The agent hung up and gazed at Katerina. "I've arranged backup just in case."


Most of the breakfast rush in Pyshechka café had deserted the place, leaving staff to clear the tables. At nine-forty A.M., Jake conducted basic surveillance. Tactical counter-measures.

Armitage sat facing the sidewalk with the wall behind him. From an al-fresco seat, he evaluated possible sniper positions.

Two points were of concern: a building balcony diagonally placed ten meters to the entry, and a corner shop with a second-level window. The agent sipped water from a bottle.

A boat churned along the canal, sightseers snapping photos and pointing at buildings. Jake adjusted his weight, taking in the east side. Waves broke at a junction point, the mouth leading to concrete piers. The steps led up to an outside landing. He watched the traffic embark from a tourist jet boat.

Bohdan Kolisnyk arrived at nine-fifty from the direction of the canal. Jake watched as the mercenary climbed the steps and sat at the table.

"Bohdan, thanks for coming."

The blond-haired killer smirked. "Mr Armitage, what do you want?"

"Why did you kill the prisoner held by the mafia?"

"The Russian worker that tried to sell secrets?" The

mercenary bent and placed his hand on the table. "I was hired to do a job."

Armitage took a long shot. "Did SPG Partners hire you for this job?"

The Ukrainian's eyes narrowed for a split second. Jake knew he'd guessed right.

"I work for myself: a contractor only. All projects and clients are confidential. That's the way it should be for everyone."

Armitage nodded, his mind running the angles.

The Ukrainian poured water into a glass.

"Are you going to make any more death threats?"

"To you? I don't threaten. If I kill a person, I do it and never tell you first. We are the same: both contract killers." The mercenary spoke with a strong accent. "Why do you Americans always stick your noses in Russian business?"

Jake nodded and sipped his water. "I could ask you the same thing."

"We did a clean-up as the mafia bungled another job. The data drive is gone so why are you here?"

Armitage smiled and said, "You know Greenwood and Bollov are making tens of millions of dollars from your dirty work? You're doing the hard work, killing and murdering, and they're making a fortune. I guess you are used to the prison life, huh?"

A breeze flowed across the table. Kolisnyk's eyelid flinched, just a slight movement. Perhaps a tick or a mannerism. Anger.

Maybe because the mercenary knew Jake was right.

The big man crossed his arms and said, "Is that all

you wanted to tell me? I'm going to kill you, Armitage. But slowly—and enjoy torturing you." The grin vanished.

"Let's call it a second date, Bohdan. I'm coming after you and your people. Until I reach the top of this sordid pyramid."

"We'll see about this American boasting." The Ukrainian laughed.

A flicker of black caught the vision in Jake's right eye. The masked soldier appeared from behind a pillar. Ten meters and closing. Armitage grabbed a shaker and tossed salt at the Ukrainian's face. The mercenary ducked, managing to avoid some of the spray.

The wind spread the remaining salt. Kolisnyk sprinted across the café and threw his hips over the rail, swung out toward the steps. He searched for the best escape routes. A second soldier flanked the first as they closed in.

The agent shoved the table and sprinted across the landing. He reached the side and vaulted over the stairs. The soldiers chased the Ukrainian over the embankment. At the elevated path, Jake paused and turned. Nobody was following him. He peered down the channel and saw Kolisnyk vanish into a populated section of sidewalk. Three soldiers trailed the mercenary, but the lead grew bigger by the second.

Over the vendor stands, Jake took the cobbled crosswalk. He squatted behind his car's side panel, waiting for the rest of the team. As they cleared, he clicked the key fob, jumped in and gazed out the windshield. Armitage started the vehicle and pulled into the lane.

*The contract killer has been identified. Now we're going to have some fun.*

# Chapter 22

The cell phone rang three times before Katerina answered.

"You're still alive, Jake. Thank goodness." The relief in her voice carried through on the Bluetooth loudspeaker.

"My plan worked well enough. I don't think the Ukrainian came armed. A smart move in a public place, but you never know with people like that. I asked him the hard questions and I know he's working for SPG consultants." Jake paused. "The military police turned up at the right time."

"That's a relief." An exhale came through the phone.

The agent grinned but kept his eyes on the road. A warm sensation in his stomach threatened to undo his hard image.

The Russian reporter interrupted his thoughts. "I've logged into our media server. To find as much information on these guys as possible. Both on the Ukrainian mercenary and Greenwood and Bollov." Key taps echoed in the background.

"Anything we can get will help give an edge." Jake turned right and passed onto the canal bridge. He slowed for a group of tourists who were pointing at buildings.

"By the way, about the registration for the blond Ukrainian's black Toyota. I rang and asked my contact in law enforcement. He rang some checks. The vehicle is registered to a warehouse in the western section. It hasn't been reported stolen, so I think it must be legit, as you say in America. I sent you a text message with the full address."

"Thanks, Katerina. This really helps. I'll check it soon and you sit tight and keep the balcony door shut."

"Ok, Jake. You take care out there." The call dropped.

*She's already learning the lingo. Smart lady.*

The vehicle curb-crawled over the rough asphalt. Armitage steered at twenty miles per hour, squinting at the letterbox numbers. In a clump of twentieth century neglected warehouses, he searched for the right place.

A typical Soviet-era industrial zone.

The block intersected at a ground level box that appeared to have the right number. Jake's gaze followed the gray, drab walls. Hurricane-wire fencing surrounded the boundary. A gate swung ajar with a rusted padlock that dangled in the wind. Holes marked sections where unwanted guests had entered.

The agent pulled up under a corrugated iron roof nailed to exposed beams. The structure had long since buckled with age and the elements. Graffiti covered the cinder-block flank. The building stood on a corner, brown paint peeling from the walls. A feral cat scurried along the raised cement dispatch zone and over the curb.

Jake checked the main entrance and docking bay, both locked. A windowpane sat two meters high from the ground. The agent crossed to the boundary and peeked over a steel-sheet fence. A small patch of grass and dirt was filled with loose ends and rusting machine parts.

Jake parked the car in a close side street and crossed the asphalt. A truck turned into the side street. The main entrance to the premises had a double garage door clamped to the concrete floor. Padlocks were fastened at either end.

The agent opened the mailbox flap and peered inside. A pile of letters sat neatly in the box. It appeared to be weeks of accumulated mail. Two men walked along the opposite side, chatting in Russian.

*This cannot be an important location.*

Through a grimy window, Jake spotted a barista. He crossed the street, checking for unusual behaviour. Armitage entered the takeout café and took in the warmth.

*I'm the only customer.*

"Can I have an expresso takeout, and extra strong, please?" Jake said to the attendant.

The young man nodded. Armitage watched the place through the window. The attendant handed him his order and he pulled some notes.

"Keep the change."

"Thanks." The Russian's eyes held a grateful glint.

The agent took the coffee and waited in the car, watching the front of the warehouse.

At midday, a text from Katerina chimed, breaking Jake's near trance-like state. He thumbed his cell phone scroll and a smile formed.

*She replied on time.*

He adjusted the seat and read the message—a two-hour update. A reply let her know his plans for an ad-lib stakeout on the warehouse. He needed to see if anybody watched the place or collected the mail. Otherwise this location was a dead end.

Jake opened the door and stretched on the grass. To get some exercise, he yanked his blue cap over his hair and did a few laps of the block. He walked in different directions each time, taking separate routes back to the corner. The cap obscured his face from any potential witnesses or counter-surveillance cameras. At all times he maintained constant visual on the entry point of the warehouse.

The agent chose a different shop and bought a bottle of water. He avoided going to the same place twice if possible. To make it harder for people to remember his face.

The neighborhood had little foot traffic. Minutes ticked by and Jake returned to the car.

After three hours had elapsed, Jake rubbed his lower lumbar. He considered ceasing the watch and calling it a day. A dog scampered past the lot. He thought of staying for another hour. The dashboard clock read three-fifty-three P.M. His burner flashed and he checked the screen. No text. Katerina checked in every two hours with a message, but she'd missed the last one by over an hour.

Armitage looked at the burner phone for network issues. It read a strong signal with four of the possible five coverage bars.

*I'll worry about her when this is done. She's safe under my state-of-the-art security system.*

A bird squawked and took flight. Jake shifted in the car seat. At four-ten a blue Kia Rio slowed to the curb.

The Rio parked and a young woman stepped onto the sidewalk. Dressed in smart business attire and European-branded pumps, she walked over to the warehouse mailbox. The female opened the lid and reached inside, taking the pile of letters. Her heels clicked on cement as she returned to the hatchback.

Jake recorded the registration and texted it to Katerina. He drove toward the city center. Peak hour traffic had begun, banked up the lanes. The gray clouds opened as a downpour started to fall. Rain battered the windows as he waited on the journalist's message.

The burner beeped. Katerina had found an address for the mystery female in the Kia hatchback. A corporate complex in the eastern section of Saint Peterburg's commercial zone.

Armitage took a right and punched the address into the GPS. According to the interface, he'd be there in ten minutes.

As expected, the street contained a long row of semi-modern office fronts. Jake found the number and parked outside. He took the crosswalk and examined a big sign on the canopy.

The name Pavel Sobol was highlighted in large, royal-blue letters, unmissable for any passing motorists. Jake blended with pedestrians as he strolled by the ground floor. A large billboard displayed a photo of a man in his forties with light-brown, short hair and glasses. The subject wore a cotton, button-down white shirt with a designer yellow tie. This impeccable dress code radiated a professional but conservative image.

*I wonder if this guy takes fashion lessons from Greenwood and SPG partners.*

The agent strolled past the entrance and glanced inside. A woman sat behind a desk, a corridor snaking down the center behind, her gaze switching between a computer monitor and an open notebook. Large portrait photos of men and women in business attire lined the background.

The rain reduced to a light patter. Jake moved away from the glass pane so the woman wouldn't notice him staring. He walked over the road to stand opposite the office. In front of an apartment high-rise, he read the slogan on the canopy: Rights of People Party.

*A politician. Makes perfect sense. But what's the connection? Just graft and corruption?*

A political party that went up against the current President in the last election. The agent sat behind the wheel and contemplated his options.

*If I go in now, I might run into Kolisnyk. That would*

*give him a head start.*

Armitage headed back to his apartment. He needed to discuss this matter with Katerina and work out a strategy. The new information created more questions than it answered.

One thought ran through Jake's mind over and over.

*Why would a known politician associate with a Ukrainian contract killer?*

The traffic thickened. Rain pattered the windshield. The agent forced himself to keep to the speed limit.

The lights outside Jake's side street blinked green. He exited Nevsky and scanned the concrete lot.

Underfoot, the broken path was slippery. Armitage strode through the dimly lit foyer. A siren wailed in the distance.

*I hope I'm back in time and she's ok.*

# Chapter 23

A dull shine reflected off the edges of the old apartment elevator bay. Armitage touched the button for level six. The folding doors seemed to take forever to close as he waited. He hadn't heard from Katerina in over two hours. A pit formed in his gut.

*I am energized and fully protected.*

Deep breaths. Jake took oxygen through the nose, down into the diaphragm. In and out. The butterflies in his stomach climbed to his chest like a serpent mounting a strike to its victim's head.

*This stress will kill me one day.*

The agent checked the floor on the panel. It had reached number three. He pressed the button for six again. The cabin clunked as it staggered toward the next level. At five, the elevator halted and he thought it would open. It shuddered and continued climbing.

A ping announced they'd reached his floor. He power-walked to the apartment and knocked quietly.

No answer.

*I did tell her not to answer the door.*

Armitage shoved his hand in his pocket and yanked out the key. The metal fumbled in the lock before it sank in and turned. It was unlike Jake to be so clumsy. He sprinted past the opening and into the living room.

Katerina sat curled on the sofa, typing on her keyboard. She looked up with a happy and bemused expression.

"You're back." She placed the computer aside and jumped up, threw out her arms. The agent placed the carryall on the table surface. Rain lashed the balcony door, clouds darkening overhead. He maneuvered past the island bench, shaking his head as he walked. Katerina curled her hands around his back.

Relief flooded his system as Jake exhaled. "I worried that something had gone wrong. You didn't send me a text in three hours."

"Sorry. I forgot to send the last one. What happened at the office address?"

Jake sank to the sofa, shoulders slumped. He crossed his arms. "The office is occupied by a politician by the name Pavel Sobol. This guy has got signs with his face on. One of the major parties to take on the Russian president in the last election."

Katerina's eyes widened as she took in the information. "Sobol heads the Yabloko party. They were the only challengers in the 2018 Presidential Campaign." She circled the sofa. "So the Ukrainian is working for a major politician? Plus Sobol might be also contracting the members of the star-and-dagger Russian mafia?"

The agent shook his head. "Yep. The politician is a real equal opportunity employer."

Katerina picked her laptop from the table. "I'm searching our databases for information on Sobol prior to the last election. Anything in connection to big business contracts."

Armitage opened the cupboard and started a stocktake on his armoury. Four pistols: a Browning, two battered Berettas, and his reliable P-96M. The agent counted five full magazines for the spare weapons. An AK47 had been collected. The magazine was half full, another spare ready. He placed two boxes of ammo for the P-96M on the table and loaded the three magazines.

All weapons underwent a complete check. By the time the agent had put the Beretta back together, Katerina motioned him to the computer.

"Take a look at this video." She pressed play and the screen lit up with feed. "Found it in our digital archives."

The grainy feed had a long-range take with a date near four years old. A zoom narrowed onto a man. Armitage saw a younger version of Sobol in a blue suit. People scrambled in a crowd. A press conference in full action played out Russian-style. The politician picked individuals from the audience, taking questions.

In the background, protestors picketed. The agent found it difficult to tell the difference between the supporters and the objectors. Signs bobbed in the air, mingled with fist pumps in defiance. The politician appeared on a raised podium, his hands gesturing passionately.

First and second rows were filled with reporters. Jake noticed a logo in the shape of a bell on a microphone cover. The brand of Katerina's media group. It surprised him, considering the degree of Presidential censorship on all media that was in effect.

"There's many of ours there," she said, having noticed his interest.

Armitage scanned over the crowd and noticed a banner for SPG and another primary manufacturing company.

"Interesting that SPG have outdoor signage."

"Yes. Look here at this guy." Katerina indicated a tall man behind the politician, monitoring the crowd. Surveillance. The posture upright, confident and assured. Military training. The man dressed in a loose suit and touched his collar. A mike.

Jake squinted at the face. His face lit up on realizing the identity. The longer hair and back turned to the camera meant it took longer for Jake to recognize.

"It's Bohdan Kolisnyk. He's a bodyguard for this politician?" Jake said and turned to Katerina.

"That's correct. I've done more digging and found out the Ukrainian was contracted, on-and-off, for three years as Sobol's main security. In fact, Kolisnyk is still a contractor on Sobol's protection team."

"This conspiracy is deepening by the hour." He took a red apple from the pantry and sunk teeth into the fruit. "Fantastic you could pull the archives. Great work, Katerina."

"Why would Sobol hire mercenaries to deal with international conspiracies? Did he want to influence the U.S. election? The politician didn't win the Russian election, so he's not in power," she said, rising and stretching her spine. "I mean there's always corruption and greed in Russia, but to this extent and without power? It's a massive risk when you hire contract killers." She paused, "Even in Russia."

"Maybe they thought their party would be victorious. Leverage for power back here? It's still a long shot, and why now?" Armitage paced the living zone, munching on the fruit.

"It doesn't add up. There must be more to this." She contemplated the laptop.

"We know Kolisnyk and the politician are linked."

The Russian reporter smiled and continued typing.

"I'll prepare some food. It's been an eventful day for both of us."

"While you're doing that, Jake, I'm going to search for links on Sobol. Transactions and data. There's got to be more, and the politician has employed this mercenary for five years."

The agent got changed in the bedroom and washed his face in the bathroom. The kitchen lit up as he boiled rice on the stove. He cooked half a kilo of chicken in the pan. With the meat, he added some vegetables and a basic sauce.

The pair ate in silence until Katerina spoke.

"Saint Petersburg isn't exactly the best destination to lose yourself and find yourself. Especially for an American."

Armitage chuckled and said, "I agree."

"So, tell me, Jake, if you don't mind, how does a guy like you end up here? Isn't there a wife who is missing her clothes—and you?"

The agent wiped his mouth on a serviette. "It's a long story. Originally I was in the Army Reserve when I finished high school. I did a gap year from university. As work experience, I'd dabbled with IT systems at a friend's father's company. A little bit of study and reading, and suddenly it seemed like I had a knack."

"Hacking too?"

"More like stopping hackers, but setting up systems people could understand. Non-technical staff."

Jake placed his cutlery on the plate.

"In the gap year, my cyber security skills and mixed martial arts background landed me a job in Bangkok. I continued my training in Mui Thai."

"The martial arts scene is brutal there, isn't it?"

The agent nodded. "Instructors conducted weekly tournaments. They were bare knuckle and almost no rules."

"Hardcore." Katrina sipped her drink.

"A person I contracted with on a project hacked one of our clients—the Red Bull site. There was a massive fall-out. The US government protected me, but the price was recruitment."

"So, you joined the NSA."

"That's right. In my six months at the NSA, I was stationed here seven years ago. My skill set is rather unique. A niche consultant in organizing corporate cyber security for CEOs. Putting it into a language they understand. The overall vision for integrating to the business. On returning to the U.S., DoD expanded my job description. More assignments in eastern Europe, and combat training too."

"And you're back now?" The Russian reporter smiled.

"I came back to Saint Petersburg after a separation. Her name is Melissa. She works at our U.S. headquarters in Forte Meade. A data analyst, and a really good one at that."

"What happened?"

Jake took up his fork again.

"The relationship started fast, six years ago. I'd just come back from Saint Petersburg on a one-year assignment when we got together. We were so close. Married ten months later." Jake sighed.

Katerina nodded and listened.

"Both of us really wanted a child." He paused. "We tried and tried and found out there were fertility issues. Melissa blamed herself and I tried talking her out of this."

"That must have been hard." Katerina said with a frown.

"Yes, it created tension. But we kept on trying for two years. A miracle happened." The agent finished his mouthful. A lump formed in his throat. "Mellissa fell pregnant."

"That's wonderful."

"Melissa was beaming. We were both over the moon. At our first ultrasound, every result came out perfect. On the fifteenth week, the complications began. She had cramps and pains, and too many." Jake broke his gaze as his eyes fogged.

"If you don't want to say, I'll understand." Katerina rested her fingers on his hand.

"It's OK. I can talk about it now." Jake paused and collected his thoughts. "We lost the baby the following week."

"That's tragic, Jake. I'm really sorry to hear." She shook her head.

The moon shone a crescent shape over the floor. Jake's mind focused and he supressed the knot in his chest. He took a deep breath as rawness flooded his system.

"We kept trying IVF but couldn't conceive again. The arguments occurred more often, eventually agreeing eighteen months ago to separate." Armitage shifted his position. "I guess I didn't know who I was supposed to be anymore."

"It's hard, separating." Katerina sighed, her gaze pointed at the darkness. "I'd love to have a child, but after being raised by a single mother, I cannot bear to take the risk. We had such poverty growing up."

"But you turned out well."

"Did you know over forty percent of children in Russia are raised by single mothers? The latest generation are higher than when I was a child. The men have no responsibility in this culture."

169

"It's hard in this day and age," the agent said. "That is an alarming statistic though. I can appreciate your fear."

Katerina looked away. "There's a charity support group for women that I owe my life. I'd do anything to donate money."

"I'm sure you would be a wonderful mother."

Katerina held her cup to her face as if to hide a blush.

"What motivated you to come back?"

"I decided, after speaking to a mentor, that going back on active duty might help heal things. The assistant director, Tom Johnson, recruited me when he was a field agent in Thailand. Tom acted like a father figure in those early years."

"I understand the connection." She smiled. "Here you are, a silver lining to my playbook."

"Here I am in your city again, chasing bad guys." Jake grinned. "Plus once you're in this game, it's very hard to get out. Always looking over your shoulder."

The reporter nodded. A serious look fell over her face.

"What about yourself, Katerina? Why is an attractive young reporter single now?"

Katerina's eyes diverted as her cheeks flushed a little redder with the compliment. "I was in a relationship that ended a year ago now." Her words caught in her throat. "My job is very demanding, so it's difficult to juggle a relationship. He's a doctor, so I guess we drifted apart until I told him we needed to chat. We had time apart and decided to split."

Katerina swallowed and pushed her plate. A sadness crossed her eyes as she stared over his shoulder.

Jake noticed a sudden change of mood. "Are you OK?"

"Before the doctor, I was in a relationship with another journalist. He had an assignment in Syria in a war zone. Some insurgents stormed a town, and he was caught in crossfire." Her eyes watered. "I never really got over it, I guess."

They sat in silence.

"I'm sorry for your loss, Katerina."

She lifted her head. "I feel like damaged goods sometimes. You know, like too much baggage?"

"Look at me. I'm a walking wound." Jake paused to summon the right words. "Everybody has past issues. It's how you deal with them that makes the difference. I think you came out fine. You're strong and independent. Any guy would be lucky to have you."

"Thanks. Grief makes us do strange things sometimes."

"I'll say." The heaviness in Jake's chest swelled.

She adjusted her body weight and caught his eyes, her gaze shiny with a tinge of sadness. "My grandmother told me once that the world is filled with ghosts. The longer we live, the more ghosts will haunt us." She paused, glancing at her palms. "But they're here to remind us we are alive. That our hearts beat, blood runs through our veins, we breath air into our lungs."

"Wise words. I believe it's true." Armitage swallowed a lump in his throat, his chest heavy. To distract the emotion, he picked up the empty plates and placed them in the sink. Warm water flowed over his hands and into the sink. He watched it run over the pile and carry away the leftovers.

Katerina joined him. She picked up a towel and dried the plates. Silence hung as the pair worked in unison. Not uncomfortable silence, Jake noted. As the dishes were packed away, the two moved to the sofa.

"So that's our stories. We've laid bare our souls. Everything is out in the open." She pulled her knees to her body. "No secrets."

"Nothing to hide. But I'm sorry I dragged you into this mess, Katerina." The agent's brow furrowed. "It's become very dangerous."

"It's not entirely your fault. I'm a big girl and this comes with the territory. Been in a war zone, remember? I don't like what these people represent as well. They're holding back my country with so much corruption. It's bad enough from the mafia criminals, but when politicians are involved... Where does it end?" She waved her arms.

"Glad you feel that way. I'm not going to let anything bad happen to you."

She smiled. "We better get back to this case, hadn't we?"

"You got it."

Katerina switched her computer on and continued her research. On the table, Jake checked agency databases for data on the politician Sobol.

At ten-thirty, Jake rose from the keyboard. He fetched a bottle of Vodka, poured two shots into a glass.

"Would you like some?" he said to Katerina and held up the bottle.

"No, thanks. Not this time." She rubbed her eyes. "I'm going to sleep soon, after I finish reading this piece."

"Good idea. This will be my nightcap."

A blue hue lit up Katerina's face as she hunched over the screen. The mouse clicked and she closed the computer.

"Sweet dreams, Jake. Goodnight." She kissed him on the cheek.

"Take care and sleep well."

As Katerina disappeared through the bedroom door, Jake fetched his P-96 and left it on the table. It was his preferred firearm. Reliable, accurate, and rarely seized up, unlike a temperamental Beretta.

The agent stared at the gun barrel, lost unravelling the hierarchy of this conspiracy. He left the weapon on the table, within reach of the bed, in case he needed it during the night.

Armitage carried his glass toward the balcony. He opened the sliding door. The cool breeze brushed his cheeks.

Darkness hid their mounting enemies. Jake sipped his final refill. A burn rode his throat and travelled to his chest. Relief. The night appeared clear and the stars bright. A thousand lights and colors sparkled which gave him hope. He paced the rail, watching the shadows.

The agent closed and locked the balcony doo,r leaving his empty glass in the sink. The sofa extended with a squeak. He pulled the blanket onto his body. The lights hung over an ink sky.

*I hope I can deliver my promise.*

# Chapter 24

Armitage didn't know the stranger chasing him. The man ran toward him as he reached the entrance to a tunnel. He couldn't see the stranger's face yet but he could hear the man's breathing. The darkness swallowed the tunnel as Jake wondered where it led. In the distance, a small yellow light revealed a bend.

*I don't recall this tunnel being here before.*

Jake pushed his legs to run harder as the path descended. Slowly the walls moved closer. He outstretched his right arm. His fingertips touched an uneven surface; concrete or smooth brick, he couldn't tell. The agent twisted to see his pursuer, closing in fast. The face was hidden as if a void, hair blurry, no particular color. His breathing turned ragged. He pushed himself hard but his legs ceased to function. His thighs staggered, running on the spot.

*I need to face my attacker.*

The bend in the tunnel suddenly appeared. Jake stopped, braced his feet in a fighting stance. Mui Thai bouts flashed. The stranger came closer and his features became clearer. A nose and mouth protruded. The hair appeared black. It turned brown. A gun appeared in the man's hand.

Armitage went for his belt to draw his weapon. An empty holster. He froze and couldn't move.

The hand pointed a gun barrel at Jake's face. He saw the weapon, but his hands were stuck. Only his eyes pivoted in their sockets.

*I'm helpless and cannot fight back.*

The hair shimmered and lightened. Blond. Jake saw the attacker's face.

Bohdan Kolisnyk.

The Ukrainian's gun clicked. An explosion. Orange flared. The bullet left the barrel in slow motion. Armitage watched and his stomach lurched.

Somewhere in the darkness, Katerina screamed.

"Where are you?" the agent tried to yell. He couldn't hear his words. Heart hammered. Dry throat. The bullet flew, slowly came within inches of his face.

*This is it. I'm dead.*

Armitage jolted upright in the bed. Sweat trickled on his brow. His hands gripped the mattress, knuckles white and bloodless. The sheets were damp with sweat. He felt his forehead and nose.

No bullets or gaping wound.

The clock glowed four-twenty-two A.M. His breathing slowed and the rhythm returned to his lungs. He leaned back and the sofa bed creaked.

Relief set in as Jake checked the pistol. The weapon lay on the table in the same position. He exhaled and his shoulders slumped. The burden of his nightmare dissipated and faded.

A noise fluttered from the balcony. Jake reached for the P-96, the grip real and solid in his palm. Cold steel. Control returned to his body.

Armitage padded to the glass wall, weapon held high. He slid the door slowly, inched to a crack. Stars lit up the faded outdoor setting. Empty. He peered out and saw the night and yellow dots.

The city sparkled in the background.

The agent crossed to the concrete pad and his footfall made no sound. He spotted a bird and sighed. His arm dropped. The butt of the weapon tapped the glass.

The pigeon startled, fleeing the ledge. The bird's wings glided into the inky black. The agent lowered his gaze and exhaled a lungful of air. He surveyed the street, nearby neighbors and positions within range. After three minutes, he sat back.

"All clear," Armitage whispered to himself. He stepped into the lounge and pulled the door shut.

Laying a towel on damp sheets, Jake sank onto the sofa bed. Pillow wrapped around his ears, he dozed off quickly.


The agent awoke to the smell of eggs cooking. He sat up and swivelled his head at the kitchen. Katerina smiled from over the stove, tapping rosemary over a sizzling pan. The aroma intoxicated his senses and the memory of his four o'clock nightmare vanished. He stretched and yawned.

*A much more pleasant way to wake.*

"Morning. I thought I'd surprise you and make breakfast."

"This is a lovely gesture." He gained his feet and moved over the cold floor. The crumpled gray sweatpants matched the pullover he shrugged over his head. He sat at the table and watched Katerina stir eggs over the stove plate.

The morning sun dappled the furniture orange. Out of habit, Jake peered at the balcony through the glass. A clearer day greeted him with grey-blue skies.

Katerina tumbled the food over toast and placed it on the table.

"You look a little weary, Jake. Did I hear you during the night?"

The agent adjusted his chair, picked up the knife and fork. "I woke at four. Thought I heard something outside. But nothing to be concerned about."

"You're taking on a lot with this case." Katerina said.

She sat opposite him, her fingers curled around a coffee mug. Her brow furrowed slightly as she gazed at him with the expression of a concerned mother.

"Nothing to be concerned about. I can take care of this matter," Jake said between mouthfuls of egg.

"I made contact with a colleague of mine after researching these names you gave me. This reporter did some investigating into a story earlier this year. His story was about SPG Partners and a deal Sobol managed."

"Feels promising. Do you know this guy well?"

"I've worked with him for more than five years. His name is Damien Chekov and he will meet with us in person." Katerina glanced at her phone calendar. "This morning at ten-thirty A.M."

"Great. Where?"

"An open park near the *Church of the Saviour on Spilled Blood*. There's no high-rises or rooftops in the vicinity. Except the church. The recreational park opposite has many entry points and always lots of people." She sipped from a mug.

"You're learning espionage skills well. Minimal risk and tactically very sound," Jake said, finishing the meal. He stacked the plates at the sink.

"I'm taught by the best spies." The journalist smiled and moved to the sofa. She flipped her laptop lid and folded her legs underneath.

Armitage opened his wardrobe and threw on jeans and a fresh t-shirt. He rummaged in the spare room, moving around crates and belongings. The items were stacked at the bottom in a storage unit. He carried a box into the living zone. From a shelf, he produced the spare firearms.

Katerina's brow furrowed. "Do we need so many guns?"

"Each of these boxes has different sized ammunition rounds. I had rounds stored for an occasion such as this. This gun is a P-96M and takes nine-millimeter bullets. My preferred weapon and small enough to conceal. For you, a Beretta. I've filled a spare magazine which holds fourteen." Jake closed the cardboard lid.

"Here you go." The agent held up the weapon. "It's the perfect size for you to use and hide. Can you handle this?"

She took the gun by its grip and held the pistol.

"It's for your protection, and in case. It's a decent gun and lightweight. Better to have the weapon and not need it than to need and not have." Armitage checked the magazine. He flicked the safety catch off and on again. "I'll leave this safety on, and you know how to turn it off."

Katerina placed the weapon in her inner pocket. The fold of the jacket was loose enough that it wasn't detectable to the average layperson.

"Shall we, Katerina?" Jake looked at his watch.

"Let's go and meet Damien."

# Chapter 25

Armitage and Katerina parked opposite one of the wider canals that breached Neva River. The double span footbridge spilled into a web of cobblestone laneways. A continuous procession of pedestrians and tourists scurried along the embankments. Restaurants and shops dotted the eastern border. The lunchtime crowds were building up to midday.

"Over here."

The hawker tents and canopies were brimming with product. Workers handed out flyers with their prices and hustled for business. The agent and Katerina angled at the park, weaved through the food trucks. A seller ran up and shoved a display board of bottle openers in front of Jake.

"Thanks, but no thanks." Jake swivelled around the man.

The Russian reporter snaked through the shoppers. Hurricane wire fencing reached three metres from the ground. Acres of parkland lay on the other side.

A path wound eastward ending at large, iron gates. Brick columns framed the entrance. The multi-colored onion domes of the *Church of the Saviour on Spilled Blood* loomed over the concrete space that marked the entrance.

Armitage followed Katerina after he checked for watchers. A playground, moated by a sandpit, took up the far corner. Groups of children jumped on the equipment. Jake smiled so as not to alarm the parents.

Katerina looked at his hand and took it in hers.

"Great idea." The agent nodded.

"The meeting is at ten-thirty and we have twelve minutes. Let's walk to the north side and scout for tails."

The pair covered the upper half of the park, looking out for signs of followers or surveillance. The lack of strategic opportunities for an ambush provided them a big advantage. A seven-meter perimeter fence bordered a strip of venues that sat in between the alley and the water. These were mostly restaurants, eateries and bars.

Armitage paused at a light pole. "The landscape of the grounds is flat, which is also a factor in our favour. It looks clear but we can never be too careful."

She pointed at a cluster of tables and benches bolted to a concrete base. "Let's wait there. It's nearly ten-thirty."

The nearest set wasn't occupied. They chose the one with the most privacy. A row of Oak trees formed a canopy which shaded their seats.

Katerina placed her black carry-all on the table. The sparse sunlight shone onto the grass and reflected off the morning dew. Three children ran after a black Labrador, chasing their pet over the path. One giggled and threw a toy. The dog barked as the children laughed. Their mother chatted to an adult and hadn't noticed the kids were moving to the end of the grass.

"There he is." She nodded at a figure moving to their spot. Jake shifted on the bench; his back faced the edge.

Across the grass patch, a man in his thirties headed in their direction. Chekov appeared to be of medium height and build with light brown hair. The reporter wore glasses and held a laptop case.

On reaching them, he hugged Katerina. "Good to see you."

"Hello, Damien. Thanks for coming." "Damien Chekov, this is a friend, Jake Armitage."

Jake stood. The two men shook hands and the party

of three sat around the public table.

"I haven't seen you in your office the past few days," Damien said, placing his laptop bag on the table.

"I'm working on a project with Jake, so doing intense research." She smiled.

"Must be something big. Any scoops you can give an old friend?" Chekov winked.

"Not yet, but I'll let you know if I can. That's what I wanted to ask you, Damien."

"Shoot."

"You remember the story on the politician Sobol and his connections with certain parties?"

"I do, and I wrote our three main articles for this when the story broke. Didn't you do something on a political conspiracy as well?" Chekov clicked his laptop screen.

"Yes, but it wasn't as interesting as this link. We need your help, please, with any extra detail on Sobol's association with criminals."

Chekov nodded and typed. "Let's see what I can find."

The agent smiled. "You know stuff that didn't get published or make it to print. Any detail you have would be appreciated."

"Katerina has helped me before, so anything I can do to repay her." Chekov nodded at Katerina.

The journalist cleared his throat, eyes trained on the laptop screen. "There's been extensive investigation into certain persons of interest. It began with a series of transactions here in Russia six months ago. A classified incident about which I cannot divulge all the details. I'll give you both a summary as best I can."

"Understood," Jake said.

"A group of Russian criminals were under investigation by our federal law enforcement. They had been watched for a period of twelve months. I know this because of a reliable source at the FSB, and I did my own undercover work. These criminal identities, in collusion with others, were trying to sell significant quantities of uranium. The illicit commodity had been offered on the black market, the dark or deep web, and to a variety of parties."

"Uranium?" Jake's eyebrows rose.

"Yes, Jake. These sellers claim access to enrichment plants and nuclear commodities: selling to the highest bidder." Katerina's brow furrowed.

Chekov shook his head. "In large quantities."

Katerina moved closer as park walkers neared their spot.

"The bidders came from everywhere, as you can imagine. African warlords from the Congo. Tinpot dictators from military regimes in Asia and the Middle East. Terrorists. At many stages of the investigation, I had to re-evaluate my involvement. It became too dangerous." Chekov lowered his screen and checked over his shoulder.

"I'm not surprised," Katerina said.

Chekov's eye's darted over two men strolling in the grass. "But I could not get out. At least not straight away."

"You had to withdraw slowly," Jake said.

"That's correct. I found data and information I didn't publish. I'm sure you can work out why. A few things I handed over to the FSB. Russian Federal Police. When my first article was released, many names and details were left anonymous. The story brought death threats, but they didn't want to stick their heads out too far. Early on, an undercover operative received a call from a gang of Chechen rebels who were interested in doing a deal. The seller we were watching claimed to have access to old Soviet stockpiles and suitcase nukes."

"Chechen rebels put their hand up for a buy?" the agent asked.

"Among others. These rebels were acting desperate. The same gang ripped off a Moscow bank to the tune of twenty million euros. A cyber-attack, so all digital and very sophisticated. We were very impressed with the skill level of their hackers." Chekov paused as if finding his words. "And when the uranium sellers showed a tiny sample, they had a Geiger counter device. Any machine that gives a crackle reading to prove the so-called authenticity is taken as gospel. The buyers don't know any better."

Jake's gaze met Katerina's. "We need an in with this group. See if it's connected to SPG and the data."

"I can help, but from the fringes." The journalist placed his palms on the table. "If you know about uranium, you'll also realize most of this stuff going around hasn't been detonable in decades. The samples that do show up were never weapons grade in the first place. In fact, over ninety percent of sellers can't even access waste. The status is over half-life and simply won't function."

"These guys don't care or give a warranty on their product. It's wild west cowboys with smoke and mirrors most of the time," the agent said. "They'll take the money and run."

"I agree, but they have to slow or reduce the demand in this marketplace. Take out either the sellers or buyers." Chekov rubbed his chin.

"Or both, if possible," Katerina said.

Jake looked at her and shook his head. "Easier said

than done."

The foot traffic in the park had increased with the lunchtime swell. Children rushed a nearby playground, crying and screaming on the equipment. Jake's watch read twelve o'clock.

Chekov stared at his hands in silence. The male reporter finally said, "Near the end, our target attracted the interest of major terrorist cells. These included a few jihadists and ISIS representatives. The Islamic State guys had tens of millions in cash to splurge."

"After Iraq and pillaging Syria, ISIS are now the richest terrorist group ever in existence." Jake looked at Chekov. "Some of these terrorists turn up with suitcases full of cash. Just to get hold of nuclear commodities they think are real. These psychopaths will detonate. Mark my words."

Katerina gazed at the ground. "It's unreal how many people and organizations want nuclear resources."

"I've dealt with these characters before. There's plenty of charlatans claiming to have access to nuclear product. From here to enrichment plants in Pakistan." Armitage adjusted his position on the bench.

"Here in Russia too, because of Chernobyl and our Soviet Cold War arms race," Chekov asserted "The perception that Russia has an endless supply of certain heavy metals is mostly a myth now."

"But the local demand is out of control." Jake gained his feet. He paced the table and watched people playing on the grass. A girl ran behind a boy, pink dress wavering in the light breeze.

"The demand is so hot for a potential scam." Katerina shifted.

"Most sellers are cashing in on opportunity. We

couldn't understand the extent of the industry either. Three undercover operatives have been in Saint Petersburg. Each one in a different operation, and the only transaction that got to a meet happened to be Chechen rebels." Chekov hesitated. "Sometimes these traders have uranium with partial life. Dangerous. It's only a matter of time before we have a major incident in this city."

"The Chechen gang have lots of money," Katerina added. "Members could be linked with star-dagger tattoos."

Armitage looked at Katerina. "And Sobol's involvement?" the agent asked.

"A reliable source witnessed a meeting between the politician and his bodyguard. They met with a buyer, a known figure in the criminal underworld." Chekov scanned the park. "That's most of the evidence I have on him. But I'm gathering still."

"Is the politician's bodyguard a tall, blond-haired guy in his late thirties? Ukrainian born?"

The journalist's dark, bushy eyebrows rose suddenly. "Yes, that's him. Sobol doesn't go anywhere without this guard dog."

"His name is Bohdan Kolisnyk." The agent monitored two young guys on the grass. Both had looked over at Jake's table more than once. The shorter man had a cap on his head and the other had a three-day growth on his cheeks.

"Can you please find us more information on these potential transactions with the politician?" Katerina asked Chekov. "Any extra data connected to both Sobol and his sidekick, Bohdan Kolisnyk, would be valuable."

"Sure can." Chekov nodded.

"Or links to the star-and-dagger ink crew." Jake gazed at Chekov. "We suspect these mafia thugs are foot soldiers only, but if there's more."

"I'll try to get more info. I need to examine what's left in the network. And which information can be released without serious repercussions for any of us."

"We understand you must be careful," Armitage said.

Jake glanced at the table. He stood at the same time Chekov did, and Katerina followed.

The group paused under a fir tree.

"Thanks, Chekov. I owe you for this." Katerina hugged him.

"Don't mention it. When I have more, I'll call you. Good to meet you, Jake."

Armitage offered his open palm to Chekov. "Thanks, Damien. We both really appreciate your help on this."

The male journalist waved and cut over the grass. Sunlight spread through the thick wall of leaves and pooled onto the playground equipment. Chekov walked on the gravel path which meandered toward the south entrance.

Jake watched the people and groups between their spot and the line of trees. The lush grass crunched underfoot as he swung the carryall over his shoulder. Katerina drank from a water bottle.

"I hope this doesn't get any more dangerous for him," Katerina said.

They watched the journalist scurry away to the gates. Chekov disappeared under the shadow cast by the Church of the Saviour on Spilled Blood.

The agent concentrated on the asphalt foreground.

"We're both hoping that."

A beep from Jake's burner made him check his emails,

and a new one from Chris Seaver's office, his assistant director. The email read:

Here's the number of a contact that you should speak to. Non-op CIA.

Armitage sent a text to meet him behind a laundromat at four-thirty P.M. He stood and glanced at the Russian journalist.

"You coming, Jake?" Katerina said.

# Chapter 26

The agent and Katerina carved a path toward a cluster of food trucks. The vehicles sat on a paved zone shaded by tree canopies. Jake analyzed the faces, looked for hostiles. Restaurants were in full swing serving meals, lines extended onto the sidewalks. The hawkers voiced their deals, competing against each other in a frenzied cacophony of noise.

*Nobody can find us easily in this crowd.*

Katerina squeezed his hand. "Come this way, quickly."

They nudged into the sightseers and Jake followed her uphill to a department store.

The skies darkened as a front rolled. Katerina weaved into the masses, bodies flashing either side. Armitage covered the flank, watching for any signs of unusual behaviour.

When they reached the far side of Nevksy, the Russian journalist broke to a powerwalk. A line of customers snaked from a shop. The agent scanned the crowds. No face stuck out in his memory, no one acted suspiciously.

A busker band banged a live tune. Strollers pushed and jostled for a good view.

Armitage nodded to Katerina. "Let's get back to the car, but via an indirect route."

Along the canal, people shuffled into the restaurants for finer dining than the takeout vendors. The water roared with boat tours and tourists gawking at the architecture.

The pair plunged through the huddle. Microphones blared, competing in the noisy atmosphere. They followed a second bridge and got into the car in silence.

Katerina's company was a refreshing change to Jake's usual solo habits. She reminded him of Melissa, his ex-wife, in small ways.

A chime sounded as Katerina waited at the car. Jake checked the text. The non-operative had replied:

Got it. See you at the strike point.

The ignition turned over and Jake nudged into the traffic stream.

As they drove down the embankment and onto Nevsky Avenue, Jake noticed a green car. The vehicle seemed familiar to him. He thought he'd recognised it from earlier that day.

The traffic had increased since late morning with the lunch peak, so he might have been mistaken. The agent's gut instincts rarely let him down. He'd test his theory out soon.

Armitage glanced at Katerina and said, "I think we have someone behind. It's a green Renault. They're three cars back and trying to maintain their distance."

"Got it." Katerina sank lower in the seat, peering at the rear-view. "I can see it."

"We'll soon find out if they are following."

As the lunch buyers ebbed, the cars thinned. The agent changed lanes and feigned a right turn. He clicked the blinker and pressed the brake pedal. At the last second, he steered off and veered into the center lane. The Renault synchronized their movements and returned behind. A horn beeped somewhere close. One of the three cars in-between took a side road so two vehicles separated the follower.

"I'm now sure the Renault is tailing us." Jake said.

"You're right. What should we do?"

"Find out what they want. But play a game first." The agent stuck to the speed limit and cruised for two kilometers. He checked his mirror; the Renault sat on the same speed. If he gave the impression of complacency, the watcher might think Jake didn't realize.

A traffic light flashed red and Jake slowed to a halt.

"We'll lose them soon. I'm waiting for the right moment." Armitage monitored the traffic, glancing either side. "Don't want undue attention from other road users."

"I thought you had a plan, Jake." Katerina's lip turned to a half-grin. He released the console and removed a revolver.

"Just in case." Jake placed the weapon at his side. "You may need to duck again."

Katerina nodded but her spine stiffened.

The opportunity came within five minutes of Jake's statement. A green at the next set of traffic signals with three seconds away from turning yellow. Armitage slowed as they neared the intersection.

"Hold on tight." Jake said and gripped the steering wheel in anticipation. "I'm going to try to shake them and head to a more secluded part of the city. Less people mean less risk and exposure."

Jake waited, watching the lights. He counted down from ten to three in his mind. As it hit zero, he reached five meters from the white stop line.

Armitage floored the pedal as the light changed. The bumper made it over the double lines with half a second to spare. He pulled the blinker and twisted the wheel hard left. Brakes skidded as rubber peeled on the road. The driver's window of the Renault slid down. A brown-haired man stared at their car. Stuck behind vehicles in both lanes, their tail couldn't budge.

"At least that shook them off." Katerina sat straight in the seat.

The agent eased off the accelerator. "For now."

"Hair-raising but necessary." Her eyebrows raised in unison. "The average person has nothing on your abilities."

"I'm going to Sobol's office and see if we can't get a fix on his movements. Try and identify his vehicle and avoid being seen, especially by his bodyguard." The agent steered west toward the freeway entry.

"Good idea. I'll keep data-diving."

"Let's recap on the information from Chekov." Jake said, the Toyota merging onto the freeway. He increased speed to the limit.

She nodded. "We know that Sobol trades in black-market uranium. The politician is linked to the drive and this political conspiracy."

"And this mafia group appear to be carrying out all their orders and grunt work." Armitage concentrated on the road.

"If there's more proof of the politician's involvement, we need to find it. And fast."

"That's right." The agent tapped the steering wheel. A sign directed motorists to an approaching exit.

"It's the only thing we'll have as a bargaining chip to keep you and Chekov safe."

Katerina nodded. "Establish the connection in the voting scandal. Then we can do something about the uranium transactions."

The burner beeped with a text message from the new

contact. Jake checked his cell:

I'll see you there at 4:30 today.

"We need to meet a contact the agency sent me."

# Chapter 27

The random puddles on Nevsky Prospekt reflected gray from overhead. Armitage concentrated on the church. He ignored the distractions and the noisy commuters. The canal cut a steady course to the multi-colored, domed tips of St Basil's.

As they circled the blocks close to Jake's apartment, both of them remained on edge. The pedestrian traffic had increased with the cooling breeze.

The agent noted the horizon. The afternoon gloom painted the sky in shades of gray. They slowed at a pedestrian crossing, walkers spilling onto the white lines. Jake scanned the lanes, checking each vehicle. His gaze moved to the road limit as he skimmed the car hoods. Silver and white were the most common.

A river of red brake lights snaked up toward the canal. Cafes and gothic buildings blurred in Jake's peripheral. Rain pattered the windows and he switched up the heater. He took a corner and braked at a traffic sign. People flooded the sidewalk, chattering under umbrellas. The rain did little to dissuade their enthusiasm.

Katerina sat pensive and stared out the window.

The laundromat had one customer, an overweight woman in her sixties with a gray hair bun. A broken LED flickered as she carried a large basket of wet clothes to a row of dryers.

"Told him to meet us behind the strip in the loading bays."

A light truck exited as Jake drove around. With renovations in a shop next door, the only person was a mother with a trolley loaded with groceries and baby.

"It's four-forty. I can't see anyone." Katerina's gaze fixed at the windshield.

The second text to the contact bore no answer. Ten minutes elapsed as Armitage shook his head. "Seems like a setup unless something happened. Let's head over to Nevsky and grab a bite to eat."

The sun had disappeared completely behind the clouds by the time they reached the Market restaurant. They chose fresh steaks from the grill and vegetables. At the till, Jake paid cash, the easiest tender and untraceable.

"Would you like a receipt?" the serving staff said.

"No, thanks."

Tables filled with young people and groups. Katerina and Jake ate in silence. "I like that the food is fresh and cooked in front of you," he said.

"Can't go wrong." The Russian journalist stood. "Let's go?"

"Great idea." The agent nodded and they elbowed their way to the sidewalk.

A breeze brought a chill. Jake bleeped the car alarm and noticed a black Jaguar. He motioned Katerina to come closer.

"Don't look straight away but I recognise that Jaguar."

Katerina leaned against the car casually. "I'll remember their registration."

"It will probably come up a fake or a chain of shell companies. Let's take them for a ride instead." Armitage started the Toyota as the traffic signals above glowed green. A silhouette of a figure was visible in the Jag from the front seat. The headlamps came on.

"They're checking us out."

The agent nodded. "Good." He cruised onto the main street.

The inside lanes merged; Jake took the corner slowly. The watcher held back again, giving two car lengths to their target.

"At the next freeway exit, there's an industrial zone behind these streets." Katerina pointed south to a cluster of nineteenth-century office structures.

"That's fine."

"What's the plan?"

"I want him to follow us." Armitage blinked left and steered toward the road shoulder. A raised median strip parted to a side alley. The entrance had a one-way sign and single lane only.

"You want a confrontation?"

"If they chase us down here, it's a tail for sure. I've got a different tactic this time." Armitage cruised the lane, sitting on twenty-five miles per hour. The road narrowed. Up ahead he spotted an intersection. Industrial sheds and stocking bays filled the corners. He checked the rear-view mirror.

*No-one around. Perfect.*

A black bird with half-meter wingspan fluttered out of the dense canopy. It soared high toward the yellow and orange of the twinkling city. Jake sped up to ninety, accelerating to the intersection.

In the rear-view, colors flared and blurred. Motion. A car materialized on the blacktop. The black Jaguar. The agent pushed the Toyota. He wanted maximum distance between them and the pursuer.

Another intersection grew on the horizon. Jake

hammered the motor, weaving through cars and obstacles. Wind pushed the panels. Armitage gripped the wheel, checking Katerina in his peripheral vision.

Grasping the handbrake, Jake yanked the lever. The vehicle skidded, fishtailing through a crosswalk. Commuters retreated to the curb.

Katerina clutched the solid, u-shaped hanger above her window.

The agent gripped the wheel.

Rubber squealed as the tires sought traction. Jake held steady, steering straight. The vehicle swerved and swung one-eighty degrees. The nose pointed straight ahead.

"That was close and intense," Armitage said and smiled at Katerina.

The Russian reporter grinned through clamped lips. "We have to put up a decent struggle or they won't believe we're trying to escape."

"Speaking of which..." The agent started up. He revved hard at the intersection, grasping the wheel to keep steady. Cars converged from both sides. The light turned red.

The signposts flashed by as lights spun in all directions.

"Hold on," the agent said, concentrating on the road. He spun the wheel. "We need to go off-road."

The tires mounted the sidewalk, metal scraped a traffic pole. Jake squinted through the windscreen. The vehicle found purchase as the cabin jostled. The stink of burning rubber entered the cabin. The traction kicked in hard.

The Toyota hit a flight of concrete steps.

As the car bumped and tossed, Katerina's hand returned to the grip handle.

Jake held tight. The vehicle navigated the sidewalk, tires slipping, and skidded, struggling to stick. The blood pumped through his ears.

The car jolted to the end of a stone ledge. Not losing momentum, the agent nose-dived the car at the asphalt. Wind rushed in the window crack. The rubber crashed to the ground. Lucky to land upright. Suspension jolted and shuddered. A jarring pain shot through his spine. Instinctively his right arm reached across the passenger seat.

Katerina held his forearm across her chest.

The agent watched the shadows that danced over the concrete. A scrape of metal grinding. The Jaguar came into view, angled onto the sidewalk, framed in the distance under the intersection glare. A raised terrace with steps separated the two vehicles.

"We've got the lead. Now to maintain the advantage."

"Take this one-way road here." Katerina pointed to a sharp right. The road curved and receded into a cluster of eaves.

Armitage sped up to the corner and jerked the steering wheel. He pushed the speedo to seventy. Trash fluttered over the uneven stone blocks. Cigarette smoke wafted from door jambs. He turned at the next intersection.

A familiar cluster of shops started with a dry cleaner.

"I know this street. There's an abandoned place with garage door two blocks ahead." They revved through two green lights. He arched wide and reversed into an open, iron-roofed warehouse. The electric garage door had a console on the wall.

Armitage leaped to the concrete and pressed the button. The door whirred to the floor, blocking the street view. He parked and flipped the light switch. Fluorescent yellow bathed the concrete floors and white-wall shelving.

"I know the owner won't be here until later. Discovered it on a stakeout five months ago. Wait here. You'll be safe."

The agent opened the glove box and pulled out the P-96. A door opened into a storeroom enclosed in glass. He dodged around single chairs gathered to a small table. Two desks lined the walls and padded mats lay on concrete floors. He entered a second door into the office and reception.

A tinted windowpane separated the office from the sidewalk. Jake watched the Jaguar turn and curb crawl, the driver monitoring each premises. At the second building, the Jaguar veered to the side and parked. Jake waited for the occupant, who didn't open the door. The road was quiet and no other vehicles were in sight. He ran crouched to the Jaguar and hid behind the trunk.

The agent waited. The driver cracked the window. A lighter clicked within the car. He pressed against the back panel, careful not to make any noise.

A trail of blue smoke curled in the breeze. Strong tobacco. Jake resisted the urge to cough. The window buzzed and lowered

An orange cigarette end appeared. Ash fell to the curb. Armitage hugged the car panel. He reached up and pressed the firearm to the driver's temple.

"Who are you and why are you following me?"

The graying man stared ahead with a calm expression.

"My name is Dodds. You sent me a text."

# Chapter 28

The non-official operative peered at Jake with a crinkled smile. He must have been late forties to early fifties and wore a blue button-down shirt and a pair of slacks.

"You didn't show to the meet."

"I wanted to see if you'd been followed."

"Satisfied?" the agent said. He holstered the weapon and leaned against the car. "Where do you want to talk?"

"I've got a place around on the main road we can go." Dodds gestured toward the ramp. "One exit back on the freeway."

"I'll follow you. I'm parked behind that garage door and someone's with me."

The CIA agent grinned. "Sure thing."

Katerina sat in the passenger seat with the pistol in her lap. As Jake appeared in the storeroom, her eyebrows rose.

"Did you catch up to them?"

"Yes, I found him. It's the CIA. The no-show from the meeting today."

"What?" Her eyes widened.

Armitage nodded and started the engine. "We're going to have a chat with him now."

"Where?"

"His hotel room."

He drove behind Dodds toward the ramp and they returned to the freeway. The brief rays of sun receded and were replaced by sparse, rolling clouds. A clump of hotels loomed over the traffic as they eased toward a shiny cluster of glass high-rises.

On five minutes, the CIA agent exited the nearest ramp. They were on the eastern side in a zone near the city center.

A block of semi-modern apartments mixed with Baroque buildings dominated the landscape. Katerina fidgeted with the pistol in her lap.

Armitage turned, keeping one eye on the road. "Don't stress. If it's OK with you, let me lead the conversation. I don't think he wants to harm us."

Katerina shook her head and stared forward. The road flared as they reached a large hotel. Dodds slowed and took a left into an underground lot beneath the glass tower. .

At a boom gate, Dodds clicked an electronic pass. The pole barrier ascended. The agent waved and Jake followed.

The place advertised four stars but appeared more like three and a half. A glass frontage gave way to a stone reception. Dodds jumped out and escorted them through the foyer area. The agent waved at the receptionist and entered a corridor.

The group walked in silence.

"This way." Dodd's pointed to the elevator.

The cabin rose to floor seven.

"Over here, people." Dodds held the door ajar as Jake and Katerina piled into a large room. A round dining table had pieces of paper scattered and a laptop computer. The sky darkened through a large window. Disposable cups lay on the stone surface.

"I'm Felix Dodds, by the way." The CIA agent put his hand out to Katerina.

"Katerina Venski."

"Pleased to meet you."

The spacious room had a worn patina. Faded carpet covered the lounge with a dated sofa set facing a TV. A tiled kitchenette contained a mini bar and a small fridge nestled in the corner.

"Anyone for a drink?" Dodd's stood behind the makeshift bar.

Katerina shook her head. "I'm going to use the bathroom."

"It's down the passageway, second on the left."

"Not for me, thanks," Armitage said, taking a seat. He watched Katerina disappear through a door.

"Right. Just me. It's past twelve o'clock here."

"So, Dodds, you're a company man." Jake watched the vodka pour.

"That's an old term. A NOC, to be specific. For the record, Jake, that's an attractive lady you have there. I wouldn't let her slip through your fingers."

The agent smiled. "She's a friend, Dodds, and helping out, so let's keep the chat polite."

"Sure. I get it." The CIA agent winked and lifted his glass. "I've been tailing Damien Chekov, the reporter, for three weeks. When I saw you at the park, I had my suspicions."

"Damien is my colleague at the media group." Katerina appeared in the archway. "And a good friend."

"I figured the first part. Thank you for enlightening me." The older man showed the crinkled smile again.

Armitage said, "Chekov is a suspect why?"

"The uranium, of course. There are far too many

transactions happening here in the mother country for our liking. You know our directors get edgy with nuclear weapons and resources, especially with foreign powers. I was in Pakistan before this, as their nuclear plants are still operating. The market is thriving. One year ago, my assistant director decided to send me to Russia to investigate. It's been a long, hard battle, I can tell you."

"I've been here for one year," Jake said, elbows resting on the table surface.

Dodds sipped on his drink. "So why were you two talking with Chekov? Same reason I'm tailing him?"

The agent exchanged a glance with Katerina. "Look, Dodds, you need to start giving me more answers before I'm giving you mine."

"OK, shoot. Ask me anything. If it's classified, I'll tell you."

"Who else are you investigating here in Saint Petersburg?"

"I've got leads on other people. I know the Russian mafia have been involved. It's a dirty game. See, the problem is that there's charlatans peddling this commodity. When you get down to it, barely any is useable. That's the only saving grace. But that means a hell more work to get across all the opportunists and fraudsters to get to the really dangerous guys. However, I need to know if any comes on the market enriched, as it only takes one jihadist or ISIS lunatic. And boom." Dodds threw his hands up in the air.

Jake nodded. "That's true."

"Some stuff I'm telling you is classified but I know you'd be across this, so I'm OK to talk." The agent took a slug of vodka.

"I appreciate the transparency, but that'll only get you

to second base with us."

"Fair enough. Did you go after Manny?" Dodds paused and stared at Jake.

"We got into an altercation due to his associations."

Dodds chuckled and said, "Manny blundered his way into more than one big operation. Hell, I thought his time should have been up ages ago. Don't know how he's lasted this long."

"Let's stop the dancing around, Dodds. There's a prison cult group linked to the uranium I'm investigating. A tattoo of stars and daggers. A data conspiracy that points to the U.S. Do you know anything about this?" Jake asked and crossed his arms.

"I can find out more for you." The older man moved around the sofa. "Do you want to partner on this operation?"

Armitage shook his head. "Don't know if I can trust you."

"I realize we got off to a shaky start." Dodds rolled up his sleeves and walked to the balcony. "I need some backup out here and figure you do too. Together we could blow this wide open and stop some of these corrupt individuals."

Jake nodded at Katerina. She gave a half-smile back and threw a sideway glance at Dodds.

"Hell, it's like the wild west out here." The CIA agent examined the cityscape.

"We might be interested but I need to think about this arrangement." The agent looked at the Russian journalist.

"Here is my burner number." Dodds wrote numbers on the back of a card. "This hotel serves as my base, Jake. I know we're on the same page about this voting conspiracy here in Russia. The rot goes all the way to the top. We don't want it to affect the rest of the free world. No offense, Katerina."

She nodded but stayed silent.

Armitage stared at the number. "I'll be in touch."

# Chapter 29

The clouds rolled over the darkened horizon as rain threatened the landscape. Jake stared at the navigation panel on the dash. A pack of gulls took flight toward the coast, aiming for higher ground. He entered Sobol's address in the device.

"That was an enlightening chat." Katerina stared at street.

"There's a lot of old stooges like Dodds in the intelligence world back home. I hope you weren't too offended by his brusque manners."

Katerina chuckled. "I'm fine, thanks. He's not the first of his kind I've met. This is Russia, remember."

"Good. Let's see what we can do about the politician's office location." The agent slowed at the lot.

Armitage and Katerina stood in silence as the elevator ascended. No one joined the pair as it stopped at six. They moved inside and shut the door.

"I agree. We need more evidence of a transaction first."

"You'll need to stay out sight. The politician and his mercenary bodyguard are the likely candidates for that death threat. So they'll know what you look like."

"Lucky we know about their relationship now." Katerina clicked her mouse and settled in front of the screen.

"That gives us a slight advantage."

"Good luck. Stay out of trouble."

The agent hauled a carryall, swinging it over his shoulder. "I'll see you soon." A pit in his stomach formed as he glanced over his shoulder.

*All she has is me. I'll be back in one piece.*

At the elevator bay, Jake chewed his lip. The ding chimed and the doors creaked.

*Damn it.*

Armitage sprinted down the hall. He stood in front of his entrance. A deep breath. The hinges creaked as the door swung hard at the wall.

"Jake you're back. What is it?" Katerina glanced up from the computer.

"Come with me. This is more important."

"I'm coming." She shut the lid and tucked her computer under her arm.

In the parking lot, Jake scoped for watchers. A scattering of walkers positioned on the perimeter, too far away to be a threat. Katerina shut the passenger door.

The foot traffic was slim as Jake pulled onto Nevsky under the shadow of the steeples.

Across the main drag, shoppers spilled out of the stores and restaurants. Despite the gloom and wet sidewalks, nothing could dampen the locals. Armitage turned right into a narrow lane a hundred meters from the smaller canal. The older high rises receded as he took the lane to the end.

Katerina deep dived into financial records connected to Sobol. She typed away, studying spreadsheets from different sources.

The politician's office was nestled in an upmarket part of the inner city. Jake slowed and craned his neck. The address had a modern foyer framed in tinted glass.

The agent parked on the curb outside a noodle shop and a chemist.

206

An elderly couple shuffled near the car, so Jake waited. He opened the carryall and took out a tracking transmitter. It was barely bigger than his thumbnail. He placed it in a small pocket where it would be safe.

"I'll stay in the car."

"Text me if you see anything suspicious."

Katerina nodded.

Jake reached for his fishing hat from the rear seat. He checked his casual appearance didn't appear unkempt.

"It's very effective in hiding your face," Katerina said.

"Back soon."

The sidewalk outside Sobol's office had a cluster of people jostling for front row. Jake moved to the other side of the mob and maintained visual contact on the entrance. A heavyset man was holding a camera pointed at the window. In front, an attractive brunette held a microphone. Jake weaved through the bodies.

Armitage crossed the street and sat at an al fresco table outside a cafe. He ordered an espresso. Noise increased as people swarmed onto the road. He watched the media gathering from his position fifteen feet away.

The office door clanged. Inside, a flurry of staff milled on the politician's ground floor. Handshaking between corporate types in suits played out. The agent couldn't see Sobol in the crowd. A journalist moved into position with a microphone. The woman next to the largest camera held a black sound bar.

A blue Mercedes braked twenty meters from the staff. Jake turned to the action but saw movement in his peripheral vision. The car stopped gently to let people shift. A tall, hefty driver emerged and opened the passenger side door. The man who stepped to the asphalt had light-brown hair and wore glasses.

The agent pulled the fishing hat over his brow.

The driver flanked the politician. Microphones hovered in expectation. All cameras pivoted toward the pair.

Sobol closed in on the greeting party. A roar issued from the crowd. The politician grinned and held his hands spread in a welcoming gesture. Cheers echoed from some of the people watching. Sobol reached the crew and paused for effect. He clasped his hands behind his back, straightened his spine.

The journalist with the audio piece reached out. The politician gazed over his supporters. She asked a question in Russian. The driver disappeared, not wanting to steal any of his boss's limelight.

Silence fell as the politician regarded the group.

"We cannot change the past, but we can change the future." Sobol spoke in Russian, projecting his voice to the street-side audience. The politician smiled and turned. A staffer opened the door and Sobol stepped away.

The crowd jostled for front row as the crew followed behind the Russian politician. People peered through the panes, bustling to get a glance inside. Others lost interest and broke away.

More shouts of encouragement and support rang out as the office door closed. A Russian woman appeared and addressed the supporters.

"Every vote counts," she said in Russian. "Please continue giving support to Yabloko party."

Her words placated the audience, telling them they were important. Watchers at the rear peeled off. The noise settled and numbers lowered as many of the citizens dispersed. The sky darkened. Car doors slammed and engines revved. The agent took cash from a pocket and paid the bill.

Armitage strolled toward the Mercedes. The politician's driver hadn't returned to the car. He monitored nearby pedestrians to be sure nobody had taken an interest in him. A steady stream of motorists trickled by as people exited. Jake reached the car, stopping to feign a glance into a shop window. He concentrated on the reflection, assessing the passers-by.

The rear of the Mercedes had backed close against the bumper of a Toyota. Jake stopped near the gap and pulled his smartphone from a pocket. He pretended to examine and play with the device. The agent slipped into the gap between the vehicles and dropped his hand . He bent and fastened the tracker underneath the bumper.

Armitage straightened in a fluid motion. Nobody had noticed. A couple pushing a young baby in a pram ambled along the sidewalk. Jake made brief eye contact but both adults were engrossed with baby talk.

The walk to the car was brisk, but slow enough not to draw attention. Armitage opened the door and settled behind the wheel.

"How did you go?" she asked, lowering a bottle of water from her lips.

"Great. I've attached a tracker to his Mercedes. Sobol arrived and said some words. Two minutes at the most."

"I caught some of the noise from here. A single statement is all they are allowed."

"They had a crew with a camera and sound bar. Two dozen followers on the street to add atmosphere. Pump out a press release. My timing went perfectly."

She smiled. "Did you see Kolisnyk?"

"Luckily, no. Sobol had another driver. No sign of the mercenary."

"That went to plan, and more smoothly than expected then."

The agent nodded and reached behind the seat. He held an electronic display. The length was eight-inches wide by ten-inches high. It had dials and buttons. The face resembled a GPS with a digital screen.

"This is the receiver. You can see the blue dot is the transmitter signal."

The blue icon sat stationary on the screen. "When the Mercedes moves, we'll see where they go."

She nodded and said, "Let's get further away. I feel paranoid being so close to their office."

"Good idea; you read my mind again." Jake started the engine and drove to Nevsky Avenue. They slowed outside a towering Baroque building and braked in a side alley.

The Russian reporter examined her laptop. "I found something that might be important."

"More of Sobol's financials?"

"The politician is definitely contracting the mafia. But other unusual transactions show he's in much deeper. International payments coming from offshore bank accounts."

"Can you identify the other parties involved?"

"That's the next step. The accounts are all numbers and characters."

"As you'd expect."

"Correct. But I'm narrowing it down with the help of

another hacker. Some of this is above my pay grade."

"That's handy to be connected." The Toyota crawled through the busy street.

A band played live music on a nearby boardwalk. The music flowed out of big speakers. Cover songs of British and American hits from the past three decades pumped the air.

"That's 'She Sells Sanctuary' playing now," Jake said, adjusting the monitor.

"I recognise that song too." Katerina shifted her position. "I've used this hacker on other projects. He's very reliable."

Jake shook his head. "I'm glad you're on our team, Katerina."

A young man appeared from a shop vestibule and sucked on a cigarette. Smoke trails curled in the air. The smoker threw the butt on the ground and squashed it on the sidewalk.

"Don't thank me yet. I want to find more dirt on these guys. Specific transactions that reveal the motives and network." The Russian reporter squinted at her screen. "What are we missing?"

"Seems like you've uncovered the first layer. If we could identify more associates, that would be gold."

The music faded slowly as they moved out of the busy intersection. Dodd's proposition ran through Jake's brain. He pushed it away for later discussion.

A beep interrupted Jake's thought pattern. He angled the console. The blue dot flashed as it moved across the screen. He looked at Katerina.

"South bound."

# Chapter 30

The blue icon sat on a route that ran to the city edge. Jake waited at an intersection as they confirmed the intended direction. The Mercedes weaved through lanes and minor roads, avoiding the main streets.

"They seem to be heading to the rural communities." Katerina studied the interface. "An area with large estates. Common for our landscape."

The agent chuckled. "Yes, I noticed." He moved off the shoulder and entered a lane.

"The houses are enormous in many urban areas."

"They might have a stronghold nestled in a regional pocket." Jake studied the interface, keeping one eye on the road. "Near where I caught up with Manny and the Ukrainian mercenary the other day."

"Remote to stay off the radar." Katerina shifted in her seat.

"I don't like saying, but here goes. This next showdown might be too dangerous for you. If I go out to a stronghold, there will be three or more armed hostiles." Armitage touched her hand. "I couldn't forgive myself if something happened to you."

Katerina looked out the window at the increasing flow of pedestrians. Peak evening rush continued to descend upon Saint Petersburg. She shook her head slowly and her gaze met his eyes.

"It's very risky, but you might need me. I understand, though, if you go alone." She half-smiled, but her lip curled in one corner.

"Let's wait and see where the target ends up." The agent stared at the screen.

The Mercedes reached the outer ring surrounding the suburbs. Armitage and Katerina watched as the car took it's time, driving at the speed limit.

Traffic thinned as they circled the city. Ten minutes later, the target drove into a private lane. The vehicle slowed in a driveway and stopped at a large lot.

Armitage pulled the address up on Google maps. A compound surrounded by high fencing stared back at them. He shook his head and looked at the Russian reporter.

"This is their destination. I need to drop you off, Katerina, as security is high. We'll be outgunned again and I can react faster on my own. I'll stay in contact with regular communication." Jake maintained her gaze. "A text message every hour."

"I can help and I've fired a gun. If I wait in the car, in case something goes wrong." Katerina's eyes shone.

"The problem is Kolisnyk." Jake shook his head. "He's trained at the highest military level and a complete psychopath. There will be other adversaries with at least intermediate weapon skills and tactics. Sobol spares no expense. Not just mafia criminals. There's too much money at stake to not engage more professionals." The agent paused. "It's too dangerous this time."

Katerina fell silent and stared through the windshield. She sipped her coffee and appeared lost in her thoughts.

Five minutes dragged on like an hour. Finally the journalist said, a grim expression on her face, "I realise you should go alone. Let's go back to the apartment. I'll keep digging for more financials. But please come back alive."

Armitage nodded. "Don't worry. I'm not leaving you

alone here." His stomach churned.

The street lights bled green in the rising mist. Jake turned into Nevsky Avenue and stopped at a crossing. A river of commuters swarmed the white-lined asphalt. Umbrellas bobbed in a kaleidoscope of colors. The sidewalks were full of corporate executives and workers eager to get home. Cars flashed by in both directions.

Storm clouds increased as they neared Jake's apartment block. He checked for tails in the rear-view mirror, alert for suspicious and recurring vehicles. Lights flickered in all directions. There didn't appear to be any of the same vehicles returning.

"Hold on tight. I'm going to do some counter-surveillance and check for tails. A bit of defensive driving."

The agent drove a double block and performed sudden last-minute turns. He took one-way lanes and used every available route to flush out followers. Ten minutes of his erratic steering and not a single vehicle had been spotted twice.

Jake pulled into the parking lot. He bleeped the fob and scanned the immediate area.

"You're really practised at this, aren't you?" Katerina said. "It's great because we'll be safe."

"Can't be too careful." Jake held the lobby door open.

In the elevator, they got to level four and a familiar figure entered. The agent rolled his eyes and nudged Katerina.

"Here we go. I'll use a different name for you," he whispered to the Russian journalist and winked. "Mrs. Bukin, how are you?"

"Well, thank you, Jake." The older lady hobbled into the elevator and squinted at the Russian reporter. "Who is this lovely companion with you today? Aren't you going to introduce us?"

"Olga, I'd like you to meet Mrs. Bukin." He gestured with his hand. "Mrs. Bukin, this is Olga."

"A pleasure, dear." Mrs Bukin leaned on her walking frame. "My, my, you're a sight for sore eyes. Jake's always a bachelor."

Katerina gave the older woman a peck on the cheek.

"Nice to meet you too, Mrs. Bukin." Katerina grinned and looked at Jake. "And what a lovely dress you're wearing. Vera Wang, is it?"

"Thank you. It's my favorite. But no, I can't afford fancy brands." The older lady returned her attention to Jake, raising an eyebrow. "I hope this man isn't leading you astray."

"No, he's fine: a gentleman, actually. We're working on a project together."

"Well, it's about time he had a nice young lady for company." Mrs. Bukin shook her head at the pair. Her brown eyes and aquiline nose gave the impression of an eagle examining its prey.

The three occupants held the support rails as the cabin clunked toward the roof. Armitage nodded at Katerina and his gaze wandered the walls to avoid the older lady's stare.

The elevator pinged not a moment too late. The agent stuck his hand out and held the door open.

Katerina smiled at Mrs. Bukin and waved. "Bye, Mrs Bukin. Have a nice evening."

"You too, dear." The older lady pushed off on her frame. Squeaks emitted from the walking-aid as Mrs. Bukin disappeared into the corridor.

The panel green lit on level six and Jake and Katerina stepped out. Armitage unlocked both deadbolts, pocketing the keys as they entered the kitchen.

"She's a lovely old lady." Katerina chuckled.

"Mrs. Bukin has her moments. I need a drink before I hit the road." Jake took a vodka bottle from a shelf. "Would you like one?"

"Sure, thanks."

A pair of birds dove through the darkening horizon. The agent poured the liquid into two glasses.

Drink in hand, Katerina slumped on the sofa, her gaze focused on the window as night dropped over an iron-colored sky.

Jake circled the lounge, examined his motion sensors, a basic setup installed to monitor any break-ins. He entered the corridor and removed a transparent plastic cover on the wall. A hidden camera lens pointed down the passage.

"I have a few concealed sensors and cameras located inside." He led her through to the spare bedroom. "The windows and entry are secured with a trip sensor." Armitage typed a password into a prompt box. A display flickered on the screen. Six different windows appeared showing each angle. A camera view trained on the entrance.

The agent examined each one. The platform had multiple views and Jake flicked through the various positions. He pointed to a series of video files.

"The parcels are videos of any motion. This one on the balcony captured a bird landing on the outdoor set."

Katerina nodded.

Armitage pointed to a thin, silver line on the

windowpane. "A thief would trigger the connection which alerts my burner phone." He looked up from the screen.

"But an advanced operator might hack the system to disable the notification. By loading the software, I can see if any compromises occurred. There have been no breaches in our absence."

The agent followed Katerina into the lounge.

"I'm going to keep searching for information on these people." Katerina flipped her computer and the desktop lit up blue.

"Sounds like a plan. Time for exterior counter-surveillance."

"It's never ending, isn't it."

"If you want to stay alive."

Armitage took the vodka. He opened the panel door and gazed over the balcony. Traffic noise dominated the darkness. He sat on a chair and scanned the open terraces. The neighbors within a five-hundred-yard range were the first priority. Every balcony on the top floor had furniture and plants only. No threats on six. He worked his way down to the first.

On level four, a middle-aged couple discussed a subject over two glasses of red wine. The agent had seen them regularly. Nothing unusual there.

Jake's gaze descended over the occupied balconies on three. A splattering of old outdoor furniture and pot plants. No people were in view and curtains were drawn.

A gray building opposite reached six storeys. Jake started with the top level.

The clouds clustered overhead, blocking much of the receding light. Jake sipped from the glass, swivelled to take in the east side.

In the distance, a baby screamed. Rainwater slushed over concrete into gutters from crude Soviet-era downspouts.

On the second and third floors only one elderly lady watered a plant. The closest threat had been neutralized.

The agent gave the sidewalk a sweep and covered off a phone booth on the other side of the road. A roof edge appeared vacant, as did two other possible strike points.

Satisfied, Jake returned to the lounge, pondering an emergency contact.

*I need to give Katerina a fallback position in case something happens.*

He placed his empty glass on the island bench. Something bugged him. He crossed the floor, rummaged in a drawer, found a writing pad, and wrote on the top page, printing a number and name with an address. A quick check on Dodd's business card to confirm the details were correct.

Armitage ripped the paper from the pad and handed it to Katerina. "Here's the number of Dodd's burner. If I'm not back in four hours, call him. Let him know this location is the last place you saw me. He's the closest we have to a friend."

The Russian reporter sipped her vodka. She glanced at the paper. Keys clicked as her fingers shimmered. The screen lit her face in a macabre blue. "I'm going to keep diving."

"That will be helpful. Thanks."

Katerina sighed and looked at him over the screen.

"I think we're making headway here." He held her gaze.

The reporter stopped typing. She rose, stepped

around the table, and embraced Jake.

"Please be careful. Come back in one piece and breathing." Her head shivered as he held her hair.

Jake realized again how insignificant he and Katerina were to this titan battle of superpowers. They were as fragile as autumn leaves in a rain-lashed storm.

The agent straightened and kept her head cradled on his shoulder. He took a deep breath and said, "Lock the door behind me, and the dead bolts. Please don't go on the balcony. I'll send a message every hour."

Katerina's head burrowed into his chest. She hugged him tight and pulled herself away. They locked gazes, lost in each other eyes. Jake formed a confident smile which masked his concern.

"Don't worry about me. Just stay safe. Please."

Armitage nodded and untangled, still holding her fingers. In her grasp, he felt cocooned from the situation.

Slowly Jake turned away. This time he didn't look back as he shut the door. His heart pounded on his rib cage. Blood rushed between his ears.

The second deadbolt clunked into place, the last sound Jake's ears registered. His pulse pounded in rhythm with his footfalls. The corridor seemed quiet, almost too silent. Katerina's face flashed in his mind. For the first time, he prayed he would run into Mrs. Bukin. Anyone would do, as long as it was a familiar face.

The door cracked and he stepped into the elevator.

*Stay focused and concentrate on the task.*

The agent leaned against the rail. The cables above groaned. He chanted the mantra.

*I am energised and fully protected.*

Over and over again, the words ran through his mind and strengthened his resolve.

# Chapter 31

The evening sky had merged the deep orange with black as heavy as Jake's heart. He started the car and a numb sensation coursed through his body. A nagging thought regarding the security of his apartment would now be tested.

*Would Katerina be safe?*

Traffic had eased off slightly but was still in peak hour. Armitage tried to push worries of Katerina's safety from his mind. He separated the irrational thought from his mission objective.

Compartmentalizing, experts called this process.

A quick lane change and Jake nudged the accelerator pedal. The car surged forward as if finally coming to life.

"Let's get this party started," Jake whispered as he tapped the wheel. He settled his pulse with slow, repetitive breathing.

*Separate the anxiety.*

He cracked the window and let the air rush by his face.

The Toyota ascended the freeway ramp at five-ten P.M. As he drove, the freeway became a little more foreign. As if he had become an intruder in a strange land. Motorists flashed by. He maintained the speed limit.

Jake kept his emotions in check with regular exercise and meditation. He'd found a clear mind and consciousness gave maximum effectiveness in the field. In addition, limited, ritualized weight-lifting gave him not only fitness and strength, but the flexibility he required in the field.

Katerina's recent comments had reminded him of the

pain of the past. The feelings had reduced to a dull throbbing in his chest, more like an ache. Having the reporter in his apartment had sparked old emotions at an inconvenient time.

Cars whizzed by in a blur. Jake forced himself to focus. He kept his eyes trained on the blue dot.

The blue icon sat stationary. Jake gripped the wheel and focused on the signposts. The ramp led into a thick band of residential estates. Wide properties punctuated with peeling timber palings dotted the curbs.

Armitage turned and drove deeper into larger homesteads and pastures. He steered through horses and hills. Newer homes mixed with older mansions as he struggled to read the numbers.

The agent flicked the signal indicator and entered the target's street. He curb-crawled on twenty miles per hour. A dead-end loomed on the map. Long lawn yards and fences merged into the next, some stretched for hundreds of feet.

Cattle grazed on lush pastures, moist from the recent rainfall. He drove on and checked the lot numbers. Homesteads nestled in cul-de-sacs, hidden by the sheer distance from the street.

The road came to a grass verge. Lanes circled the property on either side. The agent pulled up early. A side street ran off into a gully. In front stood a gated compound. Thick trees bloomed over the two-meter bricked walls.

A stiff breeze swirled. Jake upturned his collar against the cold front.

In a second drive-by, Jake conducted a visual assessment on the surveillance technology. By staking the surrounding features, it gave him a tactical advantage. He remained out of estimated camera range and didn't repeat the process in case the car could be identified.

The tracked Mercedes had been parked within the grounds. A gravelled zone surrounded the sprawling estate which sat on a full acre of land. Satellite maps provided an aerial view. The agent toggled over the plan of an eighteenth-century homestead that had been converted into a contemporary fortress.

Armitage took out a rifle scope he carried for these occasions. He swept the high points, looked for weaknesses. On the top of the stone boundary fence ran hurricane wire that climbed a half meter. Jake had scaled higher sheer walls, but this one had more exposure to the front windows. A thick patch of trees served as partial cover near the west corner. This would be his entry point.

The neo-classical façade gave way to mouldings and ledges than ran less than half the width of the land. If necessary, he'd use a rope. The architecture provided stable footholds for climbing.

Jake scanned the perimeter and searched for surveillance-tech. He kept to the well-covered sections. The trees and scrubs added natural cover, both for and from the house. He noticed a camera at the driveway access point. The lens pointed at the entry spot and had a limited range. Fir and birch trees dotted the edge and overlooked the boundaries. He drove to the west edge of the allotment. As on the map, the corner had the most concentrated area of foliage. Large canopies towered above the fence, draping leaves and contacting the top at many points.

A deep section of greenery on the opposite roadside was the perfect place to hide his car. He angled the vehicle under the main canopy.

The car door closed softly as Armitage dropped behind the wheel. In the carryall, he found his KJB detector. He grasped the black, hand-held device that looked like the old CB radio mikes. On the side protruded a retractable fifteen-centimeter antenna which located five separate frequencies. Armitage turned the machine to its side and tested the buttons. It detected Bluetooth, Wi-Fi, GSM, DECT and RF.

A recent tech upgrade allowed for missile alert. The device chimed if a drone with air-to-ground missile entered range.

Rare occurrence but very handy in case.

The agent pressed the switch to *on* and clipped the device to his belt. The compact, nine-millimeter P-96 tucked neatly in the crook of his back. He pulled his jacket over the top to conceal it.

Two cars drove along the residential street. Jake waited until they'd vanished. The crossing he'd chosen had overhead cover right up to the curb. He reached the boundary, casually sauntered along the grass track beside the sidewalk. The wall was three meters from the street.

The agent trailed the perimeter. No cameras were operating on this section. He walked closer to the boundary and moved the detector. The instrument range picked up waves from forty MHz to four GHz.

A light on the display remained dimmed. The agent hurried his pace as he neared the corner. A vehicle blurred past. He pocketed the detector.

*No infra-red and sensors this side, or on the interior boundary line.*

Jake climbed to the top of the brick fence and peered through the razor wire. A body of leaves hid his face from inside view. Large birch trees clumped the middle section, mixed with smaller scrubs. The forest formed a thick barrier wrapped by the gravel. He gazed across at the façade, a seventy-foot setback from the entrance gates.

No personnel guarded the porch. People moved inside

the rooms; lights flickered in the drape edges. A lack of visual security staff made him suspicious.

The top of the wall had flat sections in intervals. Jake crouched and weighed up his options. He aimed to get as close as possible to the strike point. His body ached.

Armitage placed the detector into the carryall. He balanced on the brick, poised to scale the wire.

*I need a chiropractor on my lower back.*

The agent crouched in the dark. He curled his right leg to his bottom. The stretch relieved his persistent joint pain, if only temporarily. He threw a piece of fabric on top of the deadly wire. From the street, there were no passing cars, but he'd need to be fast. He scaled the wire and entered the thickest canopy. From this high vantage point, the house appeared even larger and more grandiose.

*A noble residence filled with criminals.*

Two vehicles pointed toward a large garage. The Mercedes sat on the gravel further back on the driveway. Jake's gaze drew to the last car in the collection.

A white Ford SUV, but with a familiar registration.

The agent's pulse raced.

*The Ukrainian swapped plates. He's inside the house.*

Armitage sent Katerina a text message:

I'm scoping the target at location now. Stay safe.

# Chapter 32

A cluster of thick trunks and dense foliage hid Jake's descent. He slid sideways through the brush and landed in a bed of leaves, rolling behind a tree. Out of sight. The rifle scope revealed the side profile of Sobol's figure through the pane. The politician faced west, talking to another person.

Jake swivelled his high-powered lens over the next glass panel. European turn-of-the-nineteenth-century furniture in the form of overstuffed armchairs and sofas were positioned across thick carpet.

A second male sat in a leather chair, his elbows on a table. He could see the wiry physique. The graying man stared at a screen. Sobol appeared to be talking to him while pacing the room.

Armitage rested behind the tree base to assess the best entry point.

One long dining table ran the length of two large bay windows. Jake squinted at the surface. Two laptop computers were open, the wiry man operating the left one. A large stack of papers were piled on the surface.

The wiry man rose, smartphone in hand. A conversation ensued as he paced between walls, cell phone to his ear. He threw his spare hand in the air as he shouted into the device.

The agent took the breath of the room. A third figure appeared in the shadow of the far archway. Armitage trained on the face, but couldn't see the detail. He returned to the wiry man, who paused by the window and a large bookcase that blocked Jake's visual.

On the edge of the perimeter, Jake detected a blind spot. The security team had neglected the same patch of ground. Both their routine paths stopped two meters short of the position.

*That's my strike point.*

The agent slipped from hiding. He darted between tree trunks trying not to snap twigs. Leaves crunched as he avoided large piles. Any noise could alert the enemy. Closing in on the porch, he kept low. A camera pointed to the gravel. He remained out of range and headed to the east side.

The sun dropped behind the mountain range above. Visibility dimmed with the coming night. The agent squinted through the foliage at the mansion walls.

*I've got one hour of daylight at the most.*

Twenty feet from the façade, Jake ducked behind a hedge. The wiry listener had left the room and vanished south in a corridor leading to the rear of the property.

Sobol produced a smartphone and punched in a number. Jake tried to read his lips. A conversation in Russian lasted five minutes. The politician pulled the cell phone away from his ear and banged his fist on the thick antique table.

The top floor windows had cream blinds drawn to the bottom. Armitage's gaze swept the upper west edge, checking each opening, looking for weaknesses, ways into the compound.

A third floor held more furniture: a sofa, dark-stained timber shelving with rows of stacked books, a small table. The smaller sitting room had a wall separating the large space. These modest furnishings appeared more contemporary than the long room.

Two chairs sat at opposite walls with beds and a chest-of-drawers. This level appeared vacant, unused. Jake swept the outer walls and saw no other activity.

The next two trunks were aligned. The agent moved fast to the first one. He pressed his spine against the bark and breathed in deeply. It had been easy and quick, but all trees were not going to be so simple.

Armitage guessed the front wall was twenty meters from his current position. A line of tall birch trees created a thick barrier. From the windows, the foliage obscured the view.

Darkness cast shadows making the approach more stealthy. Jake reached the façade and slipped through a side gate. A room separated the large living zone where he'd seen Sobol and the wiry man. Jake moved around an old hot water tank bolted to the brick. Weeds sprouted from cracked concrete. He passed windows obscured by drapes.

Firearm in hand, Jake crept toward a grass expanse. He jogged, arm outstretched. The split path ended at a raised mound.

As Jake reached the corner, a rusting shipping container loomed into view. A man's voice spoke in Russian. Armitage pressed to the far side of the steel container, edging closer to the end.

"We don't have any more time to wait, or waste." The man spoke English with a heavy accent. Jake recognised the voice straight away.

*The Ukrainian.*

A semi-automatic pistol sat on the surface of an outdoor setting. Kolisnyk circled the table, his volume rising with each reply.

"Call me back." The Ukrainian clicked the button and stalked the grass patch.

The cell buzzed.

"Speak." The mercenary's dead eyes stared. He

listened and his head shook left and right.

"I've showed you a sample, that's enough."

The person on the other end talked. The Ukrainian listened. A rattle followed and the back door eased open. The wiry man appeared and sat on the nearest chair.

Armitage sank back against the wall.

The mercenary grunted and finished the call. The agent gripped his weapon to his chest. A distance of two-hundred feet and a right angle. Trees and outdoor furniture were between him and the target. Jake aimed and fired at Kolisnyk. The bullet went wide.

The agent rolled forward to the nearest tree as the mercenary stumbled toward his weapon. Wiry guy startled, seeking a weapon he didn't have handy.

Kolisnyk moved fast, reaching for the pistol on the table. Jake fired. From the distance, he could only deter. The Ukrainian yelled, jerked his hand away. The agent remained in cover, using tree trunks as barriers. A door swung out. Kolisnyk tumbled backward. Wiry was trying to get inside. Armitage carved a path opposite the opening. He aimed at the gap.

Movement to his right hampered Jake. He let the shot go anyway. The bullet hit the brick wall. He closed in on the garden. The mercenary was pinned. A blur came into his visual at two o'clock. Wiry fired from the corner. Armitage tumbled sideways. The rounds missed his leg by a narrow margin. He recovered in a kneeling stance.

The shot at the mercenary appeared clear. Armitage fired below the archway. The mercenary crawled backwards. Suddenly Wiry leaped into the crossfire. Bullets flew at Jake. He returned rounds while moving. Wiry jittered on the ground. Red bloomed twice on the man's chest.

"Damn." The agent rose to a crouch.

The Ukrainian vanished into the bowels of the property. Footsteps pounded as backup arrived. Jake ducked low. He searched for hostile attackers while sprinting, bent over among the tree trunks.

*I have to get into the house before the politician flees.*

The concrete steps marked the entrance. Less than twenty meters. Jake's feet pounded the grass. Rounds pierced the air from multiple angles. Two more shooters. Flanked from both sides. Pinned down.

The agent contemplated the wiry man's corpse near the entry. He could hear the click of magazines preparing for a war with the enemy.

A stocky man rushed from the west brandishing a Kalashnikov. Sharp clicks of metal-on-metal sounded, the hostile occupants gearing up for hell. The first shooter grasped his weapon and pointed at Jake's last position. The firearm sprayed a shower of rounds. The blast ripped through the outside wall, brick and plaster flying.

Armitage scrambled behind the garden edge. He flattened on the dirt mound, waited until the magazine ran dry. In fifteen seconds, he had his opportunity.

A chair collapsed on the concrete. Armitage sprinted at the setting. He spun, grabbed the wiry man's collar, and hoisted the corpse. The outdoor table sat upturned. A second spray from the hostile spattered the yard.

The agent braced the body as a shield and pummelled at the entrance.

Bullets riddled the upper torso, tearing skin and clothes apart. The agent pushed against the force of the automatic rounds pounding the corpse.

The shooter clicked the trigger, Kalashnikov spent

from barraging the body with ammunition. In the shattered archway, Jake yanked his P-96, shot around his human shield. The stocky man went to reload a magazine. Armitage's shot hit the hostile in the chest, second shot to the head.

Tiles clunked with the second shooter's body.

The agent swivelled to the side and dropped his body shield. Movement on his right side peripheral.

A blond flash streaked along the corridor. Long arms extended and wrapped Jake's waist. Hot trickles of pain flickered up his spine. His weapon slipped and slid along the ground. Jake fell in a heap. The Ukrainian tumbled.

Suddenly the mercenary was sitting on top of him.

Armitage threw an elbow. A bone crunched. He ducked.

A fist slammed toward Jake's cheek like a steam train. He managed to angle his head at the final second. The fist grazed his chin. He fought the pain. The Ukrainian yelped as his knuckles smashed the floor.

Jake kicked out at the man's groin and boot met genitalia. A crunch and a groan.

Kolisnyk crumpled to a heap and rolled down the corridor. The Ukrainian stood as Jake leaped to his feet, scrambling to collect the fallen weapon. He took the grip and spun around to face the mercenary. His assailant jumped into the living room. Armitage fired as Kolisnyk moved from sight. The mercenary vanished.

A round pierced the drywall above his head. The shot came from Jake's rear. He turned and saw the first shooter pointing a weapon. The man had crawled over the tiles from the outside. Jake leapt into the nearest doorway.

From cover, Jake assessed the threat. The shooter had

fatal injuries and would be struggling to aim straight. He stuck out his arm, shot at the man's position and waited. No return fire came. Jake peeked around the jamb. The man was lying unconscious.

The agent gripped the wall, steadying his feet. A wave of nausea hit. He fastened the pistol in his belt. Broken drywall lay scattered. He retreated back to the kitchen to gather his bearings.

The stocky shooter lay sprawled on the floor. He bent and picked up the Kalashnikov and the spare magazine. They fit in the carryall.

*I've lost precious time.*

Drops of blood spattered along the corridor. The trail led to the front rooms. Armitage clicked the full magazine into the pistol. Holding the weapon ready, Jake stepped into the passage. He headed north again, covered the angles. Step by step. Each entry and blind spot. He reached the archway to the living room.

It was empty.

Kolisnyk had disappeared.

# Chapter 33

The rumble of an engine vibrated through the walls.

Jake listened. It came from the rear of the property. He moved through the corridor, pointed the weapon in each doorway. The silence that followed unnerved him. It seemed that, besides him, all the occupants were dead.

Armitage stopped at the side-facing bay windows, covering all blind spots in-between. Nightfall had closed over the landscape.

The place resembled a Californian winery.

A whipping sound came from the hills. Jake plunged south. Air funnelled into the back door. He sprinted toward the rear yard. The cool breeze hit his face.

The agent pushed his legs harder, sensing an urgency. The concrete path wound past the shipping container. It gave way to a stream. He stumbled and jogged, following the man-made stone trail.

Major machinery sounded different, as did jet turbines and propellers. Jake knew the difference straight away.

The surrounding landscape descended. Rows of oak trees. Visibility diminished with the night. A chopping and thud came in loud. Breathing ragged, he pushed his legs. Lactic acid built fast in his muscles.

*It's a helicopter. Has to be a large cabin, four to six people.*

The crossover meandered above the water. The agent reached a section bordered with flora. His lungs burned. Voices carried in the breeze. Huge overhead halogen lamps pierced the night. The glow lit up the gray patch like a football stadium.

A blur of arms as signals were thrown to personnel. The cabin door slammed. A gust rustled leaves on nearby trees, the trunks swaying in unison. Both chopper feet lifted off the pad, tilting at the right clearance. The propeller blades roared, built to full momentum.

Hedges fortified the landing and hid a fence topped with razor. The agent's fingers grasped the wire grids. He strained to focus on the black sky. Jake saw a green Mi-17 chopper bank and curve around a row of pine trees.

The P-96 trigger was lead under Jake's finger. His arm hung limp against his hip. The pain in his arm vanished, lost in the moment. Numb. His blood boiled. Sobol and the mercenary got away again.

Armitage squinted against the glare. He raised his arm and took a shot in the wind.

*It's too far away.*

His fingers gripped the wire fence until a trickle of red ran down his left hand. Pain registered as the sharp wire end stabbed his finger.

*What's a tactical military helicopter doing here?*

The chopper nose dipped as the machine arched west toward the mountains. He waited while the politician and his cronies became a dot against the charcoal horizon.

Jake's injured arm suddenly felt fifty kilograms. He dropped his other hand to his side. A wave of exhaustion rushed his system, penetrating every cell. He found a clean cloth in his pocket and wiped his blood from the barrier. His DNA could not be found at the scene.

As Jake left the helipad in his wake, the adrenaline that had kept him running on edge dissipated and rapidly left his blood stream.

The ascending steps, two at a time. Air mixed with a tinge of diesel fuel filled his lungs. He climbed toward the ridge. The place had a macabre Hitchcock theme framed against the rising moon. That darkness spread across the landscape.

Jake paused and sent a text to Katerina:

I've penetrated Sobol's stronghold and neutralized the hostiles.

Armitage swapped the Kalashnikov in his carryall for the P-96. The familiar grip gave him renewed confidence.

The burner vibrated. A text message lit up:

I'm fine, Jake. Thank God you're OK!

Jake exhaled as he read the message. His pounding heart subsided as he pocketed the cell phone. The wind picked up strength. He zipped his jacket.

The path returned Jake to rear door of the mansion. A body lay nearby on the concrete. He flipped a switch and a night light pooled over the patio. The dark-haired thug's body lay twisted in a heap. His pockets were empty.

Shadows danced in the dim hallway. Jake stooped and checked the wiry man. A blank burner. He pocketed the device and gained his feet.

Armitage weaved into the corridor with his right arm bent. The house was deserted; bodies were his only company. He clicked the safety on his weapon to off and squeezed the grip in anticipation of an attack.

The floor creaked on each footfall. If a hostile was hidden, they'd hear Jake coming.

*I don't like announcements.*

He moved around the older section into the carpeted zone. Every archway, he waited and listened.

As the mansion groaned on its huge frame, Jake

cocked his weapon and mounted the stairs.

# Chapter 34

The agent climbed the steps and covered the shadow-filled corner return. He paused at the landing, anticipated movement.

No attack.

The thick carpet curled at the skirting, hidden by furnishings. Jake swept the blind spots and pointed the gun at each door. He stalked the interconnecting corridor with caution. The silence spooked him a little.

Armitage found rooms annexed off the spine. Most were bedrooms or sitting rooms with antiquated furniture. They looked used, with simple wardrobes containing minimal shirts and pants for both genders.

The upper west portion had larger bedrooms and high ceilings. Original mouldings and architraves told him the build had been top quality. The agent examined ornamental items resting on furniture tops. His eyes ran across a vase with dead flowers in a small pool of water. He searched surfaces for incriminating items such as IDs and burner cell phones. The wardrobes were devoid of tech devices. Some of the beds were made without a single crease.

At the end, Jake reached a door which spilled into a secondary recreational room. The clusters of sofas and side tables were stuffed in every available corner, giving the illusion the twelve-meter space was smaller. He passed an extravagant French recliner that could be two centuries old.

The faint odour of old cigar smoke lingered with Jake. He recognized it but couldn't put his finger on where it came from.

Armitage glanced at the furniture arrangement and style. He shook his head.

*What is it I find so familiar?*

At the south wall, Jake lowered his weapon. He kept his finger ready on the trigger. The temperature had dropped more in the last hour. He hadn't noticed until now. Despite the chill, a mild sweat sheen appeared on his brow. He swiped with the back of his hand. Shadows flicked across the drapes. He checked every niche and corner.

Empty. The agent slit the window drapes and peered out into the void.

The helicopter escapade weighed on Jake's mind. Through the top of the canopies, the streetlights flickered.

Somewhere close, Sobol and his cronies plotted their next move. Armitage released the drape.

*I need to finish and get out of here fast.*

The meticulous processing of the mansion covered the covert spots and positions. An armed assailant could be behind every piece of furniture or hidden within reach.

Jake swung the final door open. He found the archway to a basin, an adjoining washroom tacked to the side. Towels were draped on wall racks. The shower appeared to have recent usage.

Satisfied with the search, Jake doubled back through the corridor. He listened to the creaks, assessing any dangers.

The staircase moved in spots. Jake clenched his weapon grip, reached the bottom fast. Pistol outstretched, he headed to the front yard.

Armitage assessed the entrance, exposed to the crisp evening air. The carnage of another shootout lay plentiful on the stronghold grounds. Bodies were scattered from the kitchen to the back garden.

The agent took in the carnage and stretched his hamstrings. He pulled his foot into his buttocks, testing his joints. The stiffness dissipated as the muscle's veins expanded with blood.

*I have a headache.*

The scent of flora overpowered the smell of the gunfight. Jake squinted at the gravel driveway, his gaze on the exit. The gates gleamed, a maroon color in the distance. He listened for other hostiles but silence engulfed his immediate area. Within the large gardens, the trees cast dark shadows on the grassy patches. It gave the landscape a sinister appearance, as if formed of dark magic with the nightfall.

Armitage contemplated his car as he started off the porch. His pace quickened. Leaving the mansion, he took a deep breath and exhaled.

*I nearly got myself killed.*

A shiver ran down his spine. He concentrated on remembering the attacker's voice. Any clue, no matter how minor, became valuable. The loose stone surface crunched underfoot as he pressed on toward the car.

A gunshot rang out, breaking the silence.

Jake pivoted as a bullet grazed his upper arm. The impact stung. He dropped to one knee.

"Put the weapon down," a voice said with a distinctive Russian accent. "Slow. No sudden movement. Raise your arms."

*Where do I know that voice from?*

The agent placed the weapon on the stones and held up his hands.

"Turn around slowly. No fast movements or you'll eat a

bullet."

Armitage swivelled to see Bollov standing on the porch. The Russian held a pistol aimed at Jake's chest. Jake held Bollov's gaze as the two men circled.

"Don't come closer."

"I won't." The agent waved his palms slowly.

The business man crouched, picked up Jake's P-96M. The sleeves of Bollov's business shirt were bunched to the elbows. Must have been hiding inside. A basement cellar? Jake's brain started calculating the odds of covering the distance to the weapon. He'd disarm his opponent and safety the threat.

Bollov held out the firearm. The Russian kept his gaze trained on Jake.

"You've returned to visit us again? You've been causing much trouble. Not only for me, but with my associates." The consultant's eyes squinted.

"I try to spread the love around, Bollov. Specially to corrupt people such as yourself." Jake smiled at his captor.

The consultant inched from the doorway. "This is a matter of opinion." He sidestepped and waved the pistol at Jake. "Walk slowly into the house. And remember I'm right behind you."

Armitage crossed to the porch. He kept his arms raised and his eyes straight ahead. His mind worked overtime on an escape plan.

"Keep going down the hallway."

The agent ambled into the stretch, stalled to work out his new strategy. The Russian came closer, weapon trained at his back. Ahead, Jake noticed a loose board protruding two inches. Perfect chance to create a diversion. He pushed the toe of his boot and feigned a fall.

Bollov raised the gun in surprise.

In the momentary distraction, Jake jumped sideways and out of direct range. He crouched behind a large bookcase.

The Russian charged into the room and fired the weapon. A bullet went wild. In the confusion, the agent tackled Bollov gridiron style, the pistol flying. Bodies tumbled as Jake let go and rolled to the weapon.

Armitage fired. The round hit Bollov in the chest. The assailant's arms flailed. For good measure, Jake fired the second shot to Bollov's head. Double tap.

The Russian wheezed, body thudded to the floor. Jake waited as the Russian gargled, writhing in a fit. A final heave of the chest and his body collapsed. Both arms flopped asunder, a fitting end for the corrupt consultant.

# Chapter 35

Armitage rummaged in Bollov's jacket.

A quick search of the consultant's clothing produced another burner phone. Jake opened it without a security code and flicked through the menu. Criminals and thugs didn't leave contact names in their disposable cells. Smart. The numbers of associates were memorized and dialled when necessary.

The agent scrolled through the call register and found only two dialled numbers. Like the others, it had no data or information recorded.

The two numbers had been dialled in the past eight days. Each one called on multiple occasions. He put the phone in his pocket.

A faint whooping resonated through the trees. Jake squinted at the clouds. No stars in the sky. City lights shone in the distance behind him. An inky blackness with low visibility.

The beep chirped from his hip. The agent pulled up his jacket and glanced at the device clamped to his belt.

The detector light flashed green.

Ballistic early warning.

Incoming missile.

Armitage heard the whoosh in slow motion. No time to think. He glanced around the yard. One place. He sprinted at the rusted shipping container as his muscles strained. The air swirled, a vacuum forced by gravity. His stomach lurched.

The urgency pushed Jake's legs through the fire in his lungs.

In the last five meters, Jake's body slammed the opening. His belly hit the steel bottom. Winded, he forced his legs upward. He flipped to his backside, kicked at the door.

The hatch clanged.

A canvas sheet covered the floor. Armitage buried himself inside. The explosion reverberated the steel. Underneath his belly, the base shuddered. Steel whined and buckled. The container rose and undulated with the shockwaves.

The second blast rocked the ground.

Brick and timber tore. Jake cradled his head, face pressed to his elbows. His skull throbbed, crushed by the pressure. Debris pelted the container. Pain coursed into his legs braced against the door.

Thunder clapped. The earth shook. Foundry walls collapsed and tumbled. The agent braced the door, praying against a third missile.

Suddenly the container settled. Jake waited on his belly in the dim light. A crackling merged with the gathering wind. His eardrums rang and his head pounded.

A faint engine noise circled.

*They must be checking their handiwork.*

The propeller finally faded.

Armitage pushed himself to his feet. He braced the wall with his left palm, steadying a sudden head rush. His stomach lurched.

The hatch swung open, hanging off of one hinge. Orange fires lit up the dark. The agent stumbled onto the grass and took in the devastation. Even in darkness, the site looked like a war zone.

*Must have been a spike missile. Who had the military clearance for that kind of hardware?*

The explosions still echoed in Jake's head. He straightened against the mounting wind. Gained his bearings.

Smoke trails billowed off the rubble. Scorched wall shells held shattered windowpanes. Blackened timber lay in piles. The entire back half of the stronghold was missing. It had disintegrated, leaving a two-story gap.

Armitage stared at the wreckage. It resembled a hinged doll house with one half missing. A crow rustled from the front foliage, scanning for scraps.

Small fires spluttered in piles of rubble. Orange flames erupted and collapsed. Copper pipes protruded from the ruin.

*I need to get out before the police arrive.*

Jake circled patches of singed grass. He avoided embers dancing in the breeze. The narrow pathway to the side had upended. He gazed through the empty lounge bay window at the blasted furniture.

A soot-covered corpse lay crumpled near a support post.

*Bollov. What's left of him.*

Thunder clapped overhead. The agent peered up at the inky sky. A siren wailed faintly from the north.

*The cavalry will be here soon.*

He threw the carryall over his shoulder. A stab of pain made him wince. Rain pattered lightly, building momentum by the second. Armitage jogged the path to the undergrowth. A blessing that the falling darkness and the foliage hid some of the carnage. Splotches grew heavier.

Jake pulled his cap tight. He assessed the road for traffic from the cover of the perimeter fence.

A car had slowed, brake lights fuzzy in the mist. The driver waited. No other witnesses.

The agent wrestled the low-hanging foliage. He climbed into the car seat and typed a message to Katerina. The clock displayed the time. It had been three hours and ten minutes since he left the car. He'd missed only one text.

The phone beeped with a smiley face. His anxiety disappeared straight away.

Armitage fired the engine and reversed onto the street. He programmed the apartment location into the GPS and let the night air flush the cabin. As the tires crunched on loose asphalt, he let out a long breath.

Ahead, the city lights gleamed and wavered like a living entity. The agent wiped his eyes and face with a towel from the glove box. He coasted to the next set of lights. Road workers in high-vis coats held up signs to reduce speed to forty miles per hour.

Jake mulled over the events at the stronghold. The body count had risen. Kolisnyk escaped, but now the involvement of SPG had been confirmed. This political-criminal network extended to top-brass military.

Topped with American interference in Russian politics.

Two-way espionage.

This mission had reached a new level.

The road expanded as the Toyota ascended onto the freeway link.

A consultancy firm contracted by a corrupt politician. Not only exercising PR and marketing campaigns, SPG had hired mercenaries and contract killers. Lights flickered overhead as Jake changed lanes. The agent checked his side and rear-mirrors for tails.

*Counter-surveillance never ends.*

A managing partner had been heavily armed and willing to kill. The American director of SPG had been implicated by association alone. Perhaps this underworld crime and dirty politics was funded by foreign interests.

High gothic architecture cast sinister shadows over the dimly lit parking lot. Jake took a screwdriver from the console and moved around to the rear of the vehicle. Squatted by the bumper, he began loosening the license plate screws. He caught the old one as it dropped and attached the new ones to each side.

To remain hidden from enemies, it became a necessity to exchange number plates every week. This coupled with a different vehicle per two weeks.

# Chapter 36

A clang echoed through the apartment corridor. The agent unlocked his door at ten-twenty P.M. and placed the keys on the table. Katerina sat on the sofa, crouched over her laptop. She put the device aside, jumped to her feet, and embraced Jake.

"I thought you'd been injured—or worse."

Armitage returned the hug, comforting after the day's events.

"Took me longer than expected. The stronghold had armed hostiles."

"You smell like smoke." She regarded his torn sleeve with a grim expression. "Have an injury too. The Ukrainian military guy was there?"

"Yes, he made an appearance." Jake sighed and shrugged off the carry-all. It fell in a heap on the table surface.. "I need caffeine."

Armitage took a packet of coffee beans, tipped the contents into the mocha pot and fired up the stove. "The smoke is another thing."

The Russian reporter shook her head as she listened.

"Kolisnyk escaped with Sobol after we had a prolonged shootout. Bollov, the white-collar consultant and middle-aged partner at SPG, pulled a gun on me too."

"You're kidding." Katerina stopped pacing the living room and stared wide-eyed. "I thought that firm appeared dodgy. Contract killers and military experts with heavy firearms. These guys are in deep."

The agent poured dark liquid into a mug. "They're in all

the way. It's a strong network with vested interests for many high-profile people. The other American SPG partner must know what's happening. In fact, I'm starting to think they're pulling the strings."

"You think Americans are controlling this organisation?"

"If you could call it that." With cup in hand, Jake sank into an armchair opposite Katerina. He sipped. The rich bean flavour ran down his throat. He savored the taste as he leaned back into the thick cushion.

"Possibly. It's starting to make more sense from that angle. But who knows if we've reached the top of this pecking order yet?"

"You look exhausted, Jake."

Jake sighed. "That's not all. They shot two missiles at the house. I'm not sure if I was the original target. Hence the smoke."

Katerina placed her hands over her mouth. "You're joking. This is beyond insane."

"That crossed my mind. Has to be high-level military to get this level of hardware."

"Where were you when they hit?"

"Lying in a shipping container." Armitage shook dust from his hair. "I made it within seconds of the first blast. Talk about lying low."

Katerina gave a grim chuckle. "Even so. We need to blow this case wide open."

"We're both in danger. Lots this time. Top priority is getting you out of Russia." Jake shook his head.

"If you're here, Jake, I'm sticking by you." She returned to the computer and typed. Her finger moved down the screen and stopped. "I found further links to the deals while you were gone. It seems Sobol has other companies under different directors. Each trading with separate books. This is how he hides it all. Funnelling into not-for-profit slush funds."

"Now we can add money laundering to the list." The agent contemplated the data and sipped his beverage. "And tax avoidance. The politician needs cash to fund his political campaigns and extra-curricular activity. That must run into the millions per month."

"Yes, it seems this way. I've run some checks on suspicious entities. These accounts are so encrypted and hidden behind firewalls, they make Swiss accounts look like child's play. It's the last batch that are the key. If we can find the destination of some of these payments, it may reveal answers about what's going down here. There's way more at stake than we originally thought. Perhaps in the hundreds of millions of dollars."

"I agree. Tracing these transactions would reveal the other big players in this game." Armitage paused. "Sobol is using an offshore bank. In a city with little or no financial reporting and regulation. They usually operate in a developing country."

Katerina nodded. "I'm narrowing it down. It's hard to break the firewalls. This thing is so big, they've hired both private and government army to protect their interests."

"You're doing great." The agent carried his mug to the balcony window and stared out over the city. Lights blinked and flashed. The main canal shimmered like a hungry snake slithering toward its prey.

"There's so many lives at stake," He heard Katerina mutter.

The screen blinked. It threw a blue hue across

Katerina's face. The reporter stretched and moved to the kitchen. She replaced the mocha pot on the stove.

"More caffeine is required if I go into the early hours again this morning."

"I hear that." The agent drained his mug and stepped away from the glass wall. "I want vodka but cannot risk the downtime."

"Sit down and I'll get the first aid kit. We need to fix you up."

"It's in the pantry." Jake lowered his body into a seat. His elbow ached as it rested on the table surface.

The hissing from the stove flame took over the silence. Katerina injected a pain killer. The site went numb as Jake relaxed his upper body. She cleaned Jake's arm with antiseptic on a pad.

"This is more than a graze." The Russian journalist applied a bandage. She secured the ends and fastened a clip.

"Lucky it's not worse."

"That should do it. I helped medical staff in Syria a few years back."

"Thanks, Katerina. I'm going to lie on the sofa for a minute." Armitage pressed play on the sound bar he'd set up in the corner.

"I'll get some shut eye after a coffee and a shower." She rubbed her eyes.

"We both need it. You can use a spare t-shirt if you like."

"Thanks, I have a sweatsuit."

The room went hazy as Jake's eyes struggled to stay

open. Water pattered in the bathroom. A drowsiness overtook his senses as if he floated on a cloud.

Rhythmic melodies of a Yandex mix floated in the room. It had a catatonic effect on Jake's weary body. He fell into a slumber and dozed.


The agent roused to shouts from Katerina. His head swam as he shrugged off the night's grogginess. Lights sparkled beyond the glass. He angled his wrist, squinted at the watch: four-ten A.M. A throb came from the dressed wound. He touched his arm tenderly.

*I've been out for three hours.*

Shadows danced over the ceiling. Armitage gained his feet, moving toward the sofa. He straightened his spine and took a deep breath.

Katerina appeared dressed in a sweatsuit, hair ruffled, clutching her computer. Jake noticed she was always attractive, even when first woken.

A beep chimed from the computer. The Russian reporter perched over the table. Her eyes widened as she pointed at data cascading down the screen.

"I've got a hit." She crouched over the laptop, scanned the information. "I thought the source accounts were in Ukraine. But that's only a transit deposit."

"Interesting." Armitage pulled on a jacket. "I wonder where it's heading?"

A beep chimed. She peered at the screen.

"Kazakhstan."

"Two non-reporting countries. Makes sense with more arm's length than Georgia." Jake paced the lounge. "Untraceable and washed through two non-reporting bank systems. This is gold."

Katerina looked over the screen. "Remember both Kazakhstan and the Ukraine have committed to the Common Reporting Standard. Both will start reporting as of early next year."

"Good point. That could give these guys a limited window. Perhaps cryptocurrency is a possibility?"

"You could be right. I'll find out more with time."

"I'm sure, but we're on the clock and running out of time fast." The agent opened the black carryall on the dining table. On the surface he placed a Kalashnikov machine gun and a spare magazine. "I took this from one of the friendly Russians today. He won't be needing it anymore. I've got my handgun and the extra Beretta. Plenty of rounds."

"How's your arm?"

"It's aching a little, but clean and much better, thanks to you." Jake stocked the machine gun.

The reporter stared at the growing arsenal, "What's our next move, Jake?"

"I hit Kolisnyk today, but only a surface wound. He'll be back until one of us goes down. I'm going to call Dodds and check him out. The CIA would have intel on this. We know where Sobol is sending his money. The politician has a corrupt military in his pocket."

"Not to mention vast resources." Katerina crossed her arms. "They've got a lot of tech and hardware. That missile is doing my head in. I'm so thankful you're back in one piece."

"Tell me about it. I can still feel the heat scorching my body. My elbows are skinned and my back is killing me." Armitage laughed, rubbing his sleeves. "Dodds is worth a shot. I need trained back-up like the veteran agent to stand a chance."

"I'm here for ground support and minor hacking skills." Katerina closed the laptop and placed the device on the side table. She stood and headed to the stove.

"Thanks, Katerina..." Jake trailed off as he searched for his cell phone. His determination to catch the network responsible burned like an angry fire in his chest. Katerina had become a prisoner in her own city. Held to ransom by a corrupt politician, mercenaries, a bunch of corporate launderers with mafia underlings.

"No need to thank me. You've protected me so far—saved my life at least twice." She smiled, her hazel eyes reflected brown-green under the downlights.

"We haven't got our arses kicked yet. Great teamwork so far." Armitage grinned and pulled out Dodd's card. He thumbed numbers into his burner and pressed the call button.

City lights broke the darkness, revealed the cloaked skyline. As the number rang, Jake paced the floor. The adrenaline spiked his system as he thought about the battle to come.

The situation had entered overdrive and needed to come to a head, and fast.

# Chapter 37

The burner rang five times before a connection clicked.

"Dodds here." The CIA agent's Southern accent vibrated into the ear piece.

"Hi, Dodds. It's Jake Armitage."

"How the hell are you, Jake? I thought you'd never call."

"I'm good. I have important intel. Can you chat in person?"

"Sure thing." The American paused and answered, "Where are you thinking?"

"What about the club off Nevsky called Charlie's? It's open till six A.M. Just near the junction of the middle canal. It's a secluded place under street level."

"I know it. Can be there in twenty."

"See you." The agent clicked off.

"Will you tell him about last night?" Katerina tucked her legs underneath her body.

"Just parts. He's CIA and something is not on the level" Jake shook his head. "They always keep hidden agendas."

The receding moonlight spilled through the tinted windows, dappling the floorboards a blue-white sheen. Jake studied the patterns as he searched for inspiration.

"I hear you." She wore a grim expression.

A magazine glinted on the table surface and caught Jake's eye. It reminded him of the urgency. He hastened to the carry-all. The current state of affairs required a beef up on home security.

The agent picked up the Beretta and slid back the

chamber. One left. A box of ammunition lay opened on the surface. He loaded the magazine and pushed the piece into the handle.

"What do we know about Dodd's activities?" Jake asked, shoving a camera detector in an inner compartment. Two more loaded magazines went on his belt as he zipped the pocket.

"Not enough," Katerina said, tapping the keyboard. She concentrated on a steady stream of data. "I looked for any information on Dodd's operations in your database, but couldn't find anything useful. All my usual sources, such as government sites, came up zero. But I'm sure it's an alias, and a recent one."

"That's fine." Armitage kept further comments to himself so as not to rattle Katerina.

"I'll do this meet and let you know as soon as I have something." Jake placed a square device on the table. "I've programmed this GPS tracker in my burner so you can ping and track my cell phone. If I don't return in two hours, trace me and send someone."

"Ok." Katerina stared at the device.

The agent pushed the Beretta pistol across the surface. "You may need this too."

Jake smiled and lingered over her figure. The aroma from her hair made him wish they could have been in a more relaxed environment. He touched her outstretched hand as he passed by the sofa. Her fingers were soft. As the connection broke, he paused.

"Jake, please..." Katerina's mouth curled and worry flashed across her face. "Please take care. I won't say come back alive again." She looked away. "You know how I feel."

Armitage nodded and their gazes locked. Her eyes

seemed glazy and watery, but perhaps the light played tricks on his vision. He displayed his most confident face. His heart raced with fear.

Katerina wrapped her arms around Jake's waist. For a moment, he held her close. The warmth from her body made it hard to contemplate the frosty morning that awaited him. She buried her head in his clothes and sighed. His ribcage expanded, synced with her breath against his chest. Time seemed to stop. He wished there wasn't so much danger waiting outside.

Saint Petersburg loomed over their little world, cold and unforgiving, as if waiting patiently to deliver his inevitable fate. The agent gently untangled her arms and cupped her face in his palms. The journalist's cheeks were damp and her hazel eyes shone a brilliant shade of coppery emerald.

"It's going to be alright. We'll get through this."

The Russian reporter stared up Jake, searching for reassurance. He let go of her face and grasped her hands. They were soft and firm in his palms as he pressed her fingers. He released them and straightened. Katerina crossed her arms and hugged herself.

"Remember, if I prank call you, go set the tracer in the case." He turned the button on the top and tuned in a channel. "That way you'll know where I am."

Katerina nodded.

A breeze fluttered from the passageway. The agent closed the door behind him and headed to the elevator. He rehearsed the plan as the cabin descended to the ground.

The parking lot appeared deserted. Jake twisted the vehicle into the tunnel of gothic architecture. Facades hung impossibly high, casting monster-shaped shadows over his path. He veered south-west, the turn spilling into a cluster of semi-dilapidated buildings. A group of pigeons fought over scraps.

Armitage clicked the car alarm fob a few blocks from the venue. He wanted to take the rest on foot to assess the meeting place.

The concrete glistened with the recent drizzle. Jake turned his collar up to keep the cold at bay.

Iron downspouts snaked vertically on every building throughout Saint Petersburg. Overflow storm-water streamed from the chutes over cracked concrete, flooding the sidewalks. The crude engineering from a bygone time marked the city's architecture.

At the nearest junction to the meet, Jake checked for unusual activity. His gaze flicked over the shop fronts. A quick surveillance assessment of vulnerable positions, which were few in the early hours before dawn. He checked all balconies and high vantage points for snipers.

The agent paced from the flank of a dry cleaner storefront. A café sat thirty meters away, windows covered with blinds. He relied on limited street signage as the road melted to sharp corners enveloped in shadows.

The venue was tucked away behind a chicken shop. Music bounced from the walls.

Armitage approached the shady entrance. It sat under a neon sign hung from a half-rusted chain that blinked 'CHARLIE'S'. Music pumped from the doorway, a dark hole that descended on concrete steps into the ground.

A group of twenty-something clubbers spilled past the doorman. Jake waited in line under a wonky overhang. He watched the exiting group light cigarettes and disappear into the next bend. His behaviour may have seemed odd to the average citizen. The agent scanned the highest building, an apartment block due east, which also proved negative re any potential threats.

The nearest bouncer ushered a pair of women into the gap. Armitage stepped over a watery stream as a meaty hand hovered in front of his face. He paused. A heavily-tattooed doorman stepped from the shadows. Security asked for his ID in Russian. Jake produced his fake driver's license. After ten seconds of scrutiny, the man shoved the ID in his hand.

Strobe lights shimmered as Jake cut a path through the dance floor. At five-thirty A.M. the bar had a spattering of customers moving their feet to the beats. He passed a group of youths huddled around a table of boutique beers. The checkered floors gave way to dated boards and blackened walls. A pair of tall model types in cocktail dresses giggled at him from the bar. The agent scanned the worn décor, flaws hidden in the half-darkness.

A man behind turntables sipped a beverage. Live DJ. The music switched to drum-and-bass. An employee wiped vacant tables with a damp cloth. Her stained apron was threadbare and the drywall seemed ready to collapse at any moment under the weight of the venue's seedy atmosphere.

Armitage settled behind a table. He watched the venue for Dodds. Female employees converged on the corner booth and offered to fetch drinks for a tip. He gave a one-thousand ruble note to one and ordered a vodka. Dancers flooded the space, busting new moves as the lights roamed.

The same lady appeared and placed his order on the table. Jake gave her more money for a tip and sipped until he saw a familiar face through the smoky haze.

Dodds appeared from the dance floor and strolled up to the table. A quick handshake was exchanged. The CIA agent placed his drink on the surface, lit a cigarette, and settled opposite Jake.

"Good to hear from you, Jake." Dodds blew a blue trail from the corner of his mouth, flashed a set of stained teeth Jake could see even in the strobe light. "What do you have?"

Armitage's gaze took him in, unsure whether this discussion consisted of good judgement. He shook his misgivings off and decided to take the risk. "Have you heard of a politician named Sobol?"

Dodd's eyes narrowed and he leaned forward. "Hell, yes. Everybody in Russia has heard of Sobol. He contested the last Presidential run. What's he involved with?"

"Sobol has questionable associates and I suspect he's dirty." Jake crossed his arms. "Activity well beyond petty crime and minor offenses."

Dodds chuckled, tapped his cigarette ash. "Of course he's dirty. "All government sectors in Russia are vulnerable to corruption. But to what degree can we excuse this or turn a blind eye?"

"True. What evidence do you have on him and this illicit activity?" Jake asked. "It might help us."

"We don't need it. The CIA wants to control Sobol, but let them dig their own hole. If you get my meaning. That's until we can work out what to do with him." Dodds sipped vodka.

"Give him enough rope to hang himself?"

The older man pointed at Jake. "Now you're getting it."

"So why are you here, Dodds? I mean in Saint Petersburg."

"I'm a NOC. A non-official cover. We've been monitoring commodities and other illicit transactions here in Russia," Dodds said. "I've posed as both a foreign buyer and entrepreneur. To build connections and transact."

Armitage necked the glass and stared at Dodds. He knew exactly what the CIA wanted in Saint Petersburg. "You're trading uranium."

The CIA agent tilted his head. "You catch on fast. Have you considered working with us?"

"That's what we're doing now, isn't it, Dodds? It's not too hard to see. How deep is Sobol involved? The military too?"

Dodds shook his head. "Thing is, Jake, there's so much money in illicit commodities and nobody wants to go green until they've lined their pockets. The mother country is no exception. Chernobyl did wonders for the industry. My agency required a sleeper deep inside the network and close to the target. I've been working on this for two years. It's not easy."

"Smart...very smart." Jake paused and stared at his glass. "We need to take Sobol down."

"Easy on there. The politician has benefits by sitting in that position."

"Benefits to whom? The CIA? He's a terrorist and a threat to the free world."

"He's a threat, but even the most corrupted have their uses." Dodds spread his arms as if to emphasis his point.

"What? Like Osama Bin Laden?" The agent shook his head.

"Come on, Jake, that's a bit below the belt. We're on the same team, you and I. Anyway, Bin Laden is ancient history."

Armitage sucked on his cigarette.

"Sobol has an international consulting group that pulls

most of the shots," Dodd's continued.

Jake shifted in his seat. "Who's the group?"

"SPG partners. Have you heard of them?" Dodd's gaze met Jake's. The lighting cast a shadow across the CIA agent's face.

"SPG partners rings a bell." Jake paused as if in deep thought. "Well known in this city for some big campaigns. How deep are they in this conspiracy?"

Dodds smiled, a Cheshire cat with a secret. "All the way."

"Interesting...but doesn't change the threat."

The DJ changed sets as the bass vibrated the walls. Dodds leaned in over table. Armitage could smell the alcohol on the older agent's breath.

"Again, I need your help to take Sobol and his cronies down," Jake said and white-knuckled the table edge. "I had an incident last night. It involved the politician and his contract killer. Missiles were shot from a drone in a residential area. At a stronghold owned by Sobol or his associates."

"Hell, that's deep." Dodds raised his eyebrows.

"The first missile came when I was at the rear entrance."

Dodd's sharply inhaled. "Too close for anyone's comfort." He stared straight at Jake. "I agree we need to intervene, and fast. With your involvement, it's possible. I'll take you to their main compound.It's outside the city limits."

"When do we leave?"

"Later this morning. I can meet you outside the Winter Palace exit. Will text you." Dodds checked his watch. "You better come ready for war. We shoot to kill."

Armitage nodded. "Is there any other way?" He didn't wait for an answer.

Strobes of red and blue highlighted spaced-out patrons. Jake hustled through the dancers and ascended into the morning air. A brisk wind hit his face as he inhaled the cold breeze.

The air was almost a physical presence, a sheet of wet fabric. Fresh rain had dampened the gray, bland architecture. Armitage rubbed his hands and forged into the concrete maze of paths.

Shop signs snaked into the darkness. The agent squinted toward the receding road, listening for any approaching people. The streets were covered in inky puddles broken only by the occasional fading streetlight.

Silence stared back at Jake. Only hard-core party animals were out this early morning.

Armitage unlocked the car and sat in the vehicle. He gripped the wheel, checked mirrors for outside movement. In the watery reflection on the sidewalk, he noticed a figure across the street. Discreet. Jake made the pretence of looking at his burner phone.

The stranger dawdled on the opposite road, hidden behind a wall of brick. Jake watched with his peripheral vision. He heard faint footsteps click on the sidewalk.

*Let's see how close this one follows.*

# Chapter 38

Armitage started the engine and transitioned onto the buckled pebble-stone. He carved through the moist sheet brought about by the overnight dew. A skyscraper cast a shadow over the narrow sidewalk. He gathered a little speed and took it slow. Air inside the vehicle seemed stifled and stale.

The first sign of dawn fought the clouds. He cranked the window; the cool breeze flowed. The lane ended at a main road and he pressed the accelerator at the white lines.

A battered stop sign glinted under the streetlight. Armitage stalled on the turn, watching his rear.

*I bet this tail has a nearby car.*

As Jake exited, a late-model, gray sedan pulled out of the same lane. The tail turned onto the main avenue, confident the pursuit would continue. Jake changed to the far lane. The new tail merged behind Jake, two cars back, and sat on the speed limit. It hung a good distance, leaving a car in-between.

Armitage cruised around a plaza. Waves crashed in the canal. Seagulls swooped and screeched, pigeons cooed around commuter's legs. He checked his tail sat in position.

Street signs flashed by as Jake cut a course toward the apartment. He kept his eyes ahead, concentrating on the traffic. Colours morphed and blurred as he chewed over Dodd's words.

If this war was about uranium, they might be chasing fool's gold. It had to be more than commodities—even nuclear ones had their limit. Jake strummed the wheel with his thumbs, pushing his anxiety back into his stomach.

The agent shot a glance at his rear-view mirror. The gray sedan sat comfortably behind. Headlamps blurred in the opposite lane. Traffic had slowed, so the tail had to keep one vehicle between them.

A t-intersection appeared one hundred meters ahead. Jake pulled to a stop as the light turned red. He waited.

One second. Two seconds.

Before the left-hand traffic flow moved, Jake slammed the accelerator. The tires squealed as he launched through the gap.

Lights flashed either side of Jake's vision. The half-way line appeared. On his right, a blue sedan ploughed into view. The agent skidded and rubber melted. He veered to the opposite lane. Headlamps blinked. The trunk fishtailed, momentarily lost traction. Smoke bloomed, rising in the rear window. He adjusted the steering. Suspension shuddered.

The white line flashed past the window. Jake made it to the other side. His heart leaped up his throat.

A car horn sounded as the blue car narrowly missed a head-on collision.

The median strip separated the edge. Armitage mounted it as the car bottom scraped. Sparks flared as he merged with oncoming drivers.

He checked the mirror. The gray sedan sat at the intersection, caught behind the car with the light still red.

The next lights loomed as the previous one turned green. Jake had made a two-mile gap. In the distance, cars moved into the previous intersection. Jake pressed the accelerator. The gray sedan pushed out, changing lanes.

The agent sat on the inside lane, calculating his lead.

His pursuer hammered the stretch. Both lanes were busy which blocked the pass. The car caught up, coming level, bumper to bumper. Exhaust roared. A Ford v6 engine, better for drag racing and greater horsepower.

The two cars sat near neck-and-neck. Armitage couldn't see the driver's face, an outline through maximum-strength tinted windows.

To his right, the sedan accelerated, bumper edged forward. The passenger window whirred. A man in his thirties raised the barrel of a sawn-off shotgun pointed at Jake.

Cars had cleared the immediate section, either slowed down or pulled away. Traffic signals flickering like a hazy dream, Jake pushed the pedal. The engine revved and he pulled away. His pursuers caught up, scraped against the panels. The passenger waved him over.

"Pull over to the shoulder." The man shouted in English with a Russian accent. Over the glass lip, the thug raised his weapon. His eyes were blue-white like ice.

*The only way to find out who is in charge is to get taken.*

Armitage flicked his right blinker, slowed into the emergency lane. The sedan exited and braked ten meters in front. A cool breeze flowed through the car as he cracked his window three inches. He checked a razor blade he kept in his inner sleeve. No handle, just four inches of sharp steel.

The tall, brown-haired Russian stepped out. Under the dim streetlights, the man had a gait about him that screamed prison. This guy had hours of pumping iron under his belt.

The barrel of the shotgun glinted when the thug reached the pole. A shard of yellow lit up the Russian's face.

It traced the edge of his square jaw and illuminated his neck.

A tattoo of the dagger and star flashed as if in red neon.

The agent reached for his pistol in the compartment. Under his breath, he repeated the mantra to keep his adrenaline in check. He took his hand off the weapon.

These guys are all connected.

The gravel crunched as the thug reached the car. A gentle tap on the window with a twelve-gauge sawn-off.

"Someone wants a word with you."

Jake held up his hand and nodded. "Nice morning for a drive, isn't it?"

"Get out slowly." The armed Russian stepped sideways, allowing space for the door. "No sudden moves."

The modified shotgun carried scars and scuff marks as if scratched and aged from years of bank robberies and standovers. A relic from decades of mafia wars, no doubt. Crude but effective, and didn't take an expert marksman to deploy with deadly consequences. If shot at this close range, even the worst shooter would blow Jake apart.

Armitage released the handle with a click. He nudged the door with his left elbow, keeping his right hand in view. A large shadow fell from the thug's silhouette. Jake staggered to his feet.

The Russian was tall, north of one-ninety centimeters, and of muscular build. The agent pressed his palms on the hood as the thug patted him down with one hand. The man had the arm-reach to keep a safe distance. From the driver side, a second weapon pointed at his face.

A small hatchback came buzzing by in the opposite

direction, but sped up as it came level. The occupants would have seen the weapon, sussed out the criminality of the exchange. Nobody wanted to get involved in this kind of scene.

The tall thug tilted his head at the gray sedan. Armitage stepped away from his SUV, his legs reluctantly forced into motion.

Wind blew over Jake's face as sparks of morning sunlight lightened the gloom. A sheen of perspiration gathered on his skin, cooled by the fresh air. He repressed a shiver. A tingle shot up his spine, an electric charge.

His ex-wife's face, blurred a little. The memory faded. In its wake, Katerina's smile appeared. This warmed his chest. Jake pushed the thoughts away.

*I need to keep my cool.*

The sedan's passenger door opened. He tumbled into the rear seat. The driver pointed a Glock at his face. The shotgun guy slid alongside.

"Fasten your belt. We're going on a ride." The driver had old acne scars and appeared in his forties. His short-cropped, black hair had specks of gray on the side. No tattoos.

The shotgun barrel prodded his side. The driver pocketed his pistol and angled his head to the rear.

"Don't think of escape or my associate will blow a hole through you."

As the car rolled off the strip, Jake's vision blurred. The driver pressed the button for his side window from the front control and a screen rose.

The agent caught the stare of the brown-haired thug. "Where are we going?" Knuckles tightened on the twelve-gauge. A menacing glare meant business.

"Don't worry about this; sit back and shut up."

The dawn spread yellow over his shoulder as they veered south. A large sign indicated an exit. The vehicle steered toward a band of trees. The driver glanced in his mirror, observed his speed, and drove safely.

A cluster of warehouses loomed on a crest. Sensor lights dotted the roofs. Armitage shuffled in the seat. Not a blink from the thug holding the shotgun. They pulled into a concrete patch littered with weeds.

The driver killed the engine and turned to Jake.

"Out of the car."

The agent was frogmarched toward a large roller door. The rain formed a light blanket of mist, a white-noise machine whirring on repeat. He watched the glint of the sawn-off. The weapon bobbed with the tall guy's gait. The older thug led, the deliberate and measured steps of a confident criminal.

A narrow path to an iron door cut into the structure flank. Jake entered a faint smell of mould, rotted wood and marzipan. Inside, a decades-old industrial set-out. Shelves with manufacturing tools lined the walls. Moisture clung to the outer edges. A forklift sat in the corner facing a stack of pallets.

Crossing the vast space, they passed a stack of crates. An open lid revealed a matt-black barrel. Armitage diverted his gaze. A prod in the back forced him forward.

Overhead, a fluorescent tube flickered, highlighting the product. The nose of a missile, half-covered with canvas, flashed before his eyes. The agent blinked and darkness fell on the sight. Fatigue washed over him and his footing faltered.

The tall Russian prompted him again with a nudge, as

if aware Jake had seen the exposed missile. An entrance spilled into a corridor that forked at a junction. They turned right and walked one-hundred meters.

Armitage squinted ahead at a sliver of light in the door crack.

The dark-haired thug knocked on a panel and a click sounded. They waited as the door swung in and they entered a sterile room with thin carpet.

A heavy timber desk sat at the far side. The walls were freshly-painted white. No pictures.

A short, heavy-set man with a large brow and wide shoulders rose and put out his hand.

"My name is Tellav Ivanov and I own half of Russia." The big Russian waved toward a chair. The taller thug nudged Jake to a seated position.

"Who owns the other half? Vladimir Putin?" the agent said. He fell into the armchair.

The billionaire regarded Jake with a creased brow. He pointed to the shotgun henchman. "You can wait outside, and you," he gestured at the shorter one, "you stay here."

Armitage shifted on the patchy, cushioned back, watched the dark-haired Russian retreat to the rear wall.

"It's no secret that Russia is an oligarchy." Jake said. "You must be one of them. But what do you want with me?"

Ivanov clasped his hands behind his head. "We need to discuss important matters. Particularly your skills."

# Chapter 39

"Go ahead," Armitage said, appearing casual but remaining alert.

The billionaire crossed the carpet and paused at a shelf. With a large hand, he picked up an expensive vodka bottle and poured a tumbler.

Ivanov sipped and aimed his focus at Jake.

"Would you like one? It's Russia's finest drop of vodka."

"No, thanks. I'm more interested in why you have brought me here."

"I know this must be on your mind." Ivanov regarded the drink, drained the glass and placed it on the desk. "My associates had to bring you to me as you've caused me some trouble. No?"

"I ran into your men a few times. They're not too polite: fight first, instead of talking." The agent crossed his arms. "All self-defence on my part."

The billionaire's large face flushed a light crimson. "You come to my premises and attack my employees."

"I prefer to have a chat really." Jake adjusted his posture. "But your guys aren't the talking type."

"Then you asked questions across town with the directors at SPG."

"Those guys are pleasant enough, until they're not. You've got quite a mix of employees: mafia thugs like these guys," Jake waved his hand at the back wall, "and white-collar consultants at SPG. Equal rights employer, aren't you."

The billionaire gained his feet. "Then I have you on a surveillance camera at one of my houses. You killed more

# Simon W Clark

men, and Bollov as well."

"Bollov turned up combat-ready and hostile. That's far away from his boardroom duties, isn't it? I relieved him of his weapon, and in the process, he resisted." Jake shrugged.

"Quite the comedian." The billionaire grunted.

"The house is now rubble. Interesting friends you keep." Jake paused. "Or enemies."

The dark-haired thug cocked his weapon. Jake watched him in his peripheral vision.

"Even missiles couldn't kill you." Ivanov stared over the desk. "Although they were a bonus."

"Corrupt military as well." Jake straightened. "So why bring me to your office? Now I know your hideout."

"This is just one of my many properties." The oligarch placed both palms on the desk and squinted his eyes. "I want you to work for me."

"You want to recruit me?"

"The way you have disposed of my men shows great skill. Former military or intelligence, I assume. Now a freelancer."

"Suppose I join you. What's next?"

The billionaire chuckled. "Eliminate the competition, for a start. Clean up loose ends here with former associates."

"I need to think about it."

"In Russia, the rules of politics and commerce are different to America." Ivanov paced behind his desk. A split-system heater blew warmth into the office space. The oligarch formed a fist and scowled. "With money, you can buy anything in Russia. Even you, Armitage."

"Even politicians, I hear."

"Last chance to be on the winning side." Ivanov flexed his fingers.

"I won't join you without an insurance policy."

"Contractors don't get insurance."

"Looks like we cannot do business."

"This meeting is done." The oligarch motioned to his henchman. "Take our American friend here for a walk. You know what to do."

The black-haired thug yanked Jake's jacket. He stumbled to his feet. The taller thug joined the party as they headed south. A thick door, under a neon sign that displayed EXIT in Russian, loomed ahead. The shorter thug pushed the latch and thrust the door aside.

A rush of icy air pipped at Jake's cheeks. He squinted through the rising mist. The deserted lot, dotted with gray puddles, extended to a verge of pines.

Jake searched for an angle, an escape route. His mind blanked. They stepped across the cracked surface to the edge. The tall henchman paused at an iron lean-to. Shards of rust streaked its flank. The leader held the gun steady, just out of reach.

The tall thug stepped inside and reappeared with a shovel, a carryall and plastic sheets.

"Come on. Move." The shorter thug pushed Jake in the spine. Trees filled the wooded landscape. The Russian pointed a finger toward the thick undergrowth.

The forest expanded beyond his visual. The agent's blood rushed in his ears as he determined options. These thugs had to slip up soon and he would be prepared. He focused on a red SUV parked alone in the last bay. The only vehicle in the lot.

Both thugs were out of arms' reach.

The brush thickened as Jake's stomach tightened. He arched his shoulders, anticipated the next shove. It never came. The tall thug paused at a loose-dirt track that lay between two ten-meter conifers.

A click sounded behind Jake. Yellow pooled to his left on the leaves, brown rubble glowed eerily.

"Go on."

The agent stumbled along the loose dirt for what seemed an eternity. The path stopped at a central point. He kept his peripheral vision on the weapons. Trees around grew tall and denser, foliage casting shadows in every direction. His breath condensed to fog as the early temperature struggled to rise.

A lighter clicked. Armitage smelt smoke. He checked the environment. His mind worked overtime on plans to escape but the probability appeared unlikely. Katerina would be worried.

Armitage waited in the small clearing while the short thug thrust the shovel in the dirt.

A shiver travelled up Jake's spine.

The leader leaned against the handle and smiled at Jake.

"Start digging in this spot, American."

Jake's heart jumped into his throat.

The shovel quivered in the breeze. Armitage clenched the handle, pulled the tool from the earth. He stuck it in the ground, threw the load away. His fingers stiffened, making the dig harder. The shorter thug threw his head back and exhaled. Blue smoke trails curled and lifted into the canopy.

Jake continued the labor, his mind working overtime on an escape plan. The agent watched the smoker from the corner of his eye. The gun rested in the smoker's belt.

Metal hit a tough tree root and the impact shuddered into Jake's shoulder. He sucked in a deep breath.

The thug threw a cigarette butt on the ground and squashed it with his shoe.

An idea hit Jake. He dug the shovel deep in the dirt. It struck a stone and he arched his spine.

"Can I have one of those smokes?" Armitage said to the smoker. "Call it my last request."

The dark-haired thug removed the pack. "Why not. It's not like you'll be worried about cancer."

"That's true." The taller thug laughed at the joke. The agent swiped the back of his hand over his brow. Two meters behind the dark-haired thug, the brown-haired man held his weapon at his side.

A pigeon squawked and the sky churned. The smoker fingered a cigarette head and flicked it to the top. Jake grasped the shovel with his right hand. He stretched with his left. The pack brought the thug's arm within his space.

"Thanks."

Two feet from the offered pack, Jake leaned. The thug gave a sidelong glance at his partner. Jake's finger and thumb reached for the packet.

Smoke drifted from the thug's breath. Armitage's fingers parted, ready to take a cigarette. The atmosphere loosened in the drizzle as the henchman chuckled at his desperate expression.

Poised to take a cigarette, Jake clenched the handle. He held his eyes on the dark-haired underling, relaxed and discreetly breathing in short intervals.

The agent's fingertips hovered. Time froze. His timing had to be perfect.

Ten centimeters from Jake's forehead, the thug's face came close enough to kiss. At the last second, Jake swung the shovel from the right side. The smoker lost balance as the tool hit his outstretched arm. The man's balance collapsed.

Armitage gripped the thugs' arms, pulled his chest close, shielding his body from the tall thug. Rattlesnake fast, Jake yanked the pistol from the short captor's belt. He shot the man in the stomach.

The tall thug recovered and fired. A bullet hit the smoker in the back.

The agent looped his left hand under the opponent's right elbow. A nano-second to align and Jake pumped the trigger. The bullet's report echoed before the tall thug had time to shoot again.

A thud vibrated the earth as the big man collapsed to the dirt with a grunt.

The agent straightened and turned.

The dark-haired thug writhed on the ground. Red bloomed on the forest floor. Crouched on his knees, the dark-haired thug tried to spring to his feet.

Jake straightened his posture. He pointed and shot.

The smoker flopped to the ground.

Armitage expanded his lungs, winded and fatigued by the sudden exchange. The cold dropped on him, a barbell across his shoulders. He gasped and held his stomach. Nausea washed over him. A smell of damp earth mixed with the forest. The agent paused for a minute and lowered to the undergrowth. He grasped a handful of loose soil in his palm and squeezed.

*I am alive.*

The dirt trickled through his fingers, cool in his palm, not yet mud until a downpour came. Jake eyed the shards of dawn through the foliage.

Calm flowed over Jake. He scrambled to the bodies. In a pocket, he saw a dark outline too small to be a second firearm. Armitage pulled an old model cell phone from the dark-haired one's jeans. He pressed the screen and scrolled through the apps. The sim card appeared blank, zero contacts recorded and no call history. The tall thug owned a recent model smartphone, two numbers dialled in the past forty-eight hours.

Jake placed both devices in a pocket.

Water dripped from the leaves. The agent followed the path back to the lean-to. He kept a brisk pace to get distance from the scene. The temperature dropped with the rain patter. He wrapped his collar high around his neck.

Hurricane wire glistened against the gloom. Jake scanned the perimeter for guards. A drizzle highlighted mist over the cement foreground. The two surveillance cameras pointed inwards at the gates. Nothing monitoring the planned exit.

Armitage sprinted across the parking lot toward the noise of traffic. A main road snaked beyond the mist. He scurried onto the sidewalk. Brake lights blurred as he kept an eye on the cars. A street sign indicated inbound traffic to Nevsky.

The sidewalk headed east toward sunrise. A metro map came up in Jake's mind. He'd memorised the layout of St Petersburg five months ago. The SUV was parked on the highway roughly four kilometers from his current position.

The agent walked for five minutes, eyes trained on the traffic. A sedan curb-crawled nearby. In the sleet, a faint light on the roof indicated it was a taxi. He waved and the driver pulled into the shoulder. The cab's headlamps flashed as the vehicle slowed. A face peered from the glass. The window whirred down a few inches.

"I was stranded on the highway."

"Jump in."

The driver sat in silence, which suited Jake. Traffic thickened as they changed lanes.

"Over there." The agent pointed.

The sedan slowed as the driver stopped the meter. Armitage peeled off a one-thousand ruble note.

"Keep the change."

Jake exited the taxi and started his ignition. His head pounded from the drama in the forest. He strained against the low visibility. The climate control cranked on the heat as he pulled out onto the road.

Traffic lights switched and blinked. The agent breathed steadily, sticking to the speed limit. He punched in the apartment address. The GPS displayed fifteen kilometers to his destination.

Armitage typed a text to Katerina:

I got delayed. Coming back now. Hope you're safe.


The apartment block appeared half-empty. Early fog swirled in the headlamps. Jake pulled into his space and killed the engine. Katerina hadn't replied to his text. His heart hammered against his ribcage.

Up through the foyer, Jake powerwalked into the vaulted chamber. On mornings such as this, he likened the building to a giant fridge. He reached the elevator consoles and tapped the button.

The old mosaic patterns on the ceiling swirled and moved. Katerina's face flicked in Jake's vision. He centred his weight evenly and fought the giddy sensation. She had to be there.

The elevator pinged. The agent stepped into the cabin. His pulse radiated in his neck. He watched the panel as the lights flickered from floor to floor.

Armitage clenched his fists open and shut. The doors clanged ajar. He exited the elevator and broke into a light jog. He reached the entrance. It appeared impossibly thick, a bank vault in his mind. The bolts were still in place. Slotting in the key, he twisted the deadlock. The door creaked open as Jake pushed into the space.

The agent exhaled the air from his lungs. He reached the lounge and dumped his carryall on the tabletop. His gaze pivoted to the couch.

"Katerina, are you here?" Jake's voice echoed into the corridor.

The apartment had a stillness.

A pit formed in Jake's stomach and grew larger by the second. He rushed past the kitchen. A metallic taste flavored his mouth.

He stood at the balcony. A breeze circulated the table.

Katerina was gone.

# Chapter 40

Jake's adrenaline raced as he struggled to focus.

The microwave clock glowed eight-twenty-six A.M. as if to taunt Armitage's predicament.

*I've lost three hours.*

A dark hole blanketed the living room. He flicked the switch on the rangehood. The kitchen countertop glowed as he moved by the black stove grills.

Downlights penetrated the hallway. Jake flung open the toilet door. Nothing. He pulled his pistol and cleared the entrance to the spare bedroom. The furniture and contents sat exactly how he'd left this morning.

The agent stepped into the bathroom archway. His throat went dry. Dead silence. In his heart-of-hearts, he knew she was gone. He flicked the light off and paced to the final room. The bed covers were ruffled and the floor cleared of clutter.

Armitage fought off rising panic. He returned to the living room and slid the balcony door.

There were no notes on the counter surfaces. Jake paced between the sofa and the dining table.

*Someone locked the front, so perhaps she left voluntarily. But why? Unless she came to find me?*

The agent crouched over the table surface and checked the cell tracker. Her burner phone had been tagged by him earlier and he pressed the dials to get a read. The icon was near invisible so he changed frequencies and tried to get a more accurate location. The console had a weak signal but not strong enough to be accurate. He reclined in the seat and took deep breaths.

*I can't track her yet but perhaps the signal will strengthen outside.*

The carryall lay slumped on the stone countertop. Armitage rummaged inside and grasped the small bag. He dumped the contents on the surface. The gangster's cell phones tumbled out, courtesy of the thugs in the forest. Jake stared at the old model iPhone, the tall thug's burner.

The agent picked up the cell. It had no security code. The register had a history of two separate calls. The first had been dialled five times, all within the last forty-eight hours.

*This has to lead higher up the chain.*

Armitage pushed the call button and rang the most frequently called number.

"Hello." The voice had a Russian accent and volume was faint.

Hand over the microphone, Jake muttered a few Russian words. In silence, Jake waited.

"Is our problem taken care of?"

The agent froze as he realized who owned the voice. Colonel Petrov. He shook his head. Only in Russia could corruption be this deep—and universal.

"No. I've taken out your men. Both of them." Jake didn't disguise his voice.

Silence ensued as the respondent digested the news.

The cigar smell at Bollov's stronghold triggered his memory.

*It's the same cigar smoke as Colonel Petrov's office.*

"The panther strikes."

The art deco bronze statue in Petrov's quarters flashed

before Jake's eyes. A man in a loin-cloth poised to kill a panther with a spear.

*The Hunt.*

"Is that any way to treat an old friend."

A gruff cough came through the mike. "They were mafia low-life. Expendable."

"You're working with organized crime now, Colonel?"

"The lines became blurred for the greater good."

"The lure of an oligarch's wealth became too good, even for a man with your distinguished military career?"

"You can see things how you choose." The colonel paused. "Let us live in the present. We have mutual interests, which if we collaborate, could be beneficial."

"Such as?" Jake stared out his window. His eyes focused on the outdoor furniture as his mind snapped to attention.

"I could help with your girlfriend problem."

"Which problem?" The agent cupped the cell as he swallowed. He looked left and right around the empty living room.

"Why don't you check where she is?" The words came slow and hit Jake like hammer.

Silence sat heavy on the call. The room appeared to spin as Jake placed the palm of his right hand on the table surface. Time stopped. He anchored his core.

*I am energised and fully protected.*

Armitage's pulse pounded between his ears. He straightened his posture.

*Keep it together. Don't fall apart.*

"Where is she?" He concentrated on each word to stop his teeth grinding.

The Colonel savored each word. "Somewhere safe. No need to worry. But you should follow my instructions if you want her back alive."

"What do you want?"

"I want the names of your associates here in the city. Every person undercover that knew about the flash drive." The Colonel paused. "I'll trade her life for yours."

Jake muffled the phone mike and disguised the background noise of taking a deep breath. He had no choice but to comply.

"Where do we meet?"

The Colonel paused, "Come to the canal entrance on dock eighty-five. I'll be in front of the warehouse at zero-nine-hundred hours."

Armitage lowered the burner. He texted Dodd's phone:

Change of plans. They've taken Katerina as ransom. Rendezvous 9:00 AM canal behind the warehouse zone. Stay out of sight. Bring back-up and hurry. J.A.

# Chapter 41

The morning light reflected off the inky black water, a gray spectre that floated above the surface. Jake took position in a loft above a container hold. The meeting place with Katerina's captors at the dock on the canal edge sat empty. A single barge floated, partially hidden in the clearing fog. He trained the rifle scope on a support column, red-brown brickwork.

The agent took a deep breath, assessed the implications of failure.

East of the position, the residential balconies were mostly empty. A mix of cafes and bars dotted the higher section which curved the water. Developers had seen the potential a decade ago. Behind him, shipping containers climbed in multi-colored stacks. Yellow light splintered over his shoulder._

"This position will do fine. This dock is owned by a consortium. A chain of shelf companies that leads back to..." Dodds lay flat on the sloped iron sheets. The roof gave a one-eighty-degree view of docking bay sixty-one.

"Let me guess. Sobol?" Armitage's right eye squinted at a mounted scope. An MP-90 rifle pointed towards the strike point. Water lapped the concrete lip at the point it met the canal verge.

"You got it," Dodds said. "We've had surveillance here recently."

"What a coincidence. They're going to come with a small army of armed hostiles."

"Hell, yes. Up here we have the higher ground and covert position." The older man scanned the landscape. "My

C.O. knows we're here. She'll be ready with backup. Don't worry, we've got this covered."

A dog barked in the distance. It faded to the hum of a twin engine. The CIA agent swept his binoculars toward the canal mouth. Empty.

"I'll turn my commo audio gear off when I get to the walkway in five minutes. Just in case they've got detectors. Hang on to this for me." He slid his favored P-96 across to Dodds.

Dodds gave the thumbs up. "The goal is simple: get Katerina away safe and unharmed."

On the bottom step, Jake checked his burner. Five to nine. The enemy would have conducted counter-surveillance. He shoved the expendable Beretta in his belt, keeping it out of sight, but easy to find. The best way for them to find it on a basic frisk. Going in unarmed would look as if he had a bigger plan.

The door clicked as Jake's foot hit the cement landing. A breeze stirred off the water. He fastened his collar higher around his neck. The containers towered above, forming a maze.

Armitage faced the entry, checked for hostiles. A lone woman walked her dog across the other side of the water. No other people in the vicinity. He walked slowly, careful not to bring attention. The water shimmered, yellow shards breaking the building gaps.

A pole marked the start of the next door. Worn timber rails ran along the support beams. Jake stood on the edge and watched the incoming boat. Dawn sun competed on the horizon with the receding moon.

"We have a craft at one-o'clock." Dodd's voice came through, scratchy and faint.

"Great work. Don't move until I give the signal. I'm putting the head-piece away."

"Over."

The agent reached the embankment at the foot of an old pedestrian pier. The motor chugged south of his position. Jake cocked his head and blocked out other potential distractions. He swivelled at the canal.

Zero visibility beyond thirty feet.

Ocean glistened on the far side. The motor revved harder, barely audible over the lapping water. He squinted at the thickened clouds overhead; an arrow shape formed in the hazy cold.

A flock of pigeons flapped over the iron bridge. The agent straightened and moved his feet to keep warm. The white front of a hull appeared from the entrance of a smaller canal. Waves smashed the side as the speedboat adjusted from the turn. It appeared as if the craft might capsize from the jolt.

Armitage plunged his hands in his coat pockets and stood firm. The boat gained momentum despite the persistent rocking of water. A driver crouched over the controls. Large henchmen surrounded the man, armed with semi-autos.

The sea could be a strange creature. Jake listened to the double motors roaring across the surface. He had a clearer view of the deck as the craft came into range. On board there were another two men at the rear. At least four soldiers, plus the driver made five. All carried firearms.

Foam swirled as the craft carved the water and slowed to berth. A rope lassoed the pole. The man at the front moved fast, landed on the cement ramp.

"Show me your hands." The slim speaker, dressed in

black, emerged from the cabin.

A Kalashnikov safety clicked as the thug in a blue beanie levelled the barrel. The third man scurried onto the landing and approached Jake.

Armitage thrust his hands in the air. He moved slow, in exaggerated gestures, so as not to alarm the kidnappers. "I'm unarmed."

The thug approached and patted him down and pulled the Beretta from his belt.

"Where is Katerina?"

The speaker turned and pointed at the cabin. A deep voice called, "Confirm you are there?"

A female voice echoed over the water. "I'm ok, Jake."

Her voice was shaken, but firm.

The fog had dissipated allowing shards of morning sun to break. Jake maintained eye contact with the slim man in black. A glint at his one o'clock flashed in the corner of his vision. Jake clenched his left fist. His heart hammered in his chest.

The speaker raised his palm. "Bring her out."

Katerina appeared from the cabin. A tall, masked figure came in her wake. Jake strained as he watched her expression.

*I am energized and fully protected.*

At two meters, the beanie hostile was nearly within strike distance. Jake waited until Katerina got to the stern.

*Come on, Dodds. Don't come too late.*

Time stopped and Jake stood motionless.

The shot fired as if in a dream. A crack echoed as the bullet broke the sound barrier. Birds squawked in panic. A wet thud. The blue beanie dropped his weapon, cried out in shock. A splash as the man fell into the water.

Jake rammed the nearest hostile. The thug dropped to the concrete as Jake pulled the Berretta from his grasp and twisted the grip. A cry came as Jake fired two shots in the thug's stomach.

The leader skidded over the deck. He screamed at the driver to start the engine.

Twin exhausts spluttered and fired to life with a growl.

An order came again. Jake held the man's body as shield. Katerina yelled but her captor held a weapon to her side.

Crouched on the platform, Jake shot from the hip. A third hostile bounced against the hull. Armitage tore the Kalashnikov from the soldier's hands and sprayed the side with rounds. The craft bucked and scraped.

The speaker swiveled at the cabin. Buttons were pushed frantically as the hull rocked. In the cabin, the driver swore. Inches from the start button, the hostile moved with incredible speed.

Armitage dropped the Kalashnikov and shoved the Beretta in his waist belt. He sprinted the last stretch of the dock and launched at the boat handrail. His fingers slipped their purchase on the moist chrome. Pain stabbed his abdomen and his nails almost ripped out to maintain grip. He dangled from the fiberglass edge. His body hugged the wet hull surface.

Katerina appeared at the entrance to the lower deck, Kolisnyk's pistol at her temple. The big Ukrainian leered, having enjoyed the violence, even on a bucking deck. Jake swung his foot to the edge.

A drizzle appeared over the water, puddled on the

craft. The agent swung his body in a pendulum movement. As he came level, he shoved his weight over the rail and dropped onto the floor. The mercenary stood eleven feet away.

The driver slid the throttle frantically. Hands darted over the console. Water churned white beneath. The boat engine fired and bucked. The craft sped from the dock.

Across the deck, the mercenary found Jake's gaze. A standoff. "Drop the weapon and come forward."

The gap closed to eight feet as Jake stepped carefully toward the kidnapper and his hostage. The Russian journalist opened her eyes. Her eyebrows arched.

"Looks like you're down on men. You don't want to lose any more." Armitage circled.

"I want an exchange." Kolisnyk tightened his grip on her neck.

*I can't get a clear head shot.*

Rain battered the cabin, sleeked off the deck. Jake stalled as he looked for an opportunity to break the stalemate. Despite the wet chill, sweat dripped over his brow, mixed with the downpour.

"Let her go first." The agent outstretched his arm. "Once she's halfway, I'll toss it."

Water sloshed as the craft rocked. The mercenary laughed and held Katerina in front. She stabilised her footing.

"Come take her."

The Russian reporter appeared angry, but Jake couldn't be sure. It could have been steely resolve he saw in her expression. The mist blurred and water kicked up in streams. He wiped his brow with a sleeve.

In that second, Katerina's torso dropped and Jake thought he'd lost her. She grimaced and made a fist with her right hand. An elbow flashed at the big man's groin. The mercenary grunted, the weapon fell and clattered on the deck.

In a fluid motion, Jake pointed the Beretta and shot Kolisnyk in the chest. He didn't have time to aim. The Ukrainian tried to dodge. His waist moved in the firing line. A wet thud as the bullet hit the mercenary in the upper thigh. Kolisnyk stumbled, eyes widened, as if in shock. Red bloomed on his jeans. The weapon slipped from his grasp and slid on the wet surface.

*I'm not sure if I have any rounds left.*

The boat slowed and the mercenary's legs buckled. Armitage circled a five-meter radius around his opponent, their gazes locked. The stain on the Ukrainian's jeans expanded as his left hand stemmed the blood flow.

The mercenary gripped a combat knife from his jacket. "Do you have any rounds in that Beretta?"

"How long do you think that wound will hold out?" the agent said. "The femur is a major artery."

A light drizzle lashed the cabin. The drops were refreshing to Jake. A trail of water cooled his face, trickled down his neck. He watched the Ukrainian, the weapon trained on his opponent's forehead.

Katerina lowered her body slowly and held a rail. She was at a safe distance from danger. Jake centered his weight as he maintained balance. His arm ached but he knew once the adrenaline left his body, the pain would be much worse.

The blond gritted his teeth. The agent watched the mercenary's knees and elbows. A grunt followed as Kolisnyk lowered his head and charged at Jake. The move took him by surprise and he braced for the impact. A surge caused the craft to buck. The mercenary shook, but maintained his path.

Armitage waited until his opponent's face was less than a foot away. The wounded Ukrainian still had the weight advantage, so Jake wouldn't engage in a wrestling match. He could smell the man's breath. It was a move of pure desperation.

At the last second Jake took the impact and rolled. He pressed his feet to Bohdan's chest, cradling the Ukrainian's weight on his heels. Jake released the razor he kept in his sleeve. His arm flashed as the slice cut at the neck. Blood squirted spurts. Jake recoiled like a jack-in-the-box.

Kolisnyk's body flopped as if impaled, a hooked fish without water. Armitage kicked his feet and extended his legs straight. The mercenary's body launched over the rail. A reverse somersault.

The agent staggered to an upright position.

Katerina rushed to help. They watched as a white froth of bubbles surrounded the Ukrainian's face. Kolisnyk's body sank. Bubbles rose to the surface. The mercenary disappeared into the murky depths.

"Are you ok?" Armitage assessed Katerina.

"Thanks to you." She hugged him tight.

The boat bobbed on the water. It jolted Jake out of their embrace. He surveyed the carnage. Three corpses riddled with bullets. Pink trails, pooled on the deck, dribbled the ridges with each jolt.

"It's not over." Jake shook his head.

Katerina sighed. "I thought not."

A bird squawked somewhere in the rising sleet. Jake

took a moment to assess the situation. The dock rose out of the gloom like a mirage. He squeezed Katerina's hand and she tightened her grip in return. They negotiated the slicked surface, toes finding the safe parts to step.

The driver retreated to a corner. "Don't kill me, please. They hired me to drive the boat. I have three children."

"Hold the gun. I'll give him a pat down."

The search revealed the driver had no concealed weapons.

Katerina handed the pistol back to Jake and picked up an object on the console. "It's true. Here's his business card."

"I need you to drive this boat to shore slowly. Please." Armitage pressed the barrel to the man's temple. "If you co-operate, I won't hurt you."

The driver nodded and took the controls.

"Good shooting. How did you take out the ones on the dock so quickly?"

"That may have been our partner." Jake indicated the driver; he didn't want to mention names. "Speaking of which." Armitage pulled the ear-piece from his pocket. The device was damp so he shook it and put it back in his ear.

"Can you hear me?" Static filled Jake's eardrum. "We've lost audio contact. I think it's broken."

Katerina grimaced and faced the dock.

The agent put his hand on her shoulder. "We need to get to a safe haven. The mercenary is dead but there's a colonel looking to cash in on all his hard work."

"Got it."

"Pull into that spot." Jake pointed at a turn in the cove

away from the site they'd launched from earlier.

The driver angled the boat toward the ramp. He held the engines at low speed.

A pole protruded from the waters, the platform three meters away from their current position. The craft eased at the cement, guided in slowly. The hull scraped into place.

Waves churned less with the sky clearing somewhat from the earlier cold front. His hands ached from the exertion of the struggle. The Russian journalist threw a rope over a post. The craft bobbed on the surface.

On a hook in the cabin, Jake found a rope. He tied the driver's hands and gagged his mouth with a cloth and tape.

Relief flooded Jake's system as their feet landed on hard ground. The agent and Katerina jogged the length of the ramp. The dock exit sat within the sound barrier wall.

"I'm sending Dodds a text."

Lost audio. Meet us at the canal behind the dock exit in ten minutes.

A public lane dumped the pair in the heart of the shipping precinct. Armitage and Katerina power-walked to the far edge. Workers huddled in groups with takeout coffee. Blue smoke trails rose above the warehouse walls.

On the walkway, the traffic churned and beeped. The agent kept his gaze straight. No-one paid them attention. The gunfire must have carried along the canals.

Light broke the clouds as Jake trudged up the lane.

"Here we are. Let's stay out of sight."

Dodds jogged from the alley. His face lit up as the CIA agent saw Jake and Katerina.

"Looks like he came through after all."

Katerina nodded.

A sudden crack boomed. The bullet echoed into the walkway. Dodd's face changed as pain transformed his features. The agent's arms spread as he floated and dropped to the stone. A wet thud.

Katerina stared at the prone bony lying face down on the stone.

Down the alley, in place of Dodd's position, a woman jogged. Her brown hair, cut in a bob, bounced as her shoes clicked on the stones. She pointed a firearm at the Russian reporter. Armitage recognised her from the profile they'd located.

*Jill Seymour, Dodd's CIA handler.*

"Get down." Jake jumped to cover the journalist. A round flew over his head. He rolled across the cobblestones, patted Dodds' jacket and retrieved his P-96. The Russian reporter had ducked and scrambled for cover. She squatted behind a garbage container.

Seagulls squawked close as he gripped his chest. No bullet.

The agent turned and touched her shoulder. "Are you hurt?"

"A little banged up," Katerina pulled herself to a seated position, "but I'll be fine."

"Good. Let's go this way." Armitage gained his feet, stuffed the weapon in his belt, and held out his palm. The Russian reporter took his hand. She trailed as he weaved past trash compactors, spilling toward the canal.

The handler appeared at the far corner. Jake slid behind a brick wall. Katerina joined him. A roadblock and fifty meters lay between them and the CIA handler. The lane had no workers in sight.

He took out the P-96 and peered around the corner.

Rounds chipped a metal sign pole as sparks flew inches from Jake's face. He shot off two rounds and slipped into cover.

Seymour broke into a run.

Voices came from a crane in the next lot. A worker stumbled into the crossfire. Armitage and Katerina crossed the alley. Stray bullets flew into the rising panic.

"Isn't that Dodd's handler?" Katerina'a eyes were wide.

The agent battled to keep his voice even. He nodded and held her firm. Eyes darted over the main gate. A woman screamed behind them.

"Yes. We need to get out of here." Jake grabbed her arm. They sprinted the length of a hurricane fence.

A brick restaurant corner hid them from the laneway visual. Katerina leaned against the wall, breathing hard.

"The handler won't be long," the agent said, checking the pistol. "She'll come from this side, I think." He pointed across to the mouth of a joining lane.

"Thanks, Jake. You saved me again." The Russian reporter took in the view of Nevsky Avenue, her breath ragged as she straightened.

"Take a second to get your composure."

Katerina exhaled before speaking. Her eyes hardened. "This way." She pointed south. "I know a route. She won't come too far into the open where there's more witnesses."

"I hope you're right."

"So do I."

# Chapter 42

The Nevsky overpass smelled of diesel and damp concrete. Katerina jogged, tugging Jake's arm, pulling him toward the vehicular traffic. The cold nipped at his fatigued body and lactic acid flushed his leg muscles. The Orthodox Church steeples pointed through the chill.

"We need to change our appearance—and fast." Armitage glanced at the street vendors. The tables dotted both sides of the canal. Many had clothing articles that would make effective disguises.

People converged from all directions, putting cover between them and the shooter.

Katerina pointed into a throng of sightseers on the opposite side of the water. The kiosks blossomed to life for the morning trades. Citizens milled as passers-by power walked the popular spot, oblivious to the chase.

"Scarves and hats might be effective." She led Jake between two family groups. A young girl hummed a Russian folk song.

Chains jangled, padlocks clicked, and chatter volume increased. The nearest vendors had babushka dolls and souvenir items that were useless for cover. Jake moved through the potential buyers scanning the commuters.

The agent browsed quickly without appearing stressed. He spotted the biggest clothing sellers over the far side.

Up ahead, a crowd of six well-fed tourists had unfolded a map, each giving their opinion in American accents. Jake checked over his shoulder for Dodd's killer.

The handler had disappeared in a swarm of early morning office workers.

"Let's get across the other side of the canal." The agent hustled by a vendor trying to sell towel sets. They broke free from the throng and rushed over the bridge.

On the east side, waiters clunked al-fresco chairs around tables outside a large café. Baristas cranked machines as a strong breakfast aroma of eggs and sausages wafted in the air.

Armitage and Katerina weaved through the growing clusters of bystanders. One more block and they'd be clear of the main throngs. Seagulls squawked over bread scraps as they passed a pharmacy and a large timber see-saw.

They stopped in the mad rush to gather their position and strategy. Armitage swept the crowd, looking for signs of contractors that might be gathering.

A bus slowed and pulled onto the walkway, screeching to a halt. The agent looked at the bus, then at the Russian reporter.

"This is our chance to create distance." Jake said.

She nodded.

The doors clanged apart and a flurry of footsteps hit the cobblestones. Noise from the chattering passengers rose, adding to the layers of camouflage.

"Let's get behind this bus," Jake whispered as they nudged their way.

The pair tailed the large, guided tour group as it spread onto the sidewalk. Shoes padded and cameras clicked. Sightseers glanced and gestured at the new environment. The pair mingled with the first dozen until they reached the Nevsky curb. They broke off and powerwalked to the other side of the canal, blending with the masses. Armitage scanned the faces but couldn't see the handler.

"This is it here." Katerina paused. She pointed at a tent. Caps and sweaters hung from hooks.

"Good work." The agent circled the wares. Racks of sweatshirts spread out in aisles.

Katerina browsed a rack of sweatshirts in different colors. They had men's and women's styles.

"Got it." Katerina held a dark gray, conservative sweatshirt up to his chest. "Looks like your size."

The agent pulled the garment over his head. "Fits great."

The Russian reporter chose a blue one for herself and found a bunch of caps. She picked two from a collection.

"Sixty euro," an assistant said. Jake handed over some notes.

The vendor gave him change and pointed to a display of can openers and key rings.

Katerina smiled and waved a finger.

"Over here." She tightened her hair into a ponytail and pulled on the red cap. The grey cap she handed to Jake had a word emblazoned in black.

"One of the city's biggest football teams." She watched as Jake placed it on his head.

Armitage smiled. "Good thinking. Let's get lost in this chaos until we are sure to shake the handler."

"Past the Church of the Saviour on Spilled Blood and weave into the park. There's another protest gathering on the road out the front. We'll be hidden by hundreds of posters and signs."

The light went green as a flow of walkers covered the crosswalk. A pair held up a sign in Russian and chanting filled the atmosphere. The agent couldn't see the handler behind them. The pair stuck to the middle of the mob until they reached the other side of the church. A catacomb of laneways took them a further block.

"I think a cab and head west. The safe house apartment might be burned."

"Not necessarily. They didn't get me there." Katerina waved at a cab which crossed two lanes and steered to the curb.

The agent gave the driver the street near the apartment.

Cars blurred as the driver spun the wheel.

"What happened and how did they find you?"

"I met Chekov, the reporter. He had crucial evidence that had to be in person. We found a restaurant downtown. Two military guys grabbed me when I walked out. Sorry, Jake."

"It's ok. I was worried. They don't necessarily know about the apartment location? They must have followed Chekov."

The Russian journalist nodded. The cab weaved through peak hour. Horns blared as the driver took a U-turn and pulled into the curb near the apartment.

Armitage paid the driver cash.

"I have an idea." Jake fished in his pocket. He held the cell phone taken from the colonel's two henchmen.

"Whose cell is that?" Katerina said.

"Bear with me and I'll explain soon."

Jake swiped into the call history and called the last dialled number. It rang five times and finally clicked.

"What do you want? Come to play more games?"

"Listen, Colonel, your trap failed. I have the Russian reporter with me. Gun battles in broad daylight on the canal are inadvisable."

"I have units combing the zone now. It's only a matter of time before we capture you both."

"Hope they're better than Bohdan. Your protégé is in the canal. As the American mafia say back home, he sleeps with the fishes."

"Kolisnyk betrayed his commander. Defected with a politician. A traitor." A pause on the line. "I will torture you both."

*I thought the mercenary was working with the colonel.*

Katerina pointed at her wristwatch and mouthed, "They'll track the position, won't they?"

"Look, Colonel, don't go shooting missiles too soon." Armitage winked at Katerina. "I guess it's goodbye. Your soldiers couldn't find us if were right in front of them."

In the background, Jake heard military commands shouted in Russian. He checked the time again: ninety seconds.

"You're busy at the base, Colonel, and I've got to fly." The agent terminated the call and smiled at Katerina.

Traffic blurred as the morning chill eased off the breeze. A siren whined. Jake bustled on to the sidewalk. Katerina followed, a frown on her face.

The streets teemed with early morning workers. Smart office attire dominated the fashion as building entries swung open everywhere. Jake pulled Katerina close as they navigated through the tight spaces.

High heels clicked on cement and dozens of smartphone conversations clustered the airwaves.

"The mercenary changed sides to Sobol's team."

"That explains the missile attack at the stronghold."

"Correct. We're going to the apartment," Jake said in her ear.

Katerina shot him a wide-eyed glance. "But they'll get a lock on it?"

The agent turned and caught her gaze. "Exactly."

# Chapter 43

Armitage drew his firearm as they reached his apartment level. The alarm hadn't registered a break-in on his app, but that could be hacked. Dust gathered around the skirting. He stepped into the corridor. A broken spiderweb danced in the breeze.

"Our enemies have powerful resources." The agent looked at the entrance.

"Do you think they've been here?" Katerina kept her voice low.

"Hopefully not."

Jake deactivated the alarm and cracked the door. Silence permeated the living room, yellow splinters highlighting the edges of the furniture tops.

The atmosphere turned surreal.

*I may never return to this apartment.*

"I'll get my things and wait here." Katerina gathered her carryall, laptop, and few clothes.

The bedrooms were empty. Armitage swept the bathroom in standard military style. His gaze fell on the far wall overlooking the vanity unit. The small, recessed window remained ten centimeters ajar. He leaned toward the frosted-glass pane. It hadn't been tampered with since he last set the delicate arm. Sometimes the best alarm is using nature and subtle checks.

In a bedroom nook, Jake unzipped a duffel bag. He shoved in jeans, three pairs of underwear, socks and t-shirts.

Armitage returned to the living room and opened a

cupboard. He took a long, black case from the shelf, resting it on the table surface next to the duffel bag. Inside, black rifle parts lay in slots. He looked over the pieces, lifting the magazine. A large box of ammunition lay open. Jake pressed the rounds into the magazine. He closed the lid and fastened the clips.

The thug's burner lay on the table.

"This is the phone I called the Colonel on an hour ago." Jake placed the cell on the surface, crossed the floor and opened the sliding door.

Katerina joined him as a breeze caught her hair. His gaze scanned the open air. The balconies opposite were vacant except for an old couple on the sixth level. An old man pottered over a house plant. His wife sipped from a teacup.

"See the roof over the road?"

The Russian journalist nodded and glanced at the rifle case.

"That's where we're going."

The door swung back as soon as Jake and Katerina exited.

A rear two-lane road snaked the length of the complex. Gray clouds overhead swelled. A light number of cars ambled by.

Armitage stood at the curb and looked up at the aging Soviet structure that stood opposite. Each apartment had a small balcony. Clothes, hung on drying racks, danced in the cool breeze.

*Let's see if my hours of counter-surveillance pay off.*

Katerina caught up and they waited for the cars to clear before crossing. The agent avoided the main lobby and took a shortcut to a narrow alley that ran down the stucco high-rise opposite his apartment. Faded yellow paint peeled from the neglected brick façade.

A homeless man stumbled from behind a large bin. He grasped a grimy bottle of vodka, belched, and disappeared around the corner.

"In through here so surveillance cameras can't pick us up." Armitage pushed a heavy timber door that appeared to have seldom use. He led down a narrow corridor of whitewashed walls.

Stains and mold dotted the paint. It spilled into an archway tucked behind the kitchen. Pans banged as meals were prepared. A chef yelled commands in Russian. The food preparation was in full swing for the ground-level restaurant.

Jake motioned at an obscured opening behind a stack of pallets.

"This way to the fire exit. Stairs are safer and more anonymous than elevators."

Katerina followed close behind.

The passageway ended at a cement landing. A flight of stairs hugged a spiral. They ascended quickly, anxious to reach the roof. Open, slatted windows pushed cool air in intervals. Katerina reached the fifth floor and Jake slowed.

"Are you ok?" The agent caught his breath. His leg ached around the knee joint, the injury from the mansion gunfight four days ago.

"Fine, thanks, Jake." The Russian journalist bent her torso and placed her hands on her hips. "Don't worry about me. Let's keep going." She squeezed his hand.

A gush of rain sprayed Jake's face as they burst onto the roof. He held up his arm as a barrier for Katerina, who sheltered in his wake. The asphalt-covered surface was slick with rainfall and puddles. It appeared vacant and neglected. In the center, an iron lean-to for the handyman. The latch had a rusty padlock. Armitage pointed at a protruding ledge at waist height.

"We'll sit under the escarpment. The view is sheltered from the weather. Take this if you'd like to look out for them."

The Russian reporter held the spare scope to her eye, moving her gaze over the balconies.

"I've found your level and the apartment. I can see Mrs Bukin watering her plants."

"God bless her." Jake sat cross-legged and faced the rear of his high-rise. The roof was no more than ten meters higher than his apartment level. This gave a height advantage while not a hindrance to accuracy.

The agent unclipped the case and clicked rifle parts together. He assembled the weapon, piece by piece, and placed the tripod on the gravel.

A storm front cast the sky dark and gloomy. The Russians were used to such a climate. The pedestrian traffic had thinned and locals were going about their day with the usual expressions.

The laser rangefinder crawled over the stucco and paused at his balcony. It showed the distance as two hundred and twenty-three feet. Armitage rotated the elevation and adjusted the rifle to zero. He swept the cross-hairs over the lower floors, checking for irregularities. Any watchers or followers could be disguised or appear where least expected.

The anxiety formed a ball in Jake's stomach. It crept into his chest. He took deep breaths into his lungs, careful not to alarm Katerina.

*Time has come to test myself.*

Her survival depended on who walked into Jake's apartment and his aim. If he startled the intruders too early and they were out of range, the advantage would vanish.

The agent glanced at Katerina who moved two meters to his right. She concentrated on the traffic flow over Nevsky Prospekt. Her brow creased and head swivelled, eyes furtive on the apartment building.

"We'll be fine. Don't stress," Jake said.

Katerina nodded and relaxed her grip. She sunk to the gravel against the ledge. "It's unfortunate the situation has come to this, but we have no choice," she said and shook her head.

"It's us or them."

A tabby cat scurried along the south side near the exit. The feline disappeared behind a brick wall. Jake touched the Russian's shoulder. Her mouth turned upward at the corner, nearly a smile. He rested his palm on her for a minute and she closed her eyes. The cold wind flickered through the barriers, competed with the thin rays of yellow that pierced the clouds.

Armitage lay on his stomach and peered at the windows. Once the reticule centered over the balcony, he increased the magnification of the scope and scanned his balcony rail. He flickered over the awning and into the landing. The circle landed on his worn outdoor setting. A bird crossed his sight, squawked at another feathered friend. Worn tiles puddled with the remainder of recent rainfall. The view traced the open glass and zoomed on the smartphone.

"Come on, Colonel, track the phone. Send your thugs and the double agent."

The agent shrugged off the fatigue and negative thoughts. He figured he didn't have the luxury of whimsical doubts.

Thirty minutes dragged on. The downfall eased. No hostiles had appeared in his apartment. Armitage shifted weight onto his left elbow. An ache formed in his neck.

For the fourth time, Jake swept the block and waved the reticule over the staff entrance for good measure. Nothing unusual. He swivelled at the adjacent building. Three young women loitered outside the coin laundry. The females chatted and laughed, young and carefree.

Not watchers.

Armitage panned right. A middle-aged worker in a navy suit, white button-down, and shiny black shoes held a cell phone to his ear. The professional corporate paced the concrete, gesturing in the air.

An elderly couple shuffled past, clutching each other by the elbows as they moved. The office worker had not shifted out of view and showed no signs of suspicious behaviour.

Patience was the most undervalued quality of espionage work. The waiting took up the most time. A target watched for hours or even days. But it kept Jake alive. To move too soon or late could be fatal. Surveillance and counter-surveillance had to be done right.

The gravel crunched as Katerina moved between exhaust fan chutes. Armitage noticed her frayed nerves in his peripheral vision. He focused to the north end; three hotel patrons held cigarettes, gestured as they spoke. The group appeared unconnected. The lead talker used a butt dispensary attached to the stucco wall.

Tire brakes screeched and drew Jake's focus to the road. A Range Rover pulled into the shoulder. The bumper came to a halt opposite the staff door of his apartment complex. A heavy window tint obscured the rear passenger.

The front window lowered. Armitage pointed the scope.

A striped shoulder badge. Military uniform. Sergeant or higher.

The agent's heartbeat hammered his chest. Gut instinct told him to think twice about plan B. He retreated from the roof edge. Pressed against the cold stone, he gripped the rifle butt.

The breeze chilled Jake's bones suddenly. He listened to Katerina's footfalls: soft scrape on loose stones. Russia had become the absolute enemy. The whole country conspired against not only him, but her.

One of their own.

The targets thought they were the hunters, Jake and Katerina the prey.

They were wrong.

# Chapter 44

The driver's window descended halfway. Jake sucked in breath. The cross-hairs zoomed to the face as a piece of litter fluttered by the door panel. He could see a small brown ponytail bob behind the driver's shoulder. Female passenger.

A slick military operation.

Armitage panned to the passenger. The female turned. Her mouth moved in speech, gaze pointed toward his apartment block. He aimed through the slim gap. Best to stay out of sight, just in case.

The bullseye passed a silhouette outline that revealed a solid male in the rear seat. Jake increased to maximum magnification. The tinted glass made it near impossible to make out the person in the rear.

"You should see this."

Katerina stopped short and stiffened.

The agent motioned her to the ledge. She checked the vehicle.

"It's the Russian army, isn't it?" Katerina lowered. "They're trying to eliminate us with everything they have."

"Nothing we can't handle from here." The agent smiled and flicked from his abandoned apartment to the car.

The driver pivoted to the rear. A high-ranking officer sat behind, giving commands. The passenger turned her head: darkened sky and limited visibility shadowed her profile.

Two soldiers exited the vehicle and stepped to the sidewalk. Both were armed with M&P 15 rifles. First the pair secured the immediate zone of twenty meters. A third soldier appeared and stood ground.

The two soldiers entered the high rise through the fire escape.

Armitage alerted the Russian reporter with a wave.

The cell phone beeped. Jake swung the scope back to his apartment's balcony. The drape swirled in the open door. Two figures flashed across the opening.

The agent took a deep breath. His finger twitched. A round punched the first black silhouette. The body dropped from sight. One soldier down. Armitage adjusted and followed a shadow to the bedroom corridor. The second soldier moved. He pulled the trigger.

A bullet hit the dry wall. White clouded the view. Soldier two retreated to the bedroom. Visual cut with the archway intrusion. The agent waited. The enemy team must have radioed their CO. The third intruder appeared in the kitchen entrance. Jake fired and hit the shoulder. The soldier disappeared.

Armitage relaxed but remained alert. Two bodies were unaccounted for.

*I need to make the call.*

In the lens, the balcony table set appeared worn. He viewed his living room for a minute. No movement. Armitage placed the reticule on a square package under the glass. The contents were wrapped in gray material.

The agent took a breath and pulled the trigger.

A crack followed the split. The explosion formed a small orange fireball the size of the table: one meter square. He shielded his eyes, pulled away from the rifle. Glass shattered over the balcony. The outdoor table separated and sent debris outward.

Heat waves warped the tinted glass. The agent scanned the living space. Fire licked the gaping hole, travelled the floorboards. The kitchen lit up as furniture lay torn apart. A second body lay motionless. Jake stared at the concrete. The island bench had a jagged crack up the middle.

Katerina jogged to where roof edge ended, her eyes glued to the flames. She slumped next to Jake.

"What was that?" She gasped out of breath.

"A fail-safe—my plan B."

"Explosives." Katerina stared at the apartment. "You think I'd be used to this by now."

"We are not done yet."

Jake rotated the scope to point at the intruder's car. He took a moment to put cross-hairs on the rear passenger. Got you. The driver started up as Jake fired a round at the rear window. He inhaled.

A hole appeared in the glass. Armitage kept the reticule steady. A spider web of cracks fanned from the centre. The window imploded.

The agent squinted to maintain visual. A silhouette of the passenger slumped forward on the head rest. The car revved high. Tires squealed as the front end spun into the side alley.

"You stopped their escape." Katerina faced the street.

"Armour piercing rounds," Jake said, still fixed on the vehicle. "It wasn't the colonel."

"We will get him anyway."

Armitage pulled his rifle apart. "You have new intel?" he said and sorted the parts into two separate bags.

"Sort of." She hunched over her laptop. "There's something I haven't had the chance to tell you. When they grabbed me, I'd been chasing Sobol's money. It disappeared after the second bank."

"Did you discover where it went?"

"Chekov found some login codes." She looked up from the screen. "The money had been converted into cryptocurrency."

"Makes sense." Jake shook his head. "These guys were planning an exit strategy."

"Exactly. I think Sobol and the colonel are about to leave Russia. The transactions are all flowing in the past day." Katerina shut the laptop and tucked it under her arm.

"And cash out." The agent stood and headed to the exit. "We need to leave fast."

Katerina took the stairs.

"I parked the car a block away on an avenue."

"Let's get moving."

# Chapter 45

A fire truck braked and terminated the siren. Crimson lights strobed over the streets in all directions. Jake and Katerina left the rear exit in their wake. Two blocks from the apartment and they watched the response unfold.

The agent and Katerina stood behind a row of spectators. Ropes and tape cordoned the zone. Hose reels unwound as emergency workers in red and yellow stormed Jake's former tower.

Plainclothes police spoke to a gathering crowd. A squad car pulled up and mounted the curb. In the distance, a woman sobbed.

*I wonder if it's Mrs Bukin.*

Katerina tugged Jake's arm. Together they powerwalked to the car.

"We need to get you out of the country." Armitage pulled into the side street. "The train is the safest way."

"This time I agree. I'll catch the Allegro to Helsinki, then a ferry to Sweden."

"Great plan. You can fly out of Europe with this." Jake leaned over and took out a document.

Katerina opened the booklet. "It's a passport. Thank you so much."

"It's the least I can do, considering this mess."

She watched the traffic. "What about you, Jake?"

As the siren wails faded, Jake weaved across an intersection. The brick façade of the train station rose above a monument. He eased to a stop in a thirty-minute zone.

"Need to take care of something here. Don't worry. I'll get out as soon as possible too." Jake hesitated and bit his tongue. "I think I'm done after this."

Katerina nodded and her hazel eyes shone despite the limited sunlight. "I gave limited details on the colonel and Sobol's trading to Chekov. I don't want to put him at any more risk."

"Great. We need to delay the colonel's network in Russia when he tries to flee. I can put a word out to Interpol and the NSA to make it more challenging." The agent strummed the wheel with his thumb. "There's some cash. I want you to take it."

"I couldn't, Jake."

"Please. You'll need it to set up." Armitage reached into the back seat and passed a small bag.

The journalist unzipped it and looked inside.

"There are a few bundles of Euro notes. I could not have done this without you."

"Thanks, Jake." She smiled and put the bag at her feet.

"Best to use cash, even when you disappear into Europe."

"Got it."

A train rambled into view as Katerina opened the laptop. She pointed the screen at him. Jake stared at an account displayed on the dark web.

"That's the site where the money trail vanishes. We can hack the account but it feels too risky." The journalist smiled. "On the other hand, it's for a good cause and I don't want those bastards keeping it."

"Let's give some to a charity."

"Will they come looking for us?"

"Not after I ensure this network goes down." Jake turned to her. "What was the name of the welfare place that helped your mum?"

A tear formed in Katerina's eye. She wiped it quickly. "Translates to The Good Shepherd Organisation."

The agent tapped the keyboard. "I've got their site. I'll transfer most of this crypto into their account once it clears."

"That means some good will come of this dirty money." Katerina swallowed. She looked away.

"With another eight hundred thousand, we'll transfer that into a Swiss account. The rest I'm giving to you."

Katerina diverted her gaze. "I don't know what to say."

"Nothing needed."

"Be safe, Jake. Please." The journalist pulled on a loose-fitting hoodie and zipped it to the neck. A red scarf completed the look. The temperature in the car seemed to fog the windows. She leaned and hugged him. They embraced and held each other.

"You'd better catch that train." Armitage said finally, not letting go. She pulled free and looked him in the eyes.

"Make sure you find me if you give this life up, ok?"

The door shut as she stepped from the vehicle. The agent watched until the crowd took her from sight. He sighed and picked up his burner.

A throng of noisy commuters walked onto the street and Jake turned up the volume. The phone rang four times before it clicked.

"Hello." The voice answered.

"Zima, it's Armitage."

"Hello there. What do you have?"

"Evidence which will prove a high-ranking military officer and a politician have been engaging in serious illicit trading."

"Does this have to do with the incidents at an outer residential address?"

"Possibly, but you'll need all the facts first. I can give you all I have." Jake paused. "When can we meet in the next two hours."

"Too dangerous to come to my office. Do you know the souvenir shop next to the canal?"

"Yes. How about thirty minutes?"

"See you then."


The agent checked his watch. Eleven A.M. He sidestepped a pram and joined revellers gathered around the nearby river canal. Market sellers lined the crosswalk with tables covered in magnets and dolls.

The gated park zone straddled St Basil's Cathedral. Jake passed under the shadow of the multi-coloured domes. The atmosphere appeared upbeat as locals enjoyed the festivities that cut through the chill.

Rows of flags and commemorative towels fluttered at the souvenir entrance. A triple shopfront receded into the forecourt. Armitage moved between aisles and scanned the faces. He pretended to browse the shelves.

Zima flanked a row two across from the end. Jake nodded and pointed to the south exit. The Interpol officer led Jake to an inner shopping precinct. Neon lights advertised fried chicken adjacent to a Subway restaurant.

The agent and Zima bought two drinks and a small bucket of chicken.

The Russian officer slid into a booth and Jake positioned opposite.

"I had to make sure you were not followed." Zima said and stared over Jake's shoulder.

"Good choice."

Armitage slid a slim folder over the table surface.

"This looks juicy." The officer packed the file away.

"You'll find accounts and surveillance. With addresses and other details on this syndicate."

"I assume some of these characters have been immobilized in the recent day's activity?"

"Could very well be the case." The agent sucked coke through a straw. "Keep your source anonymous, please."

"As always." Zima nodded and rose.

"One more thing. News of this syndicate may leak in the media in the next few days, so you may want to get some arrests in quick."

"Any suggestions on where to start?"

"Look at the politician first. Sobol is still in the city, as far as I know, but may not be for long."

"Got it. Talk soon."

Zima dumped his drink container in the trash and disappeared into the crowd.


The train blew its horn as it eased from the platform. A mist blanketed the windows. Armitage watched the horizon as the locomotive left Moscow in its wake. He reread the email to his assistant director.

*I need to get this summary brief and to point.*

A man walked past his seat but didn't make eye contact. Mid-forties, average height, with gray flecks through the hair. Slumped posture indicated non-military.

*Probably not a hostile.*

Always on surveillance, the agent's gaze returned to the screen. The two-week break he'd proposed to his director could turn into a longer absence.

Green pastures and farming outcrops flashed in the background. Armitage stretched his legs with a stroll in the corridor. He remained alert to his surroundings.

Dusk fell as Jake passed from the dining car. The carpet thickened from second class to first. He barricaded the door with the only furniture he could find, a table that sat between the parallel sofa-converted beds.

The top storage shelf contained a blanket wrapped in plastic. A quick face rinse in the sink, pull the blind, and he covered himself. Jake slept with his clothes on in case he needed a quick exit. He pressed his shoes against the barricade.

*Get sleep when you can.*

Nightfall blended with the rhythmic rocking of the train. The agent lulled into a sleep as soon as his head touched the bed.


The burner beeped at six A.M. Armitage slipped from bed and pulled on his jeans. The dirty train window obscured the Ukraine capital. He slid the lock and pushed the plexi-glass.

Kiev glowed with an early morning hue. Jake breathed deep, taking in the crisp air. Grass glistened with dew, marked the first days post the Russia fallout. He ate eggs at a café on the outskirts of town. Patrons were sparse at the venue, the tranquil hum of spring in full swing. He hacked a nearby WIFI connection and plugged into the Swiss account, transferring a few thousand euro from the account into one he used.

Armitage headed to the airport. At the counter, he paid for a business flight to Barcelona in cash. These seats gave more privacy. The cabin was half-full and he slept for most of the journey. He completed Customs in the early morning, local time, and took a taxi to La Rambla.

The street and lanes were teeming with activity. Camera-toting tourists flocked as Jake weaved into the throngs. He checked for watchers as he stepped to a statue recessed over a courtyard. An apartment block cast a shadow over the original tiled foyer.

Jake took in the rustic structure. He had visited three times over the past five years.

Iron steps curled around the yellow walls. The agent took two at a time. A baby cried from an open window. He stepped into a timber archway, knocked on number thirty-seven.

A diminutive man with salt-and-pepper hair answered.

"Ramos," Jake said and stepped into the lounge.

"Come in." The host motioned to a sofa. "Please sit here."

The cushions sank under Jake's weight. A Xerox machine sat next to a desk with three printers. He watched the Spaniard gather documents. Mouldy drapes covered the windows. Downlights lit up the backyard operation. Armitage used Ramos because the Spaniard was the best identity forger he'd ever met.

"Here you go." Ramos handed Jake a pouch.

The agent flipped it open and examined the passport. A stamp from Heathrow indicated he'd flown in from London a week ago. Perfect.

Under a plastic sheath a birth certificate sat folded in quarter. Old and creased, it appeared more than authentic. He picked up a UK driver's license with a photo.

"Superb as always." Jake pulled a thick wad of euros from his pocket.

Ramos counted the money and nodded.

"Good luck, Jake."

# Chapter 46

Armitage descended the staircase and returned to La Rambla. Light dappled the leaves of historic trees lining the avenue. The weather hung over the traffic like a lavender-shaped aura. He wiped a light sheen from his brow. A great change from the cold in Saint Petersburg.

The possibilities seemed endless beyond the NSA. Apprehension sent butterflies to Jake's stomach. The next pending assignment dredged mixed emotions. He reached a strip of shops and searched the traffic. A taxi rank stood outside a Chinese restaurant and dry cleaners. The agent doubled back and hopped into a cab.

"Where to?" the driver asked.

"Take me to the hotel Turin, but do a block first." Jake stared out the window. "I'd like to take in the sights."

"You're the boss." The overweight man clicked the meter and turned the key.

Late afternoon clouds took over the sun. Satisfied no one seemed to be following, Jake said, "Drop me off here please." He walked a block to the Turin, a good three-star hotel that didn't ask questions and didn't attract the rich or the poor in large numbers, picking up a takeout coffee en route. It also had multiple alleys that ran east to west and sat between two streets' frontages. He paid and checked into a room.

Armitage swiped his card in the hotel door lock. He cracked the window latch. Coffee and pastries weaved a scent into the room. Chatter rose from the shopping hordes. He took a breath and paced the setting.

The computer glowed as Jake sat behind the screen.

Katerina's face flashed across his mind.

*I wonder what she is doing.*

The agent shook the daydreaming and focused on the task. A breeze licked his neck. He sighed and sipped his short black. The vacation agreed with him. More or less. His skin had taken a light olive hue with the warmer climate.

Last night, the loneliness had caught up to Jake for a brief moment. Without providing protection in a fast-paced environment, he had no focus. No one to care about. One contract assignment blended into the next.

*Auto-pilot. Perhaps a swim will take away the grogginess.*

The hotel pool water rushed over Jake's face. He dived deep. Cool bubbles tingled his skin. Faces from the past flickered as he surfaced. Flashback. Some friends and foes. The memories would diminish in time. A lazy freestyle took him to the far edge. His burner lit up but he ignored the device. For now.

Armitage dried his face with a towel. He checked the missed call: private number. The nudge from head office.

A rumble vibrated in Jake's stomach. He padded to the *bain marie* and chose a high-calorie snack. The lapsed diet hadn't started to show on his mid-section yet. Exterior stairs extended from the pool landing.

Jake set the pastry on the table surface. The computer came to life. A beep sounded from his inbox. He checked his anonymous, untraceable account.

A reply came in code. Director of the NSA.

The encryption took thirty seconds. The agent scanned the message. A target in Europe. Had to be completed in seventy-two hours from landing.

Flights to the city were regular. He opened a beer and took a sip. The beach where he'd finished a Grisham thriller loomed in his mind.

The message had a profile. Armitage scanned the particulars. He emailed an underground rifle specialist with specifications. No serial number—a ghost gun. He leaned in his seat.

*Will I ever be able to retire?*

The agent opened a browser. He checked flight times and booked for five-forty-five P.M. that evening. First stop Poland. He'd stay overnight to shake any followers.

Final destination Prague.

The usual protocol. Jake's carryall was ready to go and he located Ramos' fake passport. Travelled light as always.

In the lobby, Jake ordered a taxi and paid in cash. The airport lounge had few travellers. He poured a vodka and sank into a leather seat. People rushed back and forth as peak hour teetered.

On the flight, Jake fell into a light sleep. He memorized the eight other passengers. The only one that came close to a watcher's profile was a man in his forties. Casual suit jacket and jeans. No dreams came until the hostess woke him to land.

Armitage took a hire car in Warsaw. He circled the main CBD streets. The lights flickered over the old town as he took the bends. A four-star hotel named Euro Star tucked in the back streets always proved a reliable base. The agent stopped at the valet booth and entered the lobby. He showered and ate a club sandwich from room service. The final leg to Prague was uneventful.

Two days from leaving Vaclav Havel airport, Jake trained the rifle scope on the café. The target stood behind at a cash till and chatted to a customer. His finger stroked the trigger.

The sun warmed Jake's shoulders. A magpie fluttered on the gutter. He slackened his grip and slumped on the concrete.

*I'm doing reconnaissance today.*

With a heavy heart, Jake packed the weapon. The wind picked up, cooling his cheek. He took the five floors through the fire exit stairs.

A staff member carried a bag of trash to the curb. Jake pulled his blue cap visor low and crossed the tram tracks.

The noon light cast a shadow of a horse rider in a helmet. Saint Wenceslas.

The green architecture of old town Prague had a unique tinge this time of year. The Vltava River snaked behind Jake's shoulder as he paced the cobblestones. A double glass window displayed mannequins with jeans and tops. The department store. He swiveled around Asian tourists and paused at an archway.

*It's the place.*

Armitage pushed into the eighteenth-century café and scanned his left. Three tables were full. A young couple who stared into each other's eyes. He sidestepped a single man engrossed in an iPad. The third table had four students with a pile of tablets stacked. He paused at the counter.

A female with short, flaxen hair had her back turned. Jake's chest tightened with tinge of anxiety. His career hung in the balance.

"Excuse me." The agent paused. "Can you tell me where I can get a decent glass of vodka?"

The woman's shoulders tensed. She swung around. "Jake!"

Katerina pivoted and opened her arms.

Jake waited as she lifted the latch.

"Love the hair."

"How did you find me?" she gasped and stopped short. "Of course you did. What happened to your job?"

"I just quit."

She grasped his palms in hers and chuckled.

"Funny. So did I."

Printed in Great Britain
by Amazon

21117706R00192